Also by Mark Hudson
Gordan Hudde Fiction
A Deep Purple Hue
An Angry Orange Sky
A Hint of Silver
An Emerald Abyss
Nonfiction
A Retail Investigator
Sitting With Jimmy

Authored and published by Mark Hudson owner/operator of One Flyer Publishing.

A Hint Of Silver

A GORDAN HUDDE NOVEL

Mark Hudson

ISBN: 0999006606

ISBN 13: 9780999006603

I dedicate this book to my wife, who still believes in me, and also to everyone who has never given up despite impossible odds.

Chapter One

The windshield wipers screaming out in protest were the first indication to Gordan Hudde that the rain had stopped; he was too deep in thought and almost forgot that he was driving for a while. His dark-blue Toyota pickup truck was traveling east on the I-20, with the cruise control set at 75 miles per hour. He knew he would be approaching the Atlanta area soon, and he didn't want to miss the 285 N. bypasses, so he tried to pay more attention to the driving.

March in the south was a great place to be. Gordan was glad that he had taken this route as he searched for a place to call home. His entire life seemed devoted to other people's desires and whims, and, after the fiasco in Mexico last year, he was ready to officially leave working for the US government and go off into a self-imposed exile, maybe do some hunting and fishing, and get a good dog.

After driving the pickup truck loaned to him for off-roading last year, he had decided to add some upgrades to his own truck, and he was very happy with the results. The larger tires led to some major highway noise, but soon he would leave the speedier interstate and be driving slower, more-country, roads and leaving the highway roar behind. He ran his right hand down his Spartan-looking dark-black beard before returning it to the steering wheel.

He had started his search in Texas and had worked his way east, looking for the perfect place to build something new. He drove through land so green and rich that additional traffic may have been one's only warning of a larger city ahead. His research led him to the northeast part of Georgia, the piedmont plateau area, just before the Blue Ridge Mountains. Gordan thought the weather would be perfect, maybe a little too cold in winter but nothing a good wood stove couldn't handle. The summers were in the 80s pretty consistently, so maybe there would be no need for air conditioning. He would be far enough from the Atlantic coast that he wouldn't need to worry about hurricanes. The area wasn't known for tornadoes, and he would be very careful on selecting where to build. Maybe he was becoming a survivalist; who could blame him after everything he had seen in his life?

He continued north around Atlanta and headed up the I-985 until it ran out just past Lake Lanier. The land continued rising further up from the low coastal area, becoming hilly and more sparsely populated. He traveled up through Hall County and entered Pine County on the southeast end, heading up old Route 5, which was also Route 20 until just before the town of Otter. There, Route 5 headed straight through the town and continued northwest up through the mountains into the southwest corner of North Carolina and off into Tennessee. Route 20 headed north, straight up into North Carolina near the South Carolina border, the two highways creating a very soft "Y" with the split.

Gordan entered the town of Otter, population 2,805. He pulled into a Shell gas station, gravel crunching under the large wheels as he pulled up to the one landing, two pumps available on each side of the bay. Getting out and stretching, Gordan slipped his inside-the-pant holster into the back-left-center of his pants, where the Glock 26 slid easily. He slipped a dark-green windbreaker on, as the 60-degree temperature did not factor in the wind chill.

A man appearing to be in his 80s was sitting in a rocker just out of the wind and said "Howdy" as Gordan approached.

"Good afternoon," Gordan said as he stretched a little more. "Is this your place?"

"Been in the family since the invention of the combustion engine, son. Course, we was full service in those days." He smiled up through a bushy white beard that seemed to be very well kept.

The man's eyes twinkled with intelligence and energy, and Gordan was amused by the convergence of old-school human and the new equipment that surrounded him.

"I'm looking for a place to settle down, and this town looked pretty nice on a map," Gordan said.

"Yup. Hope it stays that way. You ain't one of those city fellers gonna shoot old farmer Johnson's mule during deer season, are you?" His bushy white eyebrows nearly came together when his brow furrowed.

Gordan laughed and stuck out his hand, introducing himself. "That may just depend on how hungry I am."

The old man took his hand back and began laughing, slapping his hand on his knee. "I've been asking that question for about 30 years, ever since it first happened. That's the first time anybody ever answered me that way." He chuckled some more before continuing, "Winston is the name, Jacob Winston; those city dwellers think because it's country, they can act crazy, and it don't count." He paused. "Fools."

A voice came out through the window: "Disregard the crazy old man!"

Gordan turned to go into the store and pay for gas.

"Make sure you count your change, Mr. Hudde. My great grandson Dennis wasn't born with all his facilities." Gordan couldn't see him but knew the old man was grinning.

Gordan understood this kind of humor and was grinning widely when he approached the young man behind the counter inside. Gordan noticed the security camera above the back wall; even in a small town like this, security could not be ignored.

Gordan stuck out his hand to the fair-haired young man behind the counter, thin but sturdy looking, with bright eyes of youth and health.

"How do you do, Dennis? The name's Gordan."

The young man gripped his hand tightly and said too loud, "Sorry about that outside. We were afraid the old man would scare away business, but we are the only gas station in town."

After paying to approximately fill his tank, Gordan asked about some good food nearby. Dennis informed him that the best BBQ in the south was just up the road at a small joint called "Teddy's."

Gordan continued on up Route 5 as it took a westerly course and was also called "Main Street." Nice, well-kept older homes started dotting the roadside, and he knew for sure he was in a town when he passed the small town hall/library and fire department sharing a parking lot, a hardware store, and then a small grocery store. On his left was a small, low, strip plaza with a closed movie-rental business, a soda shop, and then "Teddy's". The plaza parking was half full and consisted of a single row at the street, a double row in the center, and a single row at the storefronts. A small sidewalk ran the length of the shopping center; the overhang was wooden and appeared as if it could use a good cover of new paint. Smoke billowed up behind the place, making it appear as if there was a fire; Gordan knew that wood smokers were in use.

Gordan followed the parking lot around the western wall of Teddy's, where another row of parking was available. He parked in the last slot, where he could see the back of the plaza. Smoke was really billowing from a small shack behind the place. A 6'4" or 5" black man was coming out of the shack, carrying a large tin.

The man was wearing a white smock that tied behind his back and neck and had a baseball cap on with a University of Georgia Bulldog emblem on the front.

"How ya doing?" he called out, seeing Gordan looking over at him.

"I'm salivating just standing here!" Gordan called back.

"We'll see you in front, and we'll take care of that." He smiled broadly as he disappeared into a back door.

Gordan turned and took in a deep breath; he shook his head and said "yum" to himself as the aroma was something he could taste in the air. He noticed that many people apparently drove up and over from the road nearby that headed south and parked in the grass next to and behind the plaza. This was a good sign that they needed such overflow parking, as the other shops certainly didn't draw any crowds. Further in back, several picnic benches were stacked one on top of each other.

Gordan pushed through the old wooden door and took in the small counter and dining area. A black girl, hair in a bun and netting over it, was setting up condiments and plastic forks on a counter just past the register; she turned and gave Gordan a warm smile. She had big dark eyes, and her smock gave away a sturdy and shapely frame underneath; she was maybe 19 years old. The dark wood of the floor was shiny from years of foot traffic and cleaning.

The big man came out from the back and waved Gordan over.

"Are you Teddy?" Gordan asked.

"Well, I'm Teddy, Jr. My papa started 'Teddy's' almost 40 years ago, and I've carried on the business." He looked down at Gordan, who was 5 or 6 inches shorter.

"Nice to meet you, Teddy. I'm Gordan Hudde, and this is my first time here." Gordan extended his right hand.

Teddy pulled off the plastic glove he was wearing and gripped Gordan's hand strongly.

"That's a big mitt for a little man," Teddy said. "Running back — like you would never drop the ball."

"No football for me," Gordan replied. "You play at State?" He pointed at the man's hat.

"Na, not really. I was a big deal in high school. Messed up my knees the first year of college and never made it back"

The girl interrupted. "Don't do that, uncle — you were the best to ever come out of this town, maybe the entire state!"

"That's my niece Lila over there Gordan, and she's a little biased," he smiled, "but a teller of truths!" He turned back to Gordan and pointed at the simple menu posted on the wall.

"So, lucky for you, young man, that I took up my family business, because, Gordan, after today, you will come back every time you are here and dream about it when you're gone." He grinned.

"I'm actually here to check out some land — maybe call this place home." Gordan was all smiles, happy to be announcing these thoughts.

"Well then, step up. Step up, sir. I will ruin every other dinner you ever had or that you're ever gonna have." Teddy was honestly eager and happy to watch another newcomer try his family's special cooking.

Another couple came in and smiled at Gordan as he made his selections. He carried his two plates over to a small table and looked at the feast before him. Lila set an iced tea and several napkins on the table before he even thought about it.

She placed her now-empty hand on his shoulder and said, "The family has won 'The South's Best Barbeque' five times over the last eight years, and, last year, a TV crew filmed the place for a barbeque special!"

"Wow," Gordan said. He smiled up at Lila and added, "I'm so hungry, and I don't know where to start." He looked down at the ribs, pulled-pork sandwich, potato salad, brown and bubbly baked beans, and a piece of corn bread.

Gordan guessed that Lila went a little over the top with a deep southern drawl and said, "Sink your teeth into those ribs first, honey — you gonna cry, they so tasty." She shook her head back in forth in one direction, her right hand high in the air as she testified, and her butt shook in the opposite direction while she said "Hmmm, hmmm, hmmm." She walked away to meet incoming customers. It momentarily reminded him of another waitress not all that long ago, and he was amazed at how the sadness swept through his body like a shiver from the cold.

The ribs were a deep, dark, shiny red that ended in a crispy bronze on the ends; the pulled-pork sandwich was on the perfect roll; and the smoky flavor rolled around Gordan's mouth. He never wanted to get full, and he hadn't even started on the sides!

Teddy was busy as Gordan started out into the slowly darkening sky, but he stopped to call out to him that it was even better than advertised.

The cool, damp air was a bit of a slap to his face as Gordan held the door for a young couple and a small boy. Gordan pulled his light jacket up around his neck. The traffic on the street was slow, but what there was seemed to be heading to "Teddy's." Gordan knew that, whenever possible, he would be back here. Everyone Gordan met in the parking lot smiled and said "Hello." He was excited about the stay and was really beginning to hope that the property he would look at over the next couple of days would meet his requirements and ultimate satisfaction.

He took his time walking around the building and breath-ing in the air. He felt the breeze moving through his beard as he climbed up into his truck. He pulled out his map, and, although he'd memorized where he was going, it was just an old habit to check and recheck his position.

He saw the truck's headlights swing from the southbound road behind him and jump up as they went over the small in-clination from the road to the dirt and then land directly on the back of his own truck. Gordan looked straight out at his own shadow from the cab played out on the brick wall directly to the front of him.

The truck stopped ten feet behind him and lit him up with high beams and a row of floodlights across a roll bar; Gordan closed an eye. Suddenly it went dark and quiet. The truck behind him pulled forward and slammed into the back of Gordan's truck with a bang. Like an old bumper-car ride, it was a jolt but nothing meant to injure a person. The other truck backed off twenty feet and shut down. Gordan opened both eyes and saw that two men were now exiting the truck. Gordan opened his door and slid off the seat, pulling a 3 D-cell mag-light from a center console. He walked toward the rear of his vehicle to assess the damage.

"Shouldn't be that much damage, guys, but I don't know what you were thinking," Gordan started. Two very-large-framed men approached him; on the passenger side of the truck, the silhouette appeared to be a giant. The man directly in front of Gordan was smaller, maybe 6'4" or 5" tall, his weight difficult to determine due to an overcoat.

"Damn, Terry! Look what the city slicker did to your truck." The big man stood directly in between the two trucks Gordan estimated him to be 6'8" at a minimum. Wearing a flannel shirt with the sleeves cut off, along with a massive-looking neck allowed Gordan to guess a weight of more than 330 lbs.

"Pardon me? Gordan asked. "Did you just suggest that I did this? I didn't even have my truck running."

"I couldn't help but notice that out-of-state plate on the back of your truck there." The "little" guy, Terry, pointed at the back of Gordan's Toyota. "Smashed a taillight. Maybe you should drive American." Gordan stole a glance at the home-made steel tubing bumper on the front of the 1973 GMC four-wheel-drive pickup truck. "Yup. Looks good except some paint maybe; I'm guessing city slicker like you oughta have a couple hundred bucks on you to cover my costs." Terry smiled.

The smile told Gordan that this had been done before — and successfully. The size of the two made him believe that no one would ever argue and cough up whatever they had in wallet or purse.

"What's your name? 'Jumbo'? I'm guessing 'Big Stupid Sidekick' is too long for you to pronounce," Gordan said to the bigger man in an attempt to gauge the full extent that these local yahoos would take this.

"That there is 6'9", 350 pounds of 'Don't make me ask you again,'" Terry spoke for the big man. "Look, buddy: You have two ways to handle this. One, we stomp you good and take the money, or, two, you just give us what we want, and we all go home without the need of our medical insurance card." He had this down and was enjoying it.

"What about three, we call the sheriff?" Gordan asked.

"Everybody always wants number three, huh, Randy?" Terry said. "Well, sure, mister. You can call the sheriff. Matter of fact, he's on speed dial on my phone." Terry pulled a phone out of his loose jacket front-right pocket. "It's right here: 'Big John,' my uncle." Terry held out his phone, grinning like a fool.

Fuck. Gordan was sure his face said it all; it was just that his brain was going way faster. *Sure,* Gordan thought. *Everyone was related or at least had a relative in a small town.* But Gordan guessed that nobody picked number three. Matter of fact, Gordan guessed everyone picked number one.

Gordan went with number four.

Gordan reached up and grabbed Terry's right wrist in his vise-like grip with his own left hand. At the same time he hooked his right hand with the flashlight directly behind Terry's neck; Gordan gave a mighty heave and pulled down and toward him with everything he had. Terry let out a surprised "oomph" and stumbled forward, just as Gordan delivered a vicious knee to his liver. Gordan was surprised that Terry stayed upright and staggered back on his feet, but he had no time as he whirled to see Randy, head down and running, hands out in front of him, like a bull.

This guy was definitely not a professional fighter or football player — way too much weight out and over his center of balance. But it still was a scary sight for most people, in the dark, behind a restaurant, with nobody expecting you to call or show up anywhere soon.

Gordan stepped to his left and kicked at Randy's right foot as he was closing in; he also gave him a love tap just behind the right ear with the mag-light as the big man went stumbling past him.

Terry had dropped to a knee behind Gordan. Randy, because of the trip or because of the mag-light, rocketed over him, slamming head-first into the old GMC. Gordan ran to his own truck and pulled out a couple of zip-cuffs from behind his seat. He started forward back to the pile of big men and had a second thought; he returned to his cab and grabbed two more plastic ties.

When he returned to the side of the GMC truck, Terry had climbed out from under Randy and was on all fours wretching; Randy was not moving. Gordan put his arm around Terry, told him to breathe deep, and slipped double cuffs around his right wrist. Then, with more than a little effort, he rolled Randy over and checked his vitals. He appeared OK, and so he slipped the remaining ties over his left wrist and connected the two young men.

"You are so fucked!" Terry coughed out at Gordan. "Now, what are you going to do?" He spit on the ground afterwards.

"Any blood in that?" Gordan asked. He walked over and picked up the phone lying in the dust of the parking area. When he touched the screen, "Big John" was still queued up. Gordan took out his own phone and called the non-emergency number listed for the Pine County Sheriff's Department. When he got an answer, he asked if "Big John" was in. "Not at the moment. Can I take a message?" was the reply. Gordan said, "No" and hung up.

Gordan held up Terry's phone and hit dial.

"What do you say, nephew?" Sheriff John Schmidt said into the speaker of his personal phone as he drove.

"Is this the Sheriff of Pine County, Georgia?" Gordan asked.

"Why are you calling me on my nephew's phone? Is he alright?" Schmidt asked.

Gordan started to say he was fine when Terry screamed out behind him, "Help us, Uncle John!"

"What the hell!" the sheriff yelled into his end.

"Listen sheriff, everyone is fine." Gordan started walking away from the GMC. "Your nephew and his very large friend just tried to strongarm me outside 'Teddy's,' and I would like you to know about it." Gordan heard the siren over the phone just before he heard it within a mile or two of their location. "We're around the side," Gordan told him, and then he hung up.

Gordan slid off his windbreaker and stored it in his truck. He slid his weapon and holster under the seat and closed and locked the door.

The sheriff's car was an older model white-and-tan Chevy Caprice, and the sheriff hit the lights and siren about a block out but not the brakes until it was almost too late. Gordan stood still in the glaring high beams and held his hands out head high, obviously unarmed. He was glad the rain had kept the dust down.

A big man extracted himself from the driver's side door, probably about six foot six Gordan estimated, he wondered if there was something in the water, maybe an army experimental drug to enhance the size of the average American male.

"Put your hands on your head, and turn very slowly so that I can see your back" the sheriff commanded.

Gordan did so without any comment.

"You boys alright?" the sheriff asked Terry and Randy.

"I'm OK, I think, but I'm not sure about Randy," Terry said to his uncle.

"OK, boy." The sheriff turned his full attention to Gordan and barked out orders: "You drop to your knees, never taking your hands off your head, and then I want you to fall forward on your face. Understand?"

"Look, sheriff, I'm the victim here," Gordan started to explain when the sheriff interrupted.

"It sure as hell doesn't look like it, boy. Now, you do as I say!" His right hand dropped to a service revolver grip at his waist. "Let's not make this here situation any worse than it already is for you."

"Yeah, being the victim of a strongarm robbery by the sheriff's nephew and his jumbo-sized friend isn't bad enough. Now I'm going to get railroaded by some Podunk sheriff." Gordan was losing his patience.

"Here is the thing, sheriff. I'm about as American and law-abiding a citizen as this country can offer up, but let's just say — for the fun of it — that I don't want to play this game. Maybe you have enough reinforcements to actually take me in. I doubt it, but suppose you do. I'm going to use my one call to contact my friends in Washington, DC, and, by tomorrow, afternoon every alphabet government agency they have is going to come flooding into this lazy little county and begin looking under every rock."

Gordan paused for effect.

"Every person on this side of the state will know you fucked up by being a part of a tourist-hassling scheme, and every politician and citizen in this county will hate you. Your career will be over. It will make national TV, and lawsuits from people that these assholes pulled this stunt on before will start rolling in, and, better yet, from other assholes who have never even been to Georgia but will say it happened to them. I hate being such a dick about this, but give me a chance to tell you what happened here, or go ahead and jerk that pistol."

Gordan stood still, both hands on his head, but he had inched forward and was now about four feet from the sheriff, which was well within his reach, and he had the advantage — in his mind.

"Your call, sheriff." Gordan stared up at the big man.

Gordan saw that the sheriff was in his fifties, fair haired, big boned, a little overweight, and was breathing hard. He may have never been in a situation like he found himself now. His eyes were alert, and he began to back up, which Gordan knew was a wise move.

"Kids, I love your father, and you know I love you kids, but if you lie to me now, I'll throw the book at you and Randy like I don't know you and never have. You understand me, Terry?"

"Yes, sir." Terry responded. He was rubbing his shoulder and looking at the ground as he sat on his ass, still connected to his big, unconscious friend. "We were just looking to score some beer money; I didn't mean to hit his truck so hard. The transmission slipped a little, is all."

"This is the kind of shit that could get you killed, kid." The sheriff added, "And me fired. What do you think UNC would do with your scholarship if wind of this got out?"

Randy started making some noises, and the sheriff reached behind him and then dropped a knife near his nephew.

"Look, sheriff" Gordan interrupted. "Sorry I flew off the handle. I have ID in my back pocket, and, if the kids pay for the taillight, then live and let live." Gordan turned a bit so the sheriff would again see nothing behind him and pulled his wallet from his back pocket, retrieving his driver's license. He handed it over to the big man.

"No complaint, then?" The sheriff looked suspiciously at Gordan.

"Listen, sheriff, I'm here looking at some land. I like — or did like — the place and wouldn't want to start my life here pissing off the sheriff or his family." Gordan returned his hands high about his head.

The sheriff looked at Gordan and studied him. "You did this to these big college-aged kids all by yourself?"

"I got lucky," Gordan replied.

"Well, go ahead and stand at ease while I run your name, but don't go anywhere."

Gordan cocked his head a little. "You're ex-military — right?" The sheriff stopped and waited for a response.

"Yes, sir," Gordan said, and then the big man slipped back into the front seat. Gordan looked over at Randy, who was sitting up now; Terry was standing, stretching, and still rubbing his right shoulder.

"You going to be OK?" Gordan asked Terry.

"I hope so. That's my throwing arm," Terry replied.

"What are you, Jumbo? Defensive or offensive line?"

"Yup" was all Randy said.

"Well, big man, are you going to live?" Gordan stood over Randy.

"Yeah, I guess so." He rubbed the spot behind his right ear with an oversized, soft-looking hand. "I got a good-sized knot there."

"You should go inside and ask for some ice," Gordan told him.

"We're sorry, mister. Nobody ever said 'No' before, and it kinda took me by surprise." Terry was looking at Gordan, and Gordan felt it was a fairly sincere apology.

"Tell me: How many times you pull this stunt?" Gordan asked.

Terry dropped his voice and stole a glance over at his uncle's county vehicle. "Well maybe a handful of times, only on city folks, especially out-of-state drivers."

Gordan shook his head.

"We'll pay to fix your truck, mister. I swear it," Terry said as he watched his friend disappear into the back door of "Teddy's."

The sheriff returned with the driver's license sticking out between his fingers that were extended out to Gordan.

"Sorry for this, Mr. Hudde. I can't even begin to think what these morons were thinking. They will get your truck fixed," he added.

"Wow — that was tense there for a moment," Gordan smiled, "and please call me 'Gordan.' For all I know, we could be neighbors one day."

"Sure thing, Gordan. Can we contact you up at the Mountain Suites when they come to make good on the tail-light?" the sheriff asked.

"Yeah, but..." Gordan started to reply.

"Unless you're camping, it's the only place around." The two men shook hands.

The sheriff walked over and grabbed Terry by the neck, pulling him around the back of his truck. It appeared that he was getting a well-deserved lecture.

Gordan jumped in his vehicle and turned it over; he jumped out and found that, while the plastic was shattered, the tail-light was still on. He jumped back into the cab and headed up Main Street to the Mountain Suites. He began to wonder if maybe the next town over was full of short people where maybe he could play center on the basketball team; after all, the world has to have balance.

Chapter Two

In the state of Virginia, hundreds of miles further north, winter had not given up, and black ice was still forming on bridges and roads during the night. Gary Reavers tapped some kind of beat onto the steering wheel of his new Chrysler 300C, although no music was playing. Gary chewed Nicorette gum when he was nervous, and he was chewing now at an RPM similar to the big V-8 under the hood.

Gary hated cops, and nearly running into one at his last stop for gas in South Carolina made the rest of his trip uneasy. He took a moment to look into the rear- view mirror so that he could see himself.

"It's all good, all good," he said, and he nodded vigorously, agreeing with the man in the mirror. "Yeah, we're all OK, man. No problems. No problems." He included a smile this time. His dark-black hair dropped back into his eyes, and he took a moment to slide his left hand through his hair, combing it back over his right ear.

Gary Reavers had dropped all his bad habits and was now gainfully employed as a delivery driver. He had thought quick back there, and now he was hundreds of miles away; everything was alright. He was approaching a small farm in between Courtland and Sedley, Virginia, a beautiful, quiet, and wooded area that was not comforting to a former crack-head from New York City.

The driveway came up fast, and Reavers hit the brake just a little too late. He stopped and backed up, getting the big powder blue car lined up correctly with the driveway. He headed up past the small, rundown farmhouse and around to the back of the large, new metal barn. It was slightly uphill, and his summer touring tires sometimes lost a little traction and spun.

Reavers popped another piece of Nicorette and slid out into the 31-degree night air. His tight jeans and dark t-shirt were not enough to protect his thin 5% body fat frame from the damp, cold air. He jumped up and down several times and shook out his arms before breathing into his hands and saying out loud, "I hate this fucking place, fucking place."

"Then why don't you just leave?" a voice replied from the darkness near the side of the barn.

Reavers jumped in the air and screamed.

"Fuck you, Reggie! Think I just fucking pissed myself!" Reavers was standing in a fighting stance — knees bent, right hand low, knife held firmly in place, ready to strike. In the moment of excitement, he lost his nervous tick of repeating words at the end of his sentences.

"Alright, then." Reginald Theodore Lenard stepped closer to the steaming and ticking Chrysler, a manila envelope in his right mocha-colored hand. He had a slight cockney accent even after years of living in America. He loved to dress as if he was going to a dinner party at Oxford, and, standing in a field in

Virginia in slacks, bowtie, vest, and dinner jacket, he appeared wildly out of place. His 6'1" form was as thin and sinewy as Reavers' but not due to drugs — it was due to incredible adherence to a low-calorie diet and regular exercise. He ignored the knife because he always had a sword cane at the ready.

"Any problems?" Lenard asked as he handed Reavers the envelope.

"Not really, not really" Reavers replied as he thumbed through the contents. Satisfied, he unlocked the door and opened the driver's-side back door of the big four-door, allowing Lenard access to the back seat. Reavers stepped back and looked around, out of habit, as nobody else was within ten miles of them right now.

Lenard stood back up as straight and as tall as he could make himself; he snatched the envelope from the smaller man.

"What the fuck?" Reavers stepped back, the knife magically again protruding from his right hand.

Lenard poked him with the bronze tip at the end of the cane. "It's dead, you bloody moron. You don't get paid for delivering corpses. Otherwise, buy yourself a hearse." Lenard started walking back to the barn door.

"No, wait!" Reavers objected. "I, I ... I can get what was ordered — I can, I can," he now pleaded. "Don't pass the job to anyone else, else."

"You will have only 24 hours," Lenard said.

"Yeah, that's not a problem, not a problem," Reavers assured him, shaking his head in the negative.

Lenard turned and continued walking.

"Wait!" Reavers walked quickly to where Lenard stopped. "You guys need dead ones, too — right, right?" He leaned back and forth, his weight shifting between his feet. Years of drug abuse had destroyed tissue, and his feet had never come back to their rightful state; Reavers was a caged animal wherever he was.

Lenard turned and leaned into Reavers' face. "Look, mate. We don't send them that way, you bloody moron. Have we ever done that before?"

"Well no, no, but..." Reavers started.

"But nothing, you fucking, drug-addled fool. Get the fuck outta here before daylight, and take your problem with you." Lenard turned back and headed to the door.

"Can't you do something with it, with it?" Reavers pleaded to deaf ears as the door slammed soundly behind Lenard.

Reavers walked back to the car; he made fists of both hands, raised them over his head and began hitting himself on the top of the head like a drum, saying "Think, think, think." Meanwhile, he danced in circles.

Reavers leaned into the back seat and looked down onto the floor. The flannel blanket had been pulled back, and a small, blonde curly head was visible. Blood had dried beneath a small button nose and inside a little white ear. Reavers covered the body and tucked the blanket back underneath so that car motion would not uncover it. He slid back out and closed the car door.

"I only hit her once, I only hit her once," he said to the deep-black sky before sliding back into the car and driving off slowly, careful to not spin the tires.

Reavers headed south, his nervous ticks aside; he knew what needed to get done. He found it strange that he felt bad. He had been arrested for everything *right up to* murder before. It was true, and he always knew that, one day, he would most likely take a life, but he never thought it would be a child — a little girl at that.

He continued until he was on the 258 South and morning was an hour away. He hit the brakes too hard on the General Vaughan Bridge, and his big car slid momentarily out of control, stopping on the northbound side, still pointing south. It was quick and fortunate, and he jumped out, picking up the body and blanket and throwing it over the side and into the Nottoway River in seconds.

The blanket stayed afloat while the body dropped down into the muddy spring water that flowed faster with the thaw and wet weather. The body righted itself, and a small blond head floated downstream bobbing and moving with only the life of the river. The lungs would slowly take water, and maybe it would sink until decay brought bloating. Reavers knew none of this, as his car was moving south before there even was a splash and he began planning his breakfast. The big Chrysler engine purred along at the speed limit while he hummed "Proud Mary" by Creedence Clearwater Revival.

Chapter Three

Gordan Hudde's eyes snapped open at 05:58 hrs. He lay in the hotel bed until it said 06:00 on the button. He swung his legs over the side and stretched his oversized shoulders and arms until things began to stop creaking and popping. He dropped to the floor and did some push-ups, followed by some sit-ups, until he was warm. Then, he headed into the shower. His 3S's never took him longer than 25 minutes, as most soldiers grew used to the quick start in the mornings. It was a little longer if he needed to trim his beard, but a quick check in the mirror showed that he would get by without any fuss this morning. His beard was like something worn by a Spartan warrior — just the way he liked it.

As he came out of the bathroom, he heard a little commotion in the parking lot and peeked out the window. He threw on some sweat pants and a flannel shirt. His boots had been left open enough that his feet slid right in, without socks. Gordan stepped out into the morning light, the air even cooler on his shower-heated skin.

"Morning, gentlemen," Gordan said to the men outside surrounding his truck — the Terry Schmidt truck and two sheriffs cars were there.

Sherriff Schmidt stepped up and said, "Good morning," handing Gordan a cup of coffee. "It's black, son — don't complain." The sheriff pointed over at the deputy Gordan had never seen before. "That's Deputy Goodwin over there."

Gordan closed the distance, and the two shook hands "Nice to finally meet someone under six foot," Gordan said. Goodwin said good morning and smiled.

Gordan took a sip of the steaming coffee and said, "All good" to the sheriff. Gordan took in the two young behemoths from last night replacing the plastic of his taillight. "Awfully early for the auto-repair shop to open," Gordan noted.

"Well, I called late last night, and me and the boys took an early-morning run to Gainesville to get everything you may need. Listen up, Gordan: We make mistakes around here, but we fix 'em and do things right; if you need paint or any other touch-ups because of these here knuckle draggers, we're listening," the sheriff said. Then he stood silently, waiting for Gordan to respond.

Gordan walked up and looked at the work they were doing. It looked fine. Gordan could live with some scratches on his truck. He had planned on putting them there himself, was all.

"You guys alright this morning?" Gordan asked, stepping up and looking over their shoulders.

Big Randolph White rose up to his full height and looked down at Gordan. "My ego's all busted up worse than anything else." He punctuated his statement with a big, wide grin and an extended hand that dwarfed even Gordan's oversized mitt. "Sorry, sir."

"I'm glad nobody got hurt, and I appreciate you guys being good on your word." Gordan reached out and shook Randy's hand.

"You're a lot stronger and faster than you look," Randy added.

Gordan smiled up at him. "Old warriors got old for a reason. You should remember that."

"No need, sir. My life's crime spree is over; I can tell you that. Besides, the sheriff threatened to shoot my balls off." Randy knelt back down to help his partner.

Gordan looked over at the sheriff, who winked and smiled.

"What's your plan today, Gordan?" the sheriff asked.

"Actually I'm very happy you guys are here. I had a question about the area." Gordan gave a "wait one second" sign with his index finger, headed over to the hotel room, and came out with a map. He looked at the sheriff and then at the hood of his cruiser and added, "Do you mind?"

"Have at it" the sheriff responded.

Gordan spread a map on the hood of the cruiser and pointed out the area he would be looking at later in the morning. "You familiar with this area just north of Old Smith Creek Road?" Gordan tapped his finger on the spot, highlighted with a yellow marker.

"What — don't you believe in road maps?" The sheriff pointed out the fact that Gordan was using a topographical map.

"Well, I was interested in the elevation changes due to the possibility of the creek or local rivers flooding if I were to build." Gordan turned his right hand over, his palm facing skyward, and said, "Right?"

"No, no — that makes all the sense in the world; I guess a lot of people wouldn't go the extra step, is all," the sheriff noted. He then studied the area for a while and added, "You gonna haggle with old man Winston over this here plot, or haven't you decided yet?"

"I haven't — I mean I didn't know who owned it. Just checking it out first. But now that you mention it, you mean the guy who owns the gas station?" Gordan asked.

"And the hardware store and the lumber store and the feed and grain, for that matter," the sheriff said.

"We talking about the same funny old man outside the gas station on the east side of town?" Gordan asked.

"Yeah. You met him already?"

"Well, I needed gas," Gordan said. Then he added, "Anything I need to know?"

"He's a hard man, but fair, I think. Thing is, he's pissed that all his children run off and don't help with anything he started. Every once in a while, he threatens to sell everything off and give it to charity. A big real estate company wanted to buy some of his land a few years ago, build a golf course, and put in some ritzy homes. Ultimately, he balked; he likes the town the way it is. And don't let him fool you with the 'addled-old-man' act; he's sharp as a tack and as fit as someone half his age."

The sheriff shook his head while looking down at the map and made a satisfied "Hmmmm" sound. "That's very pretty country up there, Gordan, good hunting and fishing. It would be a real nice spot, I can tell you, but maybe a little expensive to get the town to run power up there — if it's going to be year-round living and not just a vacation cabin or something."

"Thanks, sheriff. That's all good intelligence right there." Gordan began folding the map back up.

"Good luck," the sheriff said as he tipped his hat and turned back to the two young men, now putting away their tools. "Make sure you apologize again before you go," he said, and then he slid his considerable heft into the cruiser and headed off to the east.

Randy and Terry turned to Gordan and said they were sorry again before picking up the empty plastic and cardboard left over from their endeavors and finished packing up the truck.

"I'm sincerely happy that everyone is OK and that you could fix the taillight so easily. Listen — I'm sure your uncle read you the riot act. But I have to tell you guys that, if I felt I was in fear for my life, I could have killed you both last night, and I would have been well within the law." Both men stood looking down at the ground. "Although I'm not sure I had enough rounds to put you down, 'Jumbo,'" Gordan said and tapped Randy twice on the chest over his heart, smiling up at him while shaking his head.

Randy couldn't help but to smile a little.

Terry Schmidt stepped up. "Thanks for that, too, I guess. We know it was stupid and something that could have ruined lives now — I mean other than ours."

"See you around, then," Gordan said as he headed back into his room to dress for the day.

Chapter Four

Gary Reavers was bone tired as he pulled into the small home he rented in central South Carolina. His driveway was just two worn ruts cut through green and lush grass and weeds that ran around to the back of the old farm house. He put the big sedan in park, locked the doors, and slid into the screened-in back mud room before unlocking the door and entering.

He grabbed a beer from the fridge and started to head up the old tight stairwell that led to a single bedroom. He stopped with one foot on the second stair and then second-guessed and headed into the living room. Plopping down on an old plaid sofa, he turned on the PS3 player and the TV. Once signed into his account, he sent individual messages to three different "friends" and then signed off. He staggered upstairs and slept very soundly for a man who'd just killed his first child.

◆ ◆ ◆

In the small red-brick office building in Gainesville, Georgia, for the state Child Protective Services, two women spoke through their cubicles about daily activities. The older one, a white female approximately 50 years old, seemed sad.

The black female, much younger and obviously with more energy, came around and placed her hand on the other's shoulder.

"I know. I came here with all kinds of dreams of "saving" kids, and I can't even imagine dealing with this caseload for another ten years," she said.

"Try dealing with this for another *25* years," the other replied. "I'm thinking about retiring — I really am. I just can't bear watching any more. Every day, more complaints; every day, I meet people who have no business raising a child." She placed her head in her hands and sighed deeply.

The younger woman started walking toward the electric coffee pot steaming on top of a folding table just to the left of the desks. A collage of differing brown stains showed years of drips and spills on the top. Small white specks littered a cafeteria tray that held dry creamer and an assortment of packets meant to sweeten the drinks.

"Look around you, Karen. Without you, I would be the only person actually handling cases for the whole area. We need you. I need you here. This is no time for you to give up." She returned with two cups, placing one on Karen's desk. "Double the caseload?" She visibly shook. "Oh, my — I can't even begin to think about it."

"I know," Karen said. She had no children of her own. She looked over at a wall with old Christmas cards and some crayon pictures on the corkboard from children her life and work had touched. She shook her head and managed a feeble smile. "I know you're right. Thank you — time to hit the road." She picked up a pile of file folders, balanced the cup of coffee on top, and headed to the door. "Let's go make a difference — right?"

Karen walked to her government-issue black Ford Taurus with just over 50K miles on it. 30 thousand miles more, and she could request a new one; it was a humorous thought, because they all broke down well before then. She checked to make sure the top was dry and placed the folders down, leaning in and placing her coffee into the holder. Then she added the stack to the existing one on the passenger seat.

At 5'5" tall, she was not a big woman, but her shoulders and hips had always been equal in width, and she seemed to gain extra weight only in her stomach and bottom; she exhaled deeply and groaned as she slid into the driver's seat.

She looked at herself in the rearview mirror. A Dutch-boy haircut was not how she imagined herself at 50, but it was easy to care for. She knew she had let herself go; every year the resolutions were the same, and every year, she failed them faster and faster. She just didn't care anymore, and it had just been the last couple of years that she had been able to admit it; the same went for her job.

Her trip for today would take her further north into the hills, and she just couldn't face it. She began heading out with good intentions to see how many people she could contact. She ended up driving past four different homes and stopping at none. She just drove the miles and headed home early. Nobody would know; she would fake some contact reports and some "no answer" logs and basically take the day off except for the drive. It was a pretty spring day, after all — no need to ruin it by talking to some asshole, shithead, drug-addled parents.

Chapter Five

Gordan was only about 12 miles from the hotel "as the crow flies" but easily two and a half times that via Old Smith Creek Road, which had started out heading Northwest and then meandered northeast until it actually crossed the R20 on the far east side of the county. The road currently was heading due east, and the access drive for the Winston land was due north. Gordan made the hard left into the dirt access road and came to a stop with just about his whole truck off the road.

Gordan had to hop out and pull back a double strand of barbed-wire fence that acted as a gate which blocked the dirt roadway; "No Trespassing" signs had been placed on trees on each side of the path.

Gordan kept his speed down and crept along, paying close attention to the contours of the land, the trees, and meadows out in front of him. The path took him northeast, and, as he looked north, out his side window, he could observe a bank — maybe a creek that he had crossed earlier on the main road. *Maybe Smith Creek*, Gordan thought. The land continued to climb just past the small open meadow, and Gordan parked his truck to explore further on foot. A real estate agent was supposed to meet him in just more than an hour, and he thought his truck would be an obvious rally point for anyone driving the dirt road.

Gordan approached the creek and could follow it both northeast and southwest for a hundred yards before it disappeared from view. He followed it further up and into the lush, wooded landscape. It was very peaceful, and Gordan loved being outside, listening to nature. The land just north of his truck continued upwards, and Gordan knew from his map that it should be the tip of a ridgeline that formed somewhat of a spur that pointed south. He walked about 150 yards up the hill that covered about 65 feet in elevation change. Gordan pictured leveling this area and putting a home here; looking south, he could see for twenty miles, probably see some town lights at night.

He stood facing south, eyes closed, listening to the birds and creek flow. The sun was warming the left side of his face. He heard the distinctive sound of a vehicle door close and looked down to see a person walking across the meadow. Gordan knew this would be the real estate agent, Valerie Baker, who lived and worked in the area; the two had spoken on the phone several times. She started up the hill and waved at Gordan. She had just slightly longer than shoulder-length black hair, a camel-colored leather jacket, blue jeans, and dark work boots; he guessed she was 30 years old, and, from this distance, she looked to be in good shape.

"I'll come down — you don't need to come up," Gordan called out to her.

"That's OK," she replied, smiling up at Gordan and waving. "It's a beautiful morning, isn't it?"

Gordan ran his hand down his chin and beard; it was a beautiful morning and a beautiful place to be. He heard her fall before he turned his head and looked down to see her. She rolled feet over head and then popped back up to her feet and started right back up toward Gordan.

"I'm OK!" she yelled out, a little embarrassed, before he had a chance to ask.

"Pain and adversity reveals your true character," Gordan said as she made it to his elevation and ran her hand through her hair, ensuring no grass or leaves were hung up.

"That some kind of Zen bullshit?" she said as she wiped off her shoulders and turned at the waist to look down at her pants, wiping away imaginary dirt.

"Nope, that's the bullshit a ranger black-hat used to say when he was beating the hell out of us," he said, smiling. He studied her face, which had sharp features and was darker than most people this time of year, just coming out of winter. He found her appealing. "Besides, I thought your people liked that kind of Zen-shit."

She tried to be professional but couldn't help to push back: *My people?*

"I have studied people all around the world, I would guess that you have at least *some* Chickasaw or Cherokee ancestry?" He did not turn his gaze away from her eyes, and she studied him right back.

She cocked her head a little, which Gordan felt was a confirmation, before she said, "Does it matter for some reason?" Her eyes narrowed, and she leaned back on her heels, readying herself for some kind of verbal combat.

He ignored the possible dirty look. "Attractive people are attractive people, no matter the ancestry, I guess, but I was just joking about the Zen stuff. I guess my Scottish, Irish, English, and German ancestry is too diluted to feel attached to just one."

She didn't flinch at the compliment and studied him for a few silent moments before deciding he wasn't some kind of racist. "Well there is some legend of a Jamaican voodoo princess and even a Scottish trapper in my ancestry, if you go back far enough — although my relatives are all too embarrassed to admit to *any* Caucasian blood." She really studied his face to see if the minor slight bothered him.

"I wouldn't either, but I burn before I tan," he said, matter-of-factly and still smiling at her. "You interested in selling this property?" he asked, sticking his hand out. "You did a perfect parachute-landing fall down there, you know."

"Did I?" She took his hand and shook it, applying as much of a grip as she could. Then she laughed a delayed laugh and said, "I'd bet you don't tan at all." She added, "The seller wants to sell off 300 acres that include this hill, the creek, and that meadow down below."

Gordan took his hand back. "Wow! I was thinking maybe 50 acres or a little more. That may be above my budget."

"Well, to be honest, the seller has a few sticky details that would need to be legally agreed to before selling anyway; everyone else has balked." She watched his face to see if he flinched.

"Like?"

"Like no leasing or selling of any of the property for any construction purposes other than personal use of the buyer. He doesn't want to see a golf course or hotels go up here." She studied him for a moment.

"No problem," Gordan said. "Anything else?"

"Not really — he just wants to keep the town the way it is." She started further up the last dozen feet, making it to the point's highest elevation. "What would you do with the land?"

"Well, I've just begun to explore, but imagine a switchback drive all the way to the top of this ridge coming up from the east side, over the ridge there just behind us,, with a home built right here onto the side of this hill." He turned and looked about 360 degrees. "Fully defensible from three sides."

"What?" She looked at him a little confused.

"Sorry." He shook his head. "Just something a soldier can't stop doing."

"Do you think you would be willing to put in an offer?" she asked. She looked down the east side and pointed before he could answer. "It's a little less steep on this side. Maybe we can head down that way." And then she added, over her shoulder, "My Indian pride has been damaged enough for one day." And she began heading in that direction, touching trees as she walked past them, her long, polished fingernails sliding over the wood.

Gordan followed. "I think I would like to, but let me reach out to old man Winston before I put one together." They took a few steps before he added, "Well, if this works out, next time you come over, you will be able to drive up to the top."

"There won't be a next time, Mr. Hudde, unless you mean signing paperwork at my office." She didn't look back. He was going to protest that he didn't mean it that way, but he decided to just let it go.

Chapter Six

Five-year-old Timmy Graham wiped the sleep from his eyes; he didn't recognize his surroundings for a moment and then remembered a big man dropping him on the bed in the dark. He stood up on the bed and looked out the slim, rectangular window. Bright light was shining in, and it took a moment for his eyes to adjust. A rocky landscape that disappeared into foamy white waves was as unrecognizable as the moon to a boy who'd grown up in Tennessee and had never seen the ocean.

He was still in his shorts and t-shirt that he'd been wearing yesterday; his sneakers were on the floor at the foot of the bed. Wearing the same clothes for several days was nothing to Timmy, and this was not a concern that he wasted any time on at all.

He turned and looked at his room; the bed was covered in blue sheets with rockets and stars on them. The walls were covered in pictures of dogs, kites, trains, and planes. A toilet in the corner with a stand-alone sink and a fiberglass shower stall appeared to be his very own; Timmy was impressed that he had everything in one place. The toilet called his name, and he did his business before further exploring. A small chair in front of a medium-sized TV looked like it was hooked up to a game system, and the bottom of the desk had about eight games piled high. This place was way better than the last place, and Timmy dropped to his knees and began checking out the titles. He'd never had a game system before, but he recognized some of the titles because one of his school friends had them. He picked up one of the games with a soldier on the cover and inspected it. "Cool," he said.

Timmy's stomach rumbled a little, and he looked up and focused on the door. It was bright green and had a shiny silver lever handle like they had at the school. He tried pulling down and then pushing up on the handle, but it didn't move. He pushed and then pulled, still nothing.

He began knocking on the door while calling out "Mom!" There was no reply for about a few minutes, and then Timmy began kicking the bottom of the door and screaming, "Mom, I'm hungry!" over and over. He heard someone on the other side of the door, and he stood back, not knowing what to expect.

The door opened and a man he had never seen before was standing in the frame. The man had long, blond hair, tied in a ponytail, and a goatee. His teeth showed very white when he smiled. "Whoa there, big fella!" he said, smiling down at Timmy. "You sleep OK?"

"Yeah, I guess" Timmy said, rubbing his head. "I'm kinda hungry," he added.

"Well, why don't you follow me, and we can see what's for breakfast." The adult reached down and offered his hand to the little boy.

Timmy reached up for the man's hand and asked, "Have you seen my mom around? They told me at that other place that my mom would be here."

"I'm sorry. They tell me she is still sick, and she said that she couldn't make it yet. But she wanted me to tell you to have fun. My name is Stephan, and I'm here to make sure you're happy. OK?" The adult male led Timmy from a hallway filled with green doors out into an open living-room area with many chairs and a couple of big sofas.

Timmy was just about to ask if this was like the last time he couldn't stay at home when he stopped in his tracks. Timmy pulled back on the man's hand and said, "Whoa!" Looking up at the 30-foot-high ceiling, he eyed the giant wooden beams that ran the length of the roof. An older girl was sitting on the sofa, reading. She slowly let the book drop down. Then she looked at Timmy and held up her hand, waving by only opening and closing her fingers. Timmy thought she looked sad, but he was too busy looking at the neat surfing, fishing, and boating stuff on the walls to really care.

"Check that out," Stephan said and pointed to a big hammerhead shark mounted over a bar and kitchen area a few steps up and about twenty feet over from the sofa.

"Holy cow!" Timmy bounded over to the bar and looked up at the big fish — well more than three times longer than he was tall. "Can I touch it?" he asked.

"Maybe later," Stephan said and ushered Timmy over to the other side of the bar.

A black man behind the bar said, "What will it be, little man?" and Stephan helped him into a high-backed stool at the bar.

"What can I have?" Timmy asked, looking up at Stephan.

"Timmy, this here is Trevor. Trevor is the head cook, and everything he makes is delicious. So just ask him, and see what he can do." He patted Timmy on the shoulder and stepped away to look out the window down the landscaped, sloping land to the beach and a dock, where a large yacht was pulling up to the pier.

"Really." Timmy was looking at Trevor like a kid at Christmas morning.

"Try me," Trevor said. He couldn't help but feel energy from the young child.

"I would like...a cheeseburger and a chocolate milkshake with fries?" Timmy waited for an adult to tell him to make another choice.

Trevor turned and started getting to work; Timmy noted this and said, "Awesome" almost under his breath.

If Timmy had looked, he would have noticed several people debark from the yacht outside and head into a similar, vast recreational room for adults only next door. It was very much the same, except their bar was filled with every kind of liquor — and several kinds of drugs, if one were to ask.

The "older" girl on the couch noticed, and 12-year-old Sarah DeLucia set her book down and headed back to her own green door.

◆　◆　◆

Gary Reavers sat on the edge of his single bed and stretched out his arms while he yawned. *Back to work*, he thought.

He stood up and slid his jeans on before heading down the thin stairway to the first floor. Reavers fired up his PS3 and TV, checking friend messages; he had two. Both had addresses, and he fired up his laptop to check Google Maps. One of the towns was a beach area in South Carolina. This was a time when people were eager to leave the winter behind and head to the beach. It was closer to his home, which would mean less driving but more people and a greater chance at being observed. The second was an area that he had been to several times over the last two years in rural Georgia. He would have liked to give it a year before returning but didn't want to miss out on the bonus he'd previously held in his hand.

Reavers was happy about this decision because the last time he was in the area, the damn kid just went with him without any fuss; that kid must have really hated home. He hoped this one would be just as easy.

Reavers planned his route north, up through Columbia and then west at Greenville. He grabbed a microwave bean-and-beef burrito and a bottle of water from the refrigerator. He grabbed his keys, slipped on a dark hoodie, and started for the door. He was about to lock the door behind him when he hit himself on the head. "What's wrong with you, with you?" he said before going back in and opening a kitchen cabinet. He took out a cellophane-wrapped hypodermic needle and pulled out the vial of Propofol. Opening the needle, he syphoned off 30mg and re-capped the needle, placing it back into his front sweatshirt pocket.

"Giddy the fuck up, up, up!" Reavers repeated it on purpose.

Chapter Seven

"Harvey! I am most happy that you choose to come to my home and enjoy my hospitality." Abrahim Fazal Saied placed his right hand over his heart and then turned it palm up and slowly let it slide to his right, something like a "The Price Is Right" model would do as she showed a product.

Saied's hair was very well kept and always had sheen of some hair-care product. He stood straight and tall, maybe even a little stiff, making him appear even taller than his 6'4".

Harvey was a heavy-set man and looked sloppy next to Saied, even though he was wearing a Brioni suit. His tie was loose around an unbuttoned-top-button dress shirt, and he was sweating quite profusely. At 5'6", he was very short compared to his host. You would never have been able to guess that he was a very influential figure around the world and very much respected by his peers.

Harvey stuck out his hand and shook Saied's hand with earnest sincerity. He very much appreciated being here in Saied's company, where he was treated well, without all the judgment he would receive back in the States. Sometimes he even met other "open-minded and enlightened" individuals like himself. As a matter of fact, some of the most important relationships he had developed over the last few years were right here in this beach estate.

"Saied, you are a welcome sight after last night's storm. I thought I would be swimming here at one point!" Harvey paused and looked back at his yacht. "Where is your ship?" He noted the empty area on the dock.

"I have sent it to the States for some additional... deliveries," Saied said, without a hint of a smile. "Come, let me walk you to your room," he said and led the way.

◆ ◆ ◆

Gordan started driving a little faster when he hit Route 5 heading back east into town. His vision of a home on top of a wooded hill was exciting him like nothing he had seen so far on his journeys. He slowed when he hit the Otter town limits. He certainly didn't want to have a run-in with the sheriff so soon after last night.

He didn't slow as he went past the Mountain Suites, Teddy's, or the town hall; he drove straight down the entire three miles of Main Street until he saw the older Shell sign on the north side of the road.

Gordan swung into the west side of the drive and into the gas station. The transition from road to gas station was rougher than Gordan remembered, but maybe it was the extra speed he'd carried into the turnoff. Gravel and dust were kicked up by his bigger off-road tires, and he cut it a little too close to a big light-blue sedan as it tried to travel out the way Gordan came in. It was good to feel excited about something, but Gordan realized he was moving too fast and waved at the driver, trying to apologize. He didn't see who was driving, but they didn't stop or turn around, so *Apology accepted*, he thought.

Gordan decided to pull into the two pumps he could cozy up to while pointing eastbound, trying to make up for his foolish entrance. He made sure his gas cap lined up properly and then jumped out, heading for the door.

"Need gas pretty bad there, son?" Old man Winston didn't even look up from the paper he was reading.

"Sorry about that, Mr. Winston — a little lost in thought," Gordan said as he passed.

Gordan gave the young man $40 and said "On pump...?"

"That's pump number two," the young man said. This was not the grandson, Dennis, whom Gordan had met on his last visit.

"Yeah — on two, please," Gordan said and headed out to the old man.

"I know it's not the way things are done, but I wonder if we could kick around a business proposition," Gordan said to Samuel Winston.

"Talking about it used to be how all business got done." Winston smiled up at Gordan. "Once there was no need for lawyers and piles of paper; a handshake would do."

Gordan pointed northwest and said, "I just came from your property up off Old Smith Creek Road, and I love it."

"Beautiful area, for sure," Winston added.

"I got walking up the ridge that ends a couple hundred yards off the road, and, well...I have some great ideas for a home up there." Gordan was picturing it now as he spoke.

"And..." Old man Winston pulled him out of his daydream.

"Well, I met Valerie Baker up there, and she told me you had some interesting demands for any buyer. I just wanted to throw out a few things in person before giving things over to the lawyers."

"Such as..." Winston was waiting patiently; he seemed to be interested in the excitement that Gordan was giving off.

"Well, no other building or leasing is easy. I can't see my-self with anything more than a home and barn. I also don't want to ruin the town with any golf course or anything. But, well, sir, I'm not sure I can swing 300 acres and a home and barn and everything. I was looking for maybe 50 or 80, maybe 100 acres at most, but all your other demands are easy." He stood silently now, waiting for an answer.

"Son, you say you're a soldier-boy, right? I kind-a would like to help you out, but I wanted to keep the land together so I don't have to mess around with splitting it up." Winston just looked up, no expression, waiting for whatever was to come.

Gordan stood still. He continued to look back to the north and west like he could still see the property. He ran his right hand down over his beard off his chin, deep in thought. When a potential solution came to him, his eyes lit up.

"I don't have a wife, I don't have any children, and I don't expect to have any. Why don't I draw up a will that says I will leave the property to one of your grandkids when I go?" He paused, and, before the old man could comment, he added, "If somewhere down the road I have a child, I could stipulate that any kid of mine would have to agree to the same stipula-tions to own the property or sell the property to one of your kin for the same amount of money I originally purchased it for — plus the cost of the home I build." Gordan liked it more as he heard it come out of his mouth. Hudde stood still and as tall as he could, hands in the parade-rest position, waiting for Winston to mull it over and give him an answer.

"You that serious about it?" was all the old man said.

"Absolutely," Gordan said.

"You tell your man to draw it up, and I'll look it over with that old stick in the mud I call my lawyer, and we will see; smart offer, because I'll hold down the cost to save one of my own later on." He smiled and held out his hand, adding, "In theory, anyway."

Gordan took his hand and shook it, very grateful that this might work out.

Chapter Eight

Fucking yahoos. Gary Reavers thought as dust and a few stones flew over his new car as he pulled from the country gas station. The big blue truck nearly hit him — maybe would have if he hadn't slowed down when he saw it coming.

As much as he wanted to pull around and stick his knife deep in the redneck's gut, he couldn't. As a matter of fact, that's the last thing he needed now; time and remaining anonymous were what mattered most now. He steered out west, knowing that he needed to drive about another 30 minutes before he would be close to his destination. He knew it would be getting dark about the time he would get there and, for stealth, that would be a good thing.

Reavers looked over at the Teddy's barbeque place; it was the second time he'd noticed that place while driving the countryside, and he promised himself that he would get some one of these days. It didn't take long to get to the end of this town limits, but in just those few minutes, the sun dipped down below the mountains, and darkness began in earnest.

In the cities, you could drive without your headlights on and not even notice. Here, his headlights seemed to lose the fight with darkness like he imagined in deep space or in the deep ocean. Reavers' GPS unit told him to turn south in 200 yards, and, when the road to the south came up, he was very thankful for the unit, because he didn't see any road markers. As a matter of fact, if his headlights didn't shine on it, he couldn't see anything. He needed to travel only two more miles, and he took it very slowly, looking for driveways, homes, and other markers; he was encouraged that there was almost nothing to take notice of. It was also encouraging that he had not seen another vehicle since leaving the small town.

He saw the faint porch light off to the right and slowed down even further as he passed a mailbox and a dirt driveway between the heavy brush and trees along the road. The street took a slight turn back to the west, and another driveway appeared to the south; it traveled down to what looked like a trailer. Reavers believed that the trailer would be the home of the meth-head he'd been told about. The turn in the road allowed Reavers to see the side of the home to his right that was his target. He could not see a vehicle, and his information was that an approximately eight-year-old kid would be watching his three- or four-year-old target, a blonde girl.

Seeing a place to pull off the road, maybe a farmer's route to a field, Reavers pulled in. Hopping out of the big sedan, he popped the trunk and opened a blue plastic cooler. Reaching in, he pulled out three doggie "roofie" treats wrapped in plastic. The small hamburger treats would put out a medium-sized dog for enough time for him to do his business; this made him happy because he hated the thought of having to injure a dog. He took a moment before leaving the more open area to look up and down the dark road. He took a deep breath like a diver leaving the surface of the water, and he parted some small saplings, taking his first step into the deeper darkness of the woods.

Reavers walked into the woods heading very slowly and carefully. A city boy, he didn't like this one bit because just about every animal out there scared him. But the money was just too good for him to quit; he told himself that he was almost getting good at being sneaky in the woods when his face suddenly got wrapped in a spider web, and he shook his head and waved his hand about his head, trying to make sure nothing was crawling on him. The woods gave off an odor of their own. It was something unsettling for a guy with Reavers' background. His city nose took in the green wood beginning to grow again after the winter along with leaves rotting in the warmer air after being drenched all winter and spring. Branches rubbed against each other, and new leaves whistled in the wind, making Reavers feel as if he was in an old monster movie; he didn't realize that he was the monster.

As Reavers neared the back of the small home, he leaned against a tree and just watched the back windows for a while. Crickets or frogs were making a lot of noise and was the only thing he heard over the wind and trees. He didn't see any movement, but, just like all young kids home alone, it seemed every light in the place was on. A collie mix came out a doggie door and sniffed the air; it barked at the sky and ran back and forth for a few moments, an animal happy to be outdoors. Reavers threw the first meatball near the back corner of the home and waited. The dog reacted as every dog he had run into had, eating the item the moment its snout hit it. Reavers stood and watched the small dog as it walked around a few more minutes before it stumbled and then lay down to sleep.

Peeking in the windows, Reavers found his target lying down on a small bunk bed in a room surrounded by toys. The little girl's pink footie pajamas were a stark contrast to the simple white sheets.

The back door squeaked slightly as he opened it, but the older girl hadn't moved on the couch when he tip-toed past. Reavers opened the flimsy Styrofoam-filled laminate door of the bedroom and quickly forced his gloved hand over the little one's mouth. The hypodermic needle went right through the pajamas, into the meat of the little behind with little effort. Her eyes fluttered briefly, the adrenaline trying to keep her awake. But she quickly lost the battle to the medicinal sleep.

Reavers wrapped her in her own winter princess blanket and threw the bundle over his shoulder. He got past the sister and out into the cool night air without incident. He wanted to hurry, but this was no time to twist an ankle or worse, and he picked his way carefully back to the Chrysler. He dropped his captive onto the floor of the rear seat and replaced the two doggie treats in the trunk before sliding back into the driver's seat, heading back the way he had come. Normally, he'd drive a different route from what he took into a target area, but time was short, and he needed to get to the farm in Virginia as quickly as he could to get his bonus. Damn, he wanted barbeque.

Chapter Nine

Teddy, Jr. smiled as he saw the new guy come through his restaurant door.

"It looks like I've got you Mr. Hudde — two days in a row!" He waved a big gloved hand easily eight feet high in the air without even fully extending his arm — as if anyone in the restaurant didn't know who was speaking.

Gordan shook his head sadly as he walked toward Teddy at the main counter.

"I'm afraid the proper authorities have been notified that you are getting people addicted to your product." Gordan leaned forward over the counter as if he were looking for something. "You adding drugs to your seasoning back there?"

Teddy laughed. "Mr. Hudde, why don't you swing by here in the early morning and find out, when everyone else is sleeping, I'm out back looking out for my smokers."

Gordan pulled down on his chin, "If you quit calling me 'Mr. Hudde,' I think I would take you up on that sometime — get to watch an artist at work."

"Oh, flattery will not work with me, Gordan. Maybe bring a six pack with you, and try that." Teddy winked. "I'm out back any time after 3 am."

"Load me up with one of everything." Gordan nodded down at the food along the prep tables.

"Man, I knew you'd be back — sitting over there by yourself, staring out the window, not caring about sauce all over your beard and on your shirt," Teddy said as he grabbed a plate and started to load it up.

◆ ◆ ◆

Gordan finally sat back to take a break, only to discover that, other than a few rib bones, his plate was empty. He noticed Teddy's Cousin Lila looking over at him with an amused look. He shook his head with a "What could I do?" look and began to try to clean off his fingers and beard.

Lila walked over and took a seat at the little table across from Gordan.

"It never gets old to see people so satisfied with my family's recipes," she said.

Gordan touched his mustache and lips, trying to ensure that he didn't have anything really embarrassing hanging on them. "I can't believe that you guys haven't been approached to franchise."

"Oh, we have," she said. "Jr. has turned down many offers to go big. He refuses to allow the recipes to be changed for mass consumption. Besides that, no big chain would ever take the time with the meat to live up to our Grandpa's standards."

Gordan took a deep breath and patted his stomach. "Well, now that I may live near here, I can appreciate that. I'm afraid

I may need to buy some bigger clothes." He paused, closing his eyes for a moment, savoring the tastes that he'd just enjoyed. "So, when you going to open up for breakfast?"

Lila put her hand to her heart and leaned in closer, like she was about to share a secret. "Don't ever say that to Jr. He'll likely kick your butt up and down Main Street." She smiled and chuckled a little at what must have been an inside joke. "I appreciate — and so would he — the compliment, but he never sleeps as it is, and summers are murder when all the city folks swamp us; you may not be able to get a seat in here from June till September."

"Well, thanks for the tip. I won't suggest it." He paused. "Have you ever thought about expanding?"

"They have been talking about a pavilion-style building out back for summer seating, but that's about it. Teddy says we can't really get bigger without everything getting bigger."

"Makes sense," Gordan said, taking one last swipe with the napkin at his facial hair. "I'll eat my fill till then, thank you." He smiled at her as he unrolled a $10 bill and gave it directly to her.

"Oh, thank you. But we share from the tip jar up front," she said as she pushed back at his hand, the bill protruding between his fingers.

"Oh, is that how this works? I thought that was just for the counter crew. I didn't leave enough to cover, so I'll drop it there. Goodnight, Lila." He pushed the bill down into a giant glass jar on the counter near the register through a piece of missing metal on the top. He waved at Teddy and some other young man behind the counter as he left.

Gordan walked into the parking lot and stretched his arms out as far as he could, enjoying the cool air and the way the food seemed to settle while he stood. A young couple said hello as they walked past and Gordan smiled as he returned the greeting; he wasn't quite used to the friendly atmosphere, and he could see how a person who lived here could believe that there were no threats out there in the world to worry about.

Traffic moved slowly past in both directions; nobody seemed to be in a hurry. He walked out to the sidewalk and looked east and west; a couple of kids riding bikes about a quarter mile away seemed to have no destination, but nothing else was out of the ordinary. A powder-blue sedan drove past with windows too dark to see in, but Gordan waved like he knew whoever was inside. *That's the way they do it here*, Gordan thought to himself as he walked to his truck.

"Fuck off, you fucking backwoods fuck, fuck," Reavers said, looking at the yahoo standing there, grinning like a fool and waving at a complete stranger as he passed that little barbeque place he had been eyeing. Reavers wondered if he had time to juice the kid a little more and run inside and get some, but after his last fiasco, he decided against it. "Damn, damn!"

Chapter Ten

There was no siren, but eight-year-old Pamela Tolbert knew something was wrong as she lay in her small bed and watched the lights blinking and changing color against the walls of her room. She knelt on the bed and looked out on the policeman talking to her mom. She thought she was out of tears but started crying again knowing that everything that was unfolding was her fault: Her sister had wandered off while she was babysitting.

Sheriff's deputy Larry Goodwin was trying to calm Kelly Tolbert and collect all the information he could before contacting the sheriff. He knew failure to gather details would lead to an aggravated sheriff, and nobody in the small department wanted that. The sheriff always said that, while they were a small department, they still could be as professional as anyone in the country; he demanded the best from his people, and his people wanted the best for the county and for their leader.

"Why the hell are you just standing there?" Tolbert yelled at Goodwin. She was still wearing her diner uniform, with a smock tied around her waist.

"I'm trying to get this down so that we have all the correct information, Ms. Tolbert; please help me out here. So you came home about 30 or 40 minutes after midnight?" Goodwin looked expectedly at her.

"Jesus, Larry — I told you that 20 minutes ago, and you've been eating at the diner for 8 years. Call me 'Kelly.' Now get on that radio or phone or whatever you have to do, and get some people to help; it's going to be too cold for my baby to be sleeping in the woods tonight!"

Goodwin held up his pad and turned his wrist over to look at his watch. "Kelly, I've been here about five minutes. Take a breath, and give me some information." He scanned the wooded area around the house "We'll find her." He made sure that he had good eye contact. "OK?"

"OK, I'm sorry. Can we just hurry?" She looked around at the same flashing lights that her older daughter was looking at, but she looked at them casting odd shadows throughout the surrounding trees, and suddenly she felt the evening cold; she shuddered uncontrollably.

The deputy saw this and suggested that they go inside. He called for the only other deputy on patrol tonight to give Ms. Tolbert some additional comfort that they were taking this seriously.

◆ ◆ ◆

Sheriff Schmidt pulled in behind the two patrol units already at the Tolbert home. His coffee mug started steaming the windshield right above it as soon as the vehicle stopped moving. He leaned into the vehicle and then threw his legs out the door, something he had repeated over and over for many years now. He placed the Stetson on his head and made his way toward the front door of the small home.

He didn't knock and stepped right in. He was standing in a small living room with a 30-inch flat-screen facing a love-seat, and a small, rectangular, laminated coffee table separating the two. A dirty tan carpet with stains and cigarette burns led into a small kitchen with no room for any table or chairs.

"Morning." The sheriff deliberately left off the "Good" part, just acknowledging the fact that it was morning.

"Sheriff, we have to get out there. We can't wait. My baby can't stay any longer." Kelly Tolbert began to sob, both hands up against her face, a cigarette stuck out from her fingers, a slow swirl of smoke drifting toward a yellowing ceiling.

"Kelly, I imagine the 30 minutes before you reached out to the deputy, you searched and called out all around your house. I'm guessing you found nothing out of the ordinary. Deputy Goodwin says your Pam said that nothing out of the ordinary happened last night; she put the little one to bed and then fell asleep watching TV — right?"

Kelly nodded slowly. "Yes, that's right."

"OK, then." The sheriff paused, looking as earnest as he could. "We have to take into consideration that this is a crime scene, Kelly. You need to be strong for us. We need to look over the property and the house to look for clues. Maybe you and Pam should pack a few things; we can put you up in the Suites downtown for a few nights if we have to."

"No!" Kelly stood and yelled out, "I have to be here when she comes back!"

The sheriff placed a hand on her shoulder and led her down the hall, toward the bedrooms. "Pack some things, Kelly. We will have someone here around the clock. You need to make sure Pamela is OK and let us do our job now." He started to ask but then looked in on what had to be little Debbie's room. "Don't go in or touch anything in here." He looked quickly around the small bedroom one last time before shutting the door. "Afraid of the dark?" he asked.

"Yes — how did you know?" Kelly asked.

"A night light's in every socket" he replied. Then he gently pushed Kelly toward the back room. "Can you do this, Kelly? Can we call anyone to meet you down at the Mountain Suites?"

Kelly suddenly turned and grabbed the sheriff's bicep with a firm grip. "She's my baby, sheriff. She's such a little princess. You have to do anything it takes to get her back. Promise me, sheriff — promise me!" She squeezed his arm with strength she shouldn't have been capable of.

"Kelly, I personally will do whatever it takes to find your daughter." He replaced his hat and walked out the front door. He called on his radio to get everyone in the department over to the address as soon as possible. Nobody was going home until they started figuring out what had happened here.

He called out for Goodwin, who materialized from somewhere close by. "Check on Union County. They had an award-winning search-and-rescue team. See if they are available if we need them."

"Sheriff" Goodwin acknowledged the orders and walked away, taking out his phone as he walked toward his cruiser.

Terry Tolbert drove over past the sheriff, not bothering to ask anyone to move the vehicles. She just drove over the lawn, straight to the street.

Schmidt keyed his mike. "'Bronson' — you nearby?"

"Roger, sheriff. I'm about a quarter mile behind the house."

"Head southwest until you hit the street, and head back toward the Tolbert home. Let me know if you see anything."

"Roger that." Smith still had many military quirks from his time in the army. His family had lived here for eons, and the kid was an excellent hunter. The sheriff felt confident that, if anyone in his department could find anything in the woods, it would be Ralph 'Bronson' Smith.

Schmidt walked up to Goodwin and looked at him expectantly as he ended a phone conversation.

"The guys said that they can get here in about 12 hours. Just give them a 'go' sign."

Goodwin was pleased and looked up at the sheriff to see if he approved or wanted them to start now.

"OK, good work. Hold on them for now." He patted Goodwin as he walked out into the yard and tried to find the best view from the road. He walked a little northeast out to the road and began to walk along the road. He came across the tracks from Terry and then up to the dirt driveway, finding nothing out of the ordinary. He continued walking a couple steps and then looking at the side of the road and up to house.

His radio squelched, "Sheriff, sheriff — this is Bronson, over."

The sheriff replied, "Go."

"I think I found something important, sheriff. I'm on the road, about 250 yards away from the back of the house."

"I'm on my way."

The sheriff rounded the bend and made eye contact with Bronson. He continued until he was about 25 feet away, and Bronson held up his hand.

"Sheriff, stop right there." Bronson was looking down on the opposite side of the road.

"What?" the sheriff asked.

"Right about where you are, you can make out that some-one pulled off to that side of the road. See the vegetation lying flat? Up across from me, you can make out that they cranked the wheel to do a K-turn ending where I am on this side of the road, and then they cranked the wheel back to head back the way you came. Can you see it?"

And just like that, suddenly it became obvious; the sheriff stepped carefully so as not to bother any possible evidence. He keyed his mike and called out for Goodwin.

"Yeah, boss," Goodwin replied.

"Time of the Tolbert call?" The sheriff waited for the response.

"Ah, 01:17 hours, sheriff."

"I need you to bring your car down and set up on pos-sible evidence. Get deputy Tyler to help allow cars through here — one lane only open to local traffic." He released the radio and waited.

"OK, boss. On my way," Goodwin radioed back.

Bronson called over the sheriff to the northeast side of the road, where the vehicle had been pulled over. "If you look from here, you can see that the plants have been tamped down. Something or someone definitely moved up through here, heading to or from the home. There are tire tracks a little further forward, followed by mud on the road."

"Yeah, yeah — I can see it. Good work!" The sheriff slapped Bronson's shoulder several times, happy to have his eagle eyes on his team.

Bronson was looking at the shoulder near the ditch. "Sheriff, a partial shoe print where someone went up into the woods."

Goodwin drove up in his patrol car. The sheriff gestured where he wanted his car and then tapped on the window and said "Trunk."

The trunk-hood latch made a metallic click, and then the hood rose about 60 degrees on its own. The sheriff pulled it up completely and then gazed in, while Goodwin appeared and asked if he could help.

"I got 'em," the sheriff said, grabbing two bright-orange traffic cones and a box of red evidence markers. He placed the cones out in front of the patrol car. Then he opened the box and handed a bunch of flags to Bronson. "Start here, and let's work back into the woods — see if it leads to the house."

The sheriff went back to the vehicle and brought out a large roll of crime-scene tape. He and Bronson worked their way back into the woods, marking the way to keep others from stepping in the wrong place. The trail did appear to head straight to the back of the Tolbert home.

"Fuck," Bronson said out loud. "I was looking for the kid — not a crime scene."

"Yeah," the sheriff agreed.

The shorter grass didn't expose anything new, but a toe print from a shoe that was found outside the window of the little girl's room in some raw earth seemed to. The print seemed to match the one they found near the shoulder of the road. For the sheriff, this was the final straw. He used his phone and called a number that, unfortunately, was in his quick dial.

"Yeah, yeah." He sighed deeply. "Listen — I think we have another one."

Chapter Eleven

Gordan Hudde felt an energy seeping into his life that had been missing so much since the loss of his fiancée after their whirlwind romance last year. He liked the idea of small-town life, and, even after the fiasco in Teddy's parking lot, he liked the people he had met so far. Not one to sit and wait for things to happen, he had expedited every aspect of the land purchase, and today, he would be the proud owner of 300 acres of beautiful wooded property in north Georgia. He had transferred the funds from his overseas accounts and would make a single payment to the Winston lawyer this afternoon, cementing the deal.

He had already reached out to an engineering firm to evaluate the hill he expected to build on, had a guy to drill a well, and had picked out an architect and builder from a magazine that he had read waiting for a haircut; he was calling this "Operation Home Base," and he was attacking it like he attacked everything that presented an obstacle to him.

On top of everything that appeared to be going right for him lately, the last of the clouds moved out of the sky above him, and the sun shone for the first time in two days. He stood outside the lawyer's office and looked around, breathing deeply, feeling energized by the sun's warmth. This entire experience was healing him; he knew that in making a home and calling something his, he could maybe lead a "normal" life. His old boss in the CIA, John Stevens, would scoff at this idea — in fact, Stevens had told him to his face that "normal" was not for him, that he was an extraordinary individual, and that he would never be satisfied living a quiet life. But Gordan was determined to prove him wrong. He felt positive that he would not go back to the agency.

He spied the market across the street and set a mental reminder to go look for a six-pack of beer later.

Next, he was going to arrange for a recreational vehicle or camper rental so that he could deep-six the hotel living and be on his own property, closer to keep an eye on construction and be available for possible issues. After some Internet searches and a few phone calls from his hotel room, he decided on purchasing a trailer and then having it towed in to be sold later, when the process was over.

Gordan hopped into the pickup and headed up to his property, driving back to where he thought the trailer would go. He jumped out and looked around, taking in the afternoon sun. A light breeze was making the mid-70s temperature seem a bit chilly. He looked up from the field, his field; it was like a super-high shag carpet of greens and yellows, the rich earth, spring rain, and sun making for a beautiful, low mountain meadow.

He guessed that a barn would go on this northeast edge of the meadow, a driveway sweeping around and up to the north and then back to the northwest as it would make its way to the top of the ridge where his home would sit. He thought about getting a slab poured for the barn and then dropping the trailer on it temporarily; yeah — that sounded like a smart thing to do. As Gordan looked up, he noticed how the hardwood trees thinned as the elevation rose, and pine trees grew on the highest elevation of the surrounding hills. He couldn't wait for each part of his operation to take place and advance his plans.

Gordan walked about 50 yards up the gentler eastern slope and found a large rock to sit on. He pulled on a weed, placed it into the corner of his mouth, and enjoyed watching the sunlight retreat from the meadow as it set behind him to the west. Darkness set in, and his eyes adjusted to the diminished light. He closed his eyes for about 10 minutes, and when he reopened them, the gibbous moon was giving off enough light to see easily. It was a clear night, and even with the light given off by the moon, many of the constellations could be observed. Gordan thought this would be a perfect time to check on the Teddy's barbeque operation. He picked his way down the hill to his truck and made his way back to his room at the Mountain Suites.

Gordan pulled into the parking lot at the motel. His headlights played across the only other vehicle in the parking lot — a late-model Chevy Malibu, directly across from his own room. Maybe it once was a light brown, but years of dirt and weather made the exact color difficult to identify. A light radiated around the blinds in the room directly in front of the small car. Gordan made his way into his room and retrieved the beer that he'd placed into the small refrigerator earlier in the day. It was still in the white plastic bag; he pulled it out and walked back out to his truck, the package secured under his arm.

Gordan grabbed a small cooler from the back of his truck and placed the individual bottles into the cooler; then he went over to the ice machine near the office and placed enough ice into the cooler to cover all the bottles. Happy, Gordan flipped the lid closed and went back to his truck. The blinds to the only other occupied room acted like a Newton's Cradle as someone let go on the door side blinds, and Gordan knew the room was, indeed, occupied.

Gordan started the truck, backing up first, and then heading east on Main Street until he saw Teddy's on his right. The plaza was closed, and, without any traffic, Gordan's truck slid through the parking lot like a shark; the only other movement was the moths and other bugs flying around the few parking-lot lights. He continued around to the southwest corner of the plaza, where he was able to see Teddy's shed, where the magic was made, glowing warmly in the cooling Georgia night air.

Cooler under his arm like a football, Gordan walked around and tapped on the worn wooden door frame of the shed. Teddy opened the warped old door made of planks nailed together with a larger two-by-four "X" frame; he grinned widely at Gordan.

"Son of a gun, I didn't think you'd take me up on it, Mr. Hudde. You don't know how many people I have invited, and you're one of the brave few to actually show up!"

Gordan suddenly felt like maybe Teddy asked out of a courtesy to new customers or new members of the community, and he felt a little awkward. "If this is not the right time, just let me know. I was just excited to get to see what went on behind the scenes."

"Is that beer?" Teddy asked.

"Oh, yeah — I almost forgot," Gordan said and he handed the cooler first through the door to Teddy's outreached hand. "And please call me 'Gordan' or just 'Hudde.'"

"Never turn down free beer." Teddy stepped aside and invited Gordan in. Different types of wood were stacked on the sides of the shed in separate bins. Two large preparation tables were set up end to end closer to a large iron oven that looked to Gordan like it had been pulled from an 1800s steam engine.

Teddy handed a beer over to Gordan and set the cooler on the end of one of the tables.

Gordan stepped up, beer in hand, and looked over Teddy's shoulder as Teddy poked at the wood coals glowing red.

"I love the smell of wood burning to begin with; throw in that meat smoking, and this is a slice of heaven," Gordan said.

"Just wait till I start basting the meat later in the morning — it never gets old," Teddy said, turning as he closed the iron door to the oven and adjusting the air intake valves until the coals glowed just right.

Teddy picked up his beer from the table and saluted Gordan with it before taking a long pull. "Tasty" was all he said.

"Nothing like a cold beer and fire," Gordan added, taking another pull from his own bottle.

"Well, why don't we step this up a notch, soldier boy?" Teddy grinned wide and walked back into the back door of the restaurant. When he returned, he had a one-quart mason jar; he walked back and held it before Gordan.

Gordan inspected the clear liquid and reached out and took the jar from Teddy. "Aren't you afraid of going blind?"

Teddy laughed deeply. "My ma said I was going to go blind long ago; you going to crack that or just hold it till it's warm?"

Gordan twisted off the cap. He knew better than to smell it before taking a swig; he swallowed and then breathed out, looking for flames. He whistled and reached for the beer to chase it.

Teddy slapped him high up on his back and said, "Now you a real mountain Georgian." Then he took a swig of his own.

"I can't imagine doing much of that and then getting anything done." Gordan took another swig anyway. "Let me ask you: I Googled you, man. You've downplayed how good you were in college. If you stuck it out, and your surgery went well, you were a first-round NFL draft choice, no doubt." He stood still and watched Teddy as he internalized feeling into words.

"Well, thanks for the compliment. I know I had a chance; I know I had a gift." He shook his head and looked down at his feet. "They said I may never walk again, let alone play sports. Remember that this was 20 years ago. Maybe the surgery is done better nowadays." He reached up and scratched his temple. "I was a bit angry about coming back here at first and taking up my dad's business, but I couldn't be happier now, and I think it was a blessing." He turned and looked about at his business and held his arms out at shoulder level.

"I'm surrounded by all my family, first of all, and it's very satisfying knowing I'm giving them a start in the working world; man, do you know how satisfying I find it seeing someone, especially a first-timer, eating my food, my kin's recipes?" Before Gordan could say anything, he continued, "You should have seen your face, man. Barbeque sauce dripping down that beard, stuff on your face and hands. I would bet you were thinking of absolutely nothing else at that moment. It's always beautiful to watch." Now he stopped and looked at Gordan, waiting for something back.

"I was thinking about how I could somehow eat more." Gordan said, flatly, "or I was wondering if you were open for breakfast." He smiled, knowing this was some kind of burr in Teddy's saddle.

"Aw now, don't ruin a moment with crazy talk." He took a moment to take another swig from the mason jar; then he held it out for Gordan.

"Now let me ask you sumntin." Teddy took a pull from his beer and found it empty. He held his bottle up and shook it in front of Gordan as a question as he pulled another bottle from the cooler Gordan had brought.

"Yeah, I'll take another," Gordan said. "And yes, I was in combat; that's what everyone wants to know."

Teddy twisted off the bottle cap and held the beer out for Gordan. "OK, but..."

Gordan took the beer and cut him off, nodding at him, knowing the follow-up. "Sure I've had to kill people, but it was my job, and..."

"You don't have to talk about that..." Teddy cut Gordan off, but Gordan returned the favor by walking out of the shed into the night air. Teddy followed.

"Nah, it's alright, man. It's just such a huge onion to peel if I was being honest. Let me ask you: If you practiced the restaurant day after day, year after year, wouldn't you want to try to run it? If you talked and practiced setting fires, rubbing on the spices, tending it until it was perfect, and then seeing customers like myself enjoy it, well, wouldn't that drive you a bit crazy if you never actually did it?" Gordan looked at Teddy to see how he was reacting.

"Well, nobody's going to shoot at me, I hope" Teddy said.

"I know; so that makes a soldier crazy if they want to go into combat. But you're never going to do what you trained to do? Also you don't know how you are going to react once the first shot gets fired or the first grenade gets thrown. You gonna do your job or lock up in fear? Are you going to do your job and react to what is happening or lie on the ground with your face in the dirt; nobody knows until the shit starts to happen."

Teddy was nodding at him, not knowing what to say. Gordan saved him by continuing.

Gordan's eyes glazed over, and he was obviously talking about something he had been through, bringing up some memories. "Next thing you know your team is out of ammo, surrounded and outnumbered 5 to 1, a member of your team is getting dragged off by some tangos, and your officers are telling you to stand down. Did I disobey because I couldn't stand thinking I may see a video later of that guy getting beheaded or because I didn't want to believe that my own guys would leave me to that same fate? Whatever. Then I found myself charging headlong into a building, killing everyone who tried to stop me." He paused to take another drink. His left hand made a fist, and he was clenching and opening it without knowing he was doing it.

"Let me tell you, Teddy. When they are putting medals on your chest, you start asking all those questions: *Did God give me the strength to pull that guy out? Am I lucky? Is that luck now all used up?* So do I feel bad about those I've killed? 'No' is just the simple answer I usually give, but there is a lot more to it, trust me. But I can tell you this, Teddy: I don't have PTSD, and I don't have nightmares from my experiences over there. I wake up screaming sometimes from what I lost later, something I thought I was fighting for, and when I reached out for my life, for my dream, it got taken from me." Gordan looked over at Teddy a little sheepishly, feeling a bit foolish for sharing so much.

Teddy placed a hand on his shoulder. "Man, I can't even begin to think about all that. I thank you for your service and everything. I would like to hear more." He paused — not for effect but because he saw that Gordan was indeed upset by whatever had befallen him after the war.

Teddy continued after taking his arm off of Gordan's shoulder and reaching over to offer him another pull from the mason jar. "What I was really wanted to ask is," and he paused again to gauge Gordan, "did you really take out Randy White and the Schmidt kid in my parking lot?" He stood silent, looking down at Gordan, a smile slowly spreading across his face.

"Ah, shit! First time I really unload on someone, and they aren't even interested." And Gordan started to laugh until it became a belly laugh, and he needed to hug his own stomach, tears streaming down his face.

"Hey man, I know I look like Oprah, but I ain't that deep!" Teddy said, and he joined Gordan in the laughter. Teddy wiped a tear from his cheek. "Seriously, man, that White kid's a side of beef by himself." He stood, waiting for the answer.

"I got lucky." Gordan used his canned response.

"Well, I apologize that it happened outside my place. If I had known, I would have called the sheriff myself and shut it down; damn foolish thing for kids that size, that age to be doing. They is lucky they done didn't get themselves shot, is what they is." Teddy nodded to accentuate the point.

"That's true, and I said it to the sheriff myself," Gordan added.

"Let me check out the smoker," Teddy said and walked over to the big contraption.

Gordan walked out from under a few tree branches, where he had an unobstructed view of the night sky. The stars were brilliant through the 50-degree night air, and Gordan turned to take in as much as he could see from the mountain horizon in the northwest to the sky to the southeast.

"It is beautiful country." Teddy walked back over.

"Yes sir, that it is, neighbor," Gordan said, and they toasted with the beer bottles. Sitting on the edge of a picnic table, they finished their beers in quiet, staring up at the night sky.

Chapter Twelve

Some 200 miles from the coast of Venezuela, nestled some-where between Grenada and the Barbados, Harvey Golem walked the beach in the early morning light. His excitement was building, and he enjoyed the conflicted feelings within him. He enjoyed knowing that the things he did were wrong — wrong in the society that he lived in, wrong in the context of the religion he was raised in, and illegal in every western civilization.

Harvey knew that every person he did business with would condemn him publicly if news of his behavior ever came out and was confirmed. But until then, they all would still work with him regardless of all the rumors that drifted around him like a dark cloud. He controlled so many people's fate, and they all would kiss his feet and anything else he offered while he did whatever it was that he wanted. This thought in itself made him want to touch himself.

He turned and walked back to the main adult building on the island. He asked if he could meet with Saied and then ordered a mimosa; this was as cool as the island was go-ing to be, and yet he was sweating through his short-sleeved Hawaiian shirt. His Bermuda shorts and flip-flops made him appear to be a man on vacation; his demeanor, though, was that of a man on a mission. His eyes darted about the room, and he was unconsciously tapping his foot. Maybe losing 150 pounds would help, but his size was another thing that, while it bothered the masses, it just amused him.

Abrahim drifted into the room, his graceful gait and perfect posture the inverse of Harvey and his persona.

"Good morning, Harvey." Saied bowed before his guest. "What is it I can help you with?"

"I'm going to be leaving tomorrow, so, tonight, I'll need the room." Harvey wiped the sweat from his brow with a towel.

"You are my only guest at the moment Harvey; you have the entire island to yourself." Saied smiled, nodded his head, and exited the room.

Harvey stood and wiped his palms on the sides of his shorts. He waddled over to the bar and got another drink. The bartender was prepared to engage him in polite conversation or to ignore him completely, whatever the customer wanted.

If it not for his wealth, if not for his position in business, Harvey knew that he would most likely be in prison — or worse. He knew that whatever position he had, he could not and would not deny his desires. The fact that tonight he would satisfy his darkest needs made him feel like all of his skin was on fire; pins and needles moved up and down his spine; his unnatural desires frightened and excited him all at the same time.

◆ ◆ ◆

It was just after dinner, and little Timmy Graham was ushered by the lady to his room, where she got him to take a shower — even helping to scrub him up. She gave him some pajamas that had superheroes printed on them; Timmy hoped he could keep them when he had to go to the next place. She took him by the hand and knelt before him. Her shoulder-length yellow hair looked like yarn to Timmy, and her lips peeled back to show uneven, yellow-stained teeth; she talked funny but was kind of scary. He thought she smelled bad, too.

"How would you like to meet a friend of mine, Timmy?" She held his hands between her own.

"I guess," Timmy said. "Does he know my mom?"

"I'm sure he does honey, and I know he loves to play." Her breath smelled like medicine to Timmy.

"OK." Timmy shrugged his shoulders.

The lady held his hand, and they walked through the hallway of green doors. They continued to the neat restaurant area where Timmy had been eating everything he wanted without any adults telling him "no."

They headed outside and walked between palm trees and flowers, down a sidewalk, to another set of buildings that Timmy had not been in.

"Does your friend live in here?" Timmy asked.

"Sometimes, yes. Come along, Timmy."

She opened a door, and they walked along through a building much like the restaurant area that was in the other place, except they didn't have any cool boat pictures, and they didn't have a shark, either.

They entered a hallway with several double doors. A gold carpet led down to another double set of heavy-looking doors at the end of the hall.

The lady knocked and waited.

Timmy heard someone on the other side say, "Come in."

The lady opened doors by grabbing the big bronze handles, and she stepped back so that Timmy could see inside.

A man was standing in a large, round room; Timmy immediately observed an assortment of toys all around the room. A train was running around the perimeter of the room on a track that seemed to go everywhere.

"Wow," Timmy said, taking a few steps to take in the entire room.

"This is my friend Harvey, Timmy," the lady said.

"Hey," Timmy said, heading further in to the room.

"Thank you, Nancy. That will be all," Harvey said, dismissing her with a wave of his hand.

"Is this all your stuff?" Timmy asked, looking into a playpen that held all kinds of toys from stuffed animals to animated dinosaurs and everything in between.

"It sure is, Timmy. Do you want to play?" Harvey said while tightening the waist- band of his robe, his short, heavy, and hairy legs sticking out. His flip-flops made a squeaky noise when he walked on the tile.

"Sure!" Timmy yelled out, running around the room chasing the train while trying to see everything all at once. He stumbled and fell once but was up and running before Harvey

"What are you, weird" Timmy said, trying to run away.

Harvey held the boy, forcing him face down into a giant stuffed animal. The boy's screams drifted through the walls but never reached anyone's ears. Harvey gripped the little throat and squeezed harder and harder as he was about to reach climax. His breathing was shallow and rapid; sweat beaded and ran down his back and arms; his belly giggled in a horrific cadence to the brutal thrusting. Harvey screamed into the air in animal joy at the same moment that Timmy Graham died. Timmy's last breath was breathed into a furry, life-sized panda bear.

Harvey found the pajama top and wiped his bloody, fecal-stained, and rapidly receding erection on it, throwing the soiled piece of clothing on the floor as he sat down hard on the sofa. Harvey never felt more alive than in these moments. He looked over at the dead child without any remorse, for he was a king in the jungle, and, in his jungle, cash, prestige, and power were the king makers, and he held more of all of those things than most.

Chapter Thirteen

Sheriff Schmidt turned into the small parking lot of his office and immediately observed Federal Bureau of Investigation agent Gary Sanders standing with one of his deputies outside the building. Sanders was about 5'9" and approaching 300 pounds, about five years past retirement — not exactly the kind of guy that exuded confidence. Having him standing there downing a coffee and a couple doughnuts with his man just rubbed Schmidt the wrong way right from the start; he turned into his spot and killed the engine.

"Agent," Schmidt said, nodding once at Sanders. "You have a reason for being here, Goodwin?" he said without stopping, heading into the building. He headed straight for his office, saying "Morning" to anyone he came across before getting there. Goodwin was long gone when he turned to make sure Sanders was following.

He entered the office — a glass-enclosed 10 x 12 room with a simple desk, complete with a computer monitor sitting on it; the east wall was covered by a couple of five-drawer file cabinets. Paperwork was neatly stacked into the "in" box, while the "out" box appeared empty. Schmidt turned and ushered in the agent before closing the door and pulling the blinds closed; he threw his Stetson onto the antlers of a medium-sized whitetail head that hung on the wall.

"Grab the chair," he said to Sanders. And then he pulled up his and rolled to the side so that he could see Sanders past the monitor.

Sanders sat, looking down at his iPad; he seemed agitated and looked up. "I hate these fucking things"

"Yeah — we still deal with a lot of paper," Schmidt said and nodded his head in the direction of the filing cabinets.

Sanders smiled a bit sheepishly. "As I am sure you remember, not enough time has elapsed; so many of these cases are closed within 10 days to two weeks, and there is no evidence that any borders have been crossed." He paused to make sure the sheriff was paying attention. "If this is unsolved, it would make it the third case that your county has experienced in what, seventeen months?"

"Yeah, that's right." Schmidt felt he knew what was coming and was already fighting his desires.

"The first would be one ten-year-old female blonde; the second was the four-year- old brown-haired male; this last is another female about three?" He looked up.

The sheriff nodded and sighed, "Almost four."

"The profilers say this does not sound like a serial killer and therefore believe these are all separate and unrelated issues. They even doubt that they would be linked if you are dealing with a sexual predator." Before he could continue, Schmidt interrupted.

"So why would you come here all the way from Atlanta when you could have covered this by phone?" The sheriff leaned in.

"Listen sheriff, I would like to see your crime scene and your evidence log, see if the Bureau could offer any assistance in processing. I also am heading to the surrounding counties to see if anything similar has happened without proper reporting."

"OK, Sanders — that would be helpful. I've made calls and only Banks County has said they have a confirmed abduction in the last two years. Maybe you could look for similarities for me, see if I need to go down there myself." The sheriff stood. "Anything else?"

Sanders stood, pushed and prodded at his iPad, and said "I've just sent you our most updated predator list for the surrounding area; maybe you could start doing some interviews." Sanders turned and opened the door, taking one step out before turning to look back at the sheriff, who was about to speak.

"I'll be starting a round of home or work visits tomorrow; we'll compare lists to see if anyone new moved in without reporting. Keep in touch, and thanks for the visit; let me know if there is anything we can do." The sheriff paused and grunted. "Oh, Deputy Smith is up at the scene, if that's where you're heading next." Schmidt extended his right hand; he had no intention of walking Sanders out to his vehicle. He turned to the dispatcher and said, "Mary, could you radio Bronson and

let him know that Agent Sanders will be on site in about 45?"
Then he turned and headed to get coffee of his own.

Sitting back down at his desk, he set down his mug that depicted two deer talking in the woods, one commenting on the other's bullseye birthmark. The sheriff opened his email and brought up the one from Sanders; he printed out the FBI list and compared it to the one he was working from. *What do you know?* He thought *The FBI has two names more than my own list, with possible addresses, even; maybe they're useful for something after all.*

◆ ◆ ◆

Gordan sat in his truck at the town library/County offices parking lot, windows down, in the strong afternoon sun, enjoying the goings-on of small-town life. He held the go-phone low and used the speaker instead of holding it up to his ear. His architect was grilling him about expectations.

"Have you had time to look at the pictures and drawing I sent you yesterday?" Gordan asked.

"Yes, yes, I have, and I tell you, this would be an exciting and interesting build. I've got to ask: Are you building a home or a bunker?" Stephen Webber said.

"So you see what I was looking for, then?" Gordan said.

"I think so. I'll need to fly there to check the site myself first."

"Of course," Gordan acknowledged.

"Do you have a site survey and an engineering report, and have you checked on the permits from the local town, state, whatever?" Webber asked.

"Affirmative!" Gordan was so excited by this endeavor. "I think I have everything started that needs to get done; I'm sitting at the county offices now to check on the permits, but I don't foresee any problems. Is there anything else I haven't taken into account?" Gordan asked.

"No, I don't believe there is; in fact, I'm not sure I have ever dealt with anyone on a personal build who seemed so well prepared. I think I further understand your designs." There was a pause. "I have an opening late next week. Maybe I can fly in and see this place for myself then, around Thursday, and I'll take a few days to check it all out."

"That would be great; I'll wait for your call. Thank you." Gordan hung up. He realized that he would need to learn to say "Goodbye" to people. He understood they would expect that, yet he never seemed to catch it until it was too late.

Gordan hopped out of the truck and walked into the main doors of the two-story brick building; he ignored the gun-free zone statement written on the doors in small print.

He entered the foyer and looked about. Large grey-tile floors ran up to alabaster pillars that Gordan doubted had any support responsibilities. It was very nice for a small town. It seemed that the library was in the basement, while the government offices were on the first floor. The offices ran down the left and right sides of the large hall. He finally located the county clerk's office and entered slowly, taking his time to look around to try to determine the atmosphere. He had spent a lot of time handling paperwork in the Army, and he knew how bureaucracies worked.

He walked through the door with a golden "101" painted on the frosted glass. It was not busy when he entered. In fact, as he opened the door, the few people visible through the glass separating a small waiting area and the offices further inside all stopped whatever they had been doing and looked. Two long, wooden benches were situated one in front of the other; the counter space looked like a 1940s bank. Gordan waved and spied a table laden with all kinds of tri-fold brochures explaining government requirements. He started to walk over to check out the available information before he bothered anyone.

"Can I help you with anything, honey?"

Gordan turned to see who was speaking to him. A woman with dark hair, heavily highlighted with red and piled high on her head, was standing on the opposite side of the partition, looking at him through the glass.

He approached after selecting a couple of the brochures and placed them down on his side of the counter.

"Well, how do you do?" He smiled sheepishly. "I'm Gordan Hudde; I just purchased some land and want to build a home. I need to know what the County requirements are." He took in the woman as best he could from his side of the partition; she was between 40 and 42 years old, Hudde guessed, and single, as she wore no ring. From her take-charge attitude and the way the other two women were watching, Gordan knew that she was the person who got things done around here.

"Well, welcome, Mr. Gordan Hudde. You can call me Heidi." She leaned back and to the left to accentuate her ample bust line, which held a name tag lying nearly flat on the top of her blouse, which currently was pulled dangerously taut across her chest. Gordan's mind began thinking about tensile strength as he gazed momentarily at the thread trying desperately to hold a button. She was round faced, with high cheek bones. Her big brown eyes were accentuated with a bit too much makeup, and her bright-red lips were full and pouty. Gordan guessed there was a satin tavern jacket hanging in the back with her name on it. Gordan couldn't see from her waist down. Heidi shifted her weight from her left foot to her right foot and leaned on the counter; Gordan couldn't help but notice the name tag bounce and jiggle. "Please tell me there is something I can help you with," she finished.

Gordan took a moment to acknowledge the other two ladies with a slight nod, as they were paying very close attention.

"Well, first, please just call me Gordan; second, I was thinking about quite a few things...." He paused to grip his beard on his chin and pulled down through it as he often did in thought. "But, suddenly, I seem to have forgotten just about everything." He finished with his best grin.

"Well, aren't you nice." She flipped her hand at him in an "Oh, stop it" gesture and leaned closer to the glass to look down at the brochures that he had set down there. "So you're looking for the permit process to build on your recently acquired property?"

"Yeah, that's it. We just closed, so I doubt the deeds and everything have made it to your offices yet, but I wanted to get going right away or as soon as possible, anyway." Gordan looked down at Heidi and added, "Anything you could help me get started on would be appreciated."

"Why, aren't you a go-getter," Heidi said, placing her index finger near the corner of her bright lips.

He leaned in as close as he could to the glass. "'Unstoppable' is a word they've used about me before." And he winked.

Heidi smiled broadly and waved the papers in her hand to fan her face. "Incorrigible, maybe, I would guess."

Gordan left the office in about fifteen minutes with all the documentation that would need to be filed by his architect and builders with the County; he heard some giggling and laughter after he closed the door. He was about to leave when he suddenly turned and headed down the steps to take a look at the library; it had been a long time since he had been in one. The invention of the Internet, he imagined, had diminished the popularity of libraries.

Gordan walked down the stairway and followed a sign past the bathroom emblems, past a drinking fountain, and through a door. An elderly woman looked up from a mahogany-colored wooden counter area. Gordan smiled as he walked past the desk, and the woman looked back down at whatever it was she was reading.

Long rows of metal shelving packed with books ran the length of the entire rest of the basement. Older, fluorescent lighting cast a yellow hue, and Gordan closed his eyes to allow them to adjust to the harsh contrast to the light upstairs that came from many windows. With his eyes closed, Gordan was brought back to one of the older homes he had grown up in; he could smell the musty odor of the basement, not unpleasant but with a hint of dust and moisture. He remembered tip-toeing down the long flight of wooden stairs, the light from the upstairs barely reaching the broken, cracked concrete floor, the rest of the basement in shadow. He would make a mad dash to the single light bulb at the center of the basement, swinging in the dark, due to unknown forces. He used to tell himself that failure to catch the chain and turn the light on with the first attempt would result in certain death. Back then, he was afraid because he still believed that monsters lurked where darkness was prevalent. Later, he learned that men were the worst monsters that roamed the earth, and he had become a hunter of them; now, he used the dark — and liked it.

As a child, Gordan loved Edgar Rice Burroughs and had read everything he had written, especially *Tarzan* and *John Carter.* He went through a phase where he read many of the Conan books by Robert E. Howard. Later, he developed a taste for mythology, especially Norse and Greek. He'd spent many hours hiding in a small library, just like this one, dreaming of being one of the heroes he'd read about.

"Can I help you, young man?" the elderly librarian said to him, pulling him from his thoughts.

Gordan hadn't even noticed her, pushing a small, grey metal cart with books to return to the shelf.

"No, ma'am. Thank you. I was just drifting back to my childhood, is all." Gordan smiled politely.

"It happens to many people when they come in" she said, smiling back. She began pushing her cart toward the back of the room.

"Have a nice day," Gordan said as he turned and left. He seemed to travel forward with each step back to the future as he jumped the stairs two at a time and headed back out into daylight; it gave him a chill that traveled down his spine.

His stomach rumbled as he hit the daylight. From the position of the sun, he knew that Teddy's would be open within the hour, so he drove slowly in that direction.

♦ ♦ ♦

The sun was much lower in the sky, shadows were long, and Gordan once again felt like he'd eaten too much. He started thinking that maybe he should always get take-out, because, as everyone began sitting and talking to him while he was inside, he seemed to order more and finish it. Gordan stretched, belched a barbeque-tasting gas, and patted his stomach. His first thought was to look about to see if he had disgusted anyone; his second was to wonder if he had just made enough room to order more; he shook his head "No."

Gordan walked to his truck and leaned against it, taking in the beautiful evening. He poked around his teeth with a toothpick, making sure that nothing was stuck.

"You an addict, man!" Teddy said from behind him.

Gordan turned to look at the wizard of tasty meats. "Teddy I don't know if I love you or hate you, man!" he said with a smile.

Teddy laughed. "Don't hate me 'cause I'm beautiful," quoting an old TV shampoo ad. "See you tomorrow?" He kept laughing out loud as he headed back into his barbeque shack, waving once over his head without looking.

Gordan climbed into the truck cab and turned it over, waiting a moment for his playlist to start playing. He thought he might catch some news on cable and get some early rest, maybe get up early, and get into his property early to explore.

Gordan pulled out, crossing traffic, and headed west toward the inn, just a couple of minutes away. He considered turning his headlights, on as the trees and mountains produced alternating areas of fading sunlight and shadow, making him squint.

AC/DC was just banging the bell at the intro to "Hells Bells" as he turned left into the Mountain Inn Suites parking lot. Gordan immediately observed additional vehicles on the west side of the lot, opposite his room: a brown Malibu, a burnt-orange older pickup truck, and a mini-van that was white, blue, and brown.

As he pulled in and turned into a slot in front of his rental door, Gordan saw that a tall, thin, grey-haired black man was holding up a folding chair like a lion tamer. He seemed to be holding back a tall, thin white male with maybe a "high and tight" haircut or a short Mohawk.

Gordan hit the power to the radio and then heard the muffled yelling. As he headed out of his cab, he first felt back for the comfort of his .45 in place at the small of his back. He made sure his T-shirt was over the grip.

A shorter male with shaggy dark hair was between the pickup and the Malibu, yelling, "Kick his ass, Russell!"

Gordan saw that another folding chair was in front of a room with an open door. The sky continued darkening, and the light from inside spilled out onto the sidewalk outside.

Gordan also saw the room that earlier was occupied now had a young child in it, a female, he thought, peeking out of the window, a horrified look on her face.

The black lion tamer was yelling over his shoulder, "911 Deloris! 911 Deloris!" and now Hudde could make out that he was most likely in his late 60s.

Gordan began making his way into the chaos when he noticed what he thought to be female legs sticking out from under the front of the pickup and just slightly behind the black man.

Gordan watched carefully and at no time observed either of the younger men display any weapons, although both had knives on their belts.

The taller man was screaming at the elderly man, "It's none of yer damn business, sambo — you best move along before you get you some, too."

"Watch out, Russell," the shorter, dark haired guy said as he noticed Gordan approaching carefully. "You best go away lest you want your ass kicked, pal!" he added as Gordan stepped into the area between the vehicles. Now Gordan could see a woman, maybe in her mid-30s, wearing what appeared to be waitress's outfit, her hands covering what looked to be a bloody nose, lying somewhat under the front of the pickup.

An elderly black woman came out from the open door to the right, and Gordan guessed this would be Deloris. She yelled out, "Sheriff is coming!"

"You nosey mother-fuckers should mind your own business!" The taller man took a menacing step in the direction of the older man and ripped the lawn chair from his grasp; he threw it in the direction of the parking lot, and it landed on the Malibu hood.

The woman on the ground screamed out, "Russell, stop it!"

The door to the left of the black couple's room swung open, and a seven or eight-year-old girl screamed out, "*Daaaddyyy!*" in a most blood-curling way.

"Is this faggot with you?" Russell pointed at Gordan while screaming at the woman. Before she could answer, Russell spun toward Gordan with murder in his eyes.

Gordan held up his hand in the universal "stop" sign and said, "Hold on. Let's wait for the sheriff to get here; nobody needs to get hurt any further."

"Better run, lover boy!" the shorter guy said to Gordan.

Russell stepped into Gordan's range and swung a huge right-hook haymaker at Gordan's head. Gordan was probably two to three inches shorter. He did two things way quicker than Russell expected: he ducked, and he stepped right into Russell as the right went screaming harmlessly overhead.

Gordan reached up with his right hand at the same time as he took another half step past Russell with his right foot, placing it firmly behind the taller man. Gordan took his meaty, large right hand and placed it around the throat of the lighter man. Russell made the mistake that many had made: He tried to wrestle Gordan's fingers from his throat. Gordans' grip was legendary, and his hand would not be removed without permission.

Gordan now used his legs, back, and shoulders to lift Russel off the ground about four inches, pushing him past Gordan's extended right leg and hips, throwing Russell off balance. Gordan threw Russell toward the ground with all of his considerable strength.

The sidekick, now behind Gordan, said, "You a dead man now."

The sheriff's siren seemed close.

Gordan released his grip on Russell, who was fighting for air, and threw a quick glance at the sidekick, who was giving ground and backing up from Gordan.

The small parking lot suddenly exploded with lights and sirens as first one and quickly a second sheriff's vehicle pulled into the area.

"You don't do well in parking lots, I see." Sheriff Schmidt appeared beside Gordan and looked down at the prone figure at his feet. "Russell Tolbert," the sheriff said with scorn "This is about the way I last saw you about three or four years ago."

Russell was currently coughing and trying to catch his breath.

The sheriff looked about the parking lot. His deputy Goodwin was tending to Kelly Tolbert over on the sidewalk and the elderly black couple was standing near the eight-year-old, Pam Tolbert, closer to their own room. This left the man Gordan had now nearly forgotten about.

"Oh, Charlie, don't tell me you've taken up with playing sidekick to Tolbert, here, again." The sheriff had one hand on his hip and the other firmly on the grip of a big handgun. He looked at the ground and shook his head; with his Stetson, he towered over the other man.

"I ain't done nothing wrong, sheriff; you ain't got no rights to harass me none," Charlie stated his case.

"This here your piece-of-shit pickup, Charlie? I think I'll start tonight's festivities by impounding it due to it being a hazard." The sheriff looked at Charlie. "Or maybe you should shut up until I ask you something. Why don't you start out by planting your ass right there — yeah, that's right."

Gordan began walking toward his room; everyone seemed to be otherwise occupied.

"Don't get lost, there. I need to ask you a few things," the sheriff yelled out to him when he saw him.

Gordan turned on the light to his room and turned back to the parking lot. "I'll be right here." He didn't bother closing the door; he just turned on the TV and sat on the bed, watching some talking head read the news.

About 40 minutes later, Gordan heard the sheriff bellow his name. Gordan got up and walked to the door, looking out. The Sheriff was standing near the passenger side of the orange pickup with Russel Tolbert. The sheriff waved him over, and Gordan complied, walking up to the sheriff's left, Tolbert on his right.

"This here, Russell, is Gordan Hudde; he's a retired soldier and a decorated war hero. He's decided to move here because we're all so nice and polite in these parts." The sheriff paused and looked expectantly at Tolbert. "Isn't that so, Russell?"

Russell Tolbert stepped over and extended his right hand to Gordan "I'm sorry. I was wrong, and I shouldn't lose my temper so."

Gordan shrugged his shoulders. He noticed the tattoos running up the other man's arm to his neck and even on the side of his face, "OK. We all make mistakes." Gordan looked a little questioningly at the sheriff.

The sheriff cleared his throat and put his arms around Tolbert's and Hudde's necks, bringing them in close. "Now, here is the deal I'm going to make with Mr. Hudde, and I don't want you to miss anything, Russell. So listen close. Mr. Hudde, I think I know that you don't care if you ever see Russell Tolbert ever again, but Russell here does have a history of holding a grudge and — to make things worse — of making very bad decisions. So, Mr. Hudde, I want you to know that if you see old Russell here sneaking around your property or your truck, you go ahead and kill this stupid motherfucker right where he stands, and, well, our town will build you a statue and have a parade every year on that date." He pulled Russell in very close, shutting off his air supply a little. "You got that loud and clear, Russell?"

"Yes, sir," Russell said to the ground.

"Now take Charlie and get the hell out of here. I'll contact you if I hear anything." The sheriff pushed Russell toward the truck by the back of his neck.

The passenger door slammed shut, and the truck roared off. You could track it by the blue smoke coming out of the rusted tailpipe.

The sheriff turned to Gordan while he keyed his radio. "That's it for me tonight," he said. Gordan heard several replies saying, "Goodnight, sheriff."

"Now, Teddy tells me you're a beer drinker. Got any in there?" the sheriff said and started walking toward Gordan's room.

"Ok, I guess Teddy couldn't make it in the mob — loose lips. But, yeah — I got a few. Come on." Gordan led the way.

The sheriff pulled off the cap and dropped it into the little plastic pail; he took a swig and said, "The older couple and Kelly Tolbert said thank, you by the way, for stepping in and helping." Then he paused and said, "Now don't hold it against Teddy for talking to me. He's a good judge of character, and I value his opinion."

"What did he say?" Gordan asked.

"He said that we should be happy that you picked our town." The sheriff finished the bottle and dropped it into trash as well.

Gordan looked at his half-empty bottle and raised an eyebrow "Another?" he asked, and the sheriff shook his head "No."

"Is that it?" Gordan asked.

"That's the best you can get around here, kid. Teddy is a pillar." The sheriff seemed a bit off, and Gordan noticed.

"Just say it, sheriff. I'm known to be a straightforward kind of guy."

"The night we met, you threatened me." The sheriff started, but Gordan cut him off.

"What, I didn't..."

The sheriff held up his hand. "Wait. You said that, with one phone call, you could get all the alphabet agencies of the government to come give us a colonoscopy." The sheriff paused but held up his hand to keep Gordan from interrupting again. "No, we ...I... had it coming. The thing is — could you really do it?"

The sheriff was very uncomfortable, and Gordan could see it. "I guess I could, but I was just throwing shit at the wall, seeing what would stick. You gotta know I was wondering if you knew those guys were pulling that trick — and maybe even helping them."

"I understand. I want to think I would come up with the same thing if I were in your shoes. Here is the thing, Gordan. The reason Russell was all jacked up tonight was that his littlest kid, Debbie, is missing, and that's why I cut him some slack." He paused. "The woman is his ex, Kelly, and she's here because we think her house is a crime scene."

"Oh, crap. Now I feel kind of bad, except for the ex-wife's bloody nose," Gordan said.

"Don't," the sheriff replied. "Kelly divorced him because he stabbed a guy and was in the state pen for the better part of four years. He doesn't seem to have gotten a grip on his temper, and hanging around with that Charlie Watson and his good-for-nothing brother ain't going to help him none, neither. She told me she ran into the door frame and that's what accounted for the bloody nose."

"Yeah, sure," Gordan said sarcastically.

The sheriff grabbed the one chair in the room and slid it over. He sat down with a thud. "Damn it, but their kid is the third kid in just over two years, and I need to do something. Gordan, if you have any friends, any connections that could help... I'm begging here." He let out a deep sigh and looked down into his hat.

"Jeezus, sheriff, I'm sorry. I had no idea," Gordan said. "What about the FBI?"

"I'm smarter than I am proud, Gordan. I called them right after we came up empty with the first child. They send me reams of documents about 'profiling' and tell me to get back if anything pops up. They choose which cases are theirs very carefully, and, frankly, our cases don't fit the criteria."

"You kidding me? Didn't they send anyone?" Gordan asked.

"Nah. I wish I *was* kidding you. Oh, sure — they sent a guy. He's an alright man, but he's older and not really very, um..."

Gordan let the sheriff search for the right word, and the sheriff looked up and said "passionate."

Gordan remained silent, waiting for the sheriff to continue.

"The guy comes up from Atlanta and spews all kind of statistics. For instance, did you know that more than 200,000 kids get reported missing in America every year?"

Gordan thought the sheriff was waiting for a response, so he said "No."

"Yeah, and of them about 90% are found within the first two weeks — runaways, parental abductions, and such get solved." The sheriff was really studying Gordan.

"That leaves 10 percent, Gordan; that is somewhere near 2000 kids each year disappearing. That leaves me and my three kids out in the cold; I'm having difficulty sleeping at night. I don't know what else to do, and I'm having a difficult time looking at *myself* in the mirror, let alone some kid's parents." He ran his hand over his thinning hair and looked earnestly at Gordan.

"I'm not a cop, sheriff." Gordan immediately wanted to take it back, but he continued leaning into the sheriff's direction and maintaining eye contact.

"You must know somebody, or you must have worked with somebody that you could reach out to, right?" The sheriff was obviously grasping for straws, and it was awfully courageous for him to ask.

Gordan reached out and placed his hand on the sheriff's shoulder, saying "I *do* know people, sheriff, but I'm just thinking about if I could help you in any other ways."

The sheriff looked up. "If you can, we'll take it."

"Look, sheriff. Every time I've ever looked for someone, it was an adult, and I knew who they were and where they were last seen." Gordan pointed out. "Maybe if I can review your paperwork — you know, a different set of eyes?"

"Well, we know who the kids were, and where and when they were taken," the sheriff responded. "I could swear you in — put you on the payroll to make if official."

Gordan sat, running his hand through his beard. "Similarities among the missing children?" he asked.

"Not really," the sheriff replied. "Three kids, age's range from three to ten, two girls and one boy."

"I'll make some calls tonight and meet you at 0600hrs tomorrow morning at your office. Oh, and sheriff, I don't want any money." Gordan watched the sheriff put on his Stetson, and Gordan thought maybe he stood just a little taller when he was standing at the door.

"What are you? Some kind of rich kid?" the sheriff asked.

"Something like that." Gordan closed the door and went to one of the drawers. He pulled a go-phone package out and cut the phone from the plastic. He needed to make some calls.

Chapter Fourteen

Abrahim Saied didn't get up when Harvey Golem came out for breakfast. "I trust you rested well?" Saied said to the fat man, with absolutely no interest in hearing the answer.

Golem was eyeing the table of breakfast foods, ignoring the colorful fruits as his fat but fastidiously clean fingers selected several Danish and a cup of coffee.

"Ah, Saied. Every time I come here, my lust for life returns to reinvigorate me just long enough until the next trip." Golem paused to drop several cubes of sugar into his coffee. "As I told you, my trip needed to be short. The set demands my presence, and the charity has asked that I give a lecture in Orlando on Friday."

"It is good that you return refreshed from your short stay here, then." The reserved man rose without effort and placed his hand over his heart. "May Allah deliver you safely." Saied bowed ever so slightly and then left Golem to his breakfast.

During that moment, Golem checked the ocean and saw that it appeared calm. He was happy, as the yacht would take him to St. Thomas, where he would then catch a flight to Florida.

Saied stopped and watched the boat grow smaller to the north. It was another successful trip by an important, wealthy person and another opportunity for his operation to remain important in the American mainland.

Also holding all this video evidence on a man of Golem's stature for potential viewing by the people in the social circles in which Golem circulated would no doubt be very important one day, Saied thought.

A shorter, stockier man — even more touched by the sun and also from the Arabian Peninsula — Saied's right-hand man, Malik Saad, appeared from behind him.

"Malik, what news?" Saied looked expectantly at the man.

"The body has been fed to the fish as with all the others and the room cleaned for the next guest. A copy of the video has been retained," Saad told him.

"Very good, Saad. Have I ever told you that these people are so guilt ridden from their appetites that I feel almost penitent taking their money?" Saied turned and placed his hand on Saad's right shoulder as they returned to the main sitting room.

"Until I look at our bank accounts, that is," he chuckled as they went into Saied's own office area.

"You know my feelings, my friend," Saad said as he sat down in a plush chair. "I would wish we would lure them all here and slit their throats while they sleep — until we threw so many bodies in the ocean that we could walk to the American mainland."

"Religion and politics will be your undoing, Saad. Relax, and enjoy your time here." Saied sat at a table and pulled up his banking on a laptop. After finding the page he desired, he turned the laptop so that Saad could see it. "Where else could you live but here, take as little risk as we do, and enjoy these numbers? If it bothers you so, denounce all your properties you're currently collecting rent on, and head to Afghanistan to fight. Or, better yet, go back to London and blow yourself up in the Tube!"

"No — you know I'm not one of those. Sometimes I just tire of being a baby-sitter," Saad replied.

"Well, then quit moping around. Go work out, or go fishing. Go fuck one of those pretty girls we brought you from America." Saied looked at Saad, waiting for him to make a comment. "Stop listening to your mother."

"Ah, those harpies. They are either screaming or crying — nothing in between," Saad said.

Saied got up and looked out the window at the beautiful scene. "Cut out their tongues or feed them to the sharks, and we will get some that are more agreeable." Saied slapped Saad on the back. "Whatever is your will — just cheer up!"

"I know, I know," Saad said. "Maybe I'll go watch a movie or something." He got up and started to leave the room.

"Look at where you are, man. We could still be stuck in gloomy old London with five days of sunshine a year!" Saied called out to Saad as he headed down the open hall door.

Chapter Fifteen

Gordan looked around at the meager office of the sheriff, a Styrofoam cup steaming in his right hand.

"OK, Gordan. Stand up, and raise your right hand" the sheriff said as he reentered his office.

"Ah, shit, sheriff. I'm just not that into 'dress-right' dress anymore," if you know what I mean. No offense." Gordan stood, though.

"I'm way too short staffed for this, Gordan. I don't need a deputy to boss around. I'm looking for a second set of eyes. Let's call you an advisor to the County." The sheriff still stood, holding a badge and looking at Gordan expectantly.

"I certainly don't need a badge or a uniform," Gordan stated.

"Listen, kid. You're gonna run into more Russell Tolberts and other circumstances out there, and if you could flash a badge, it may save you some trouble. Not everyone in these parts is as affable as Teddy or old man Winston." The sheriff rested his case.

"Yeah, I get it. But no uniform," Gordan said, reaching for the badge.

The sheriff pulled the badge up and away from Gordan. "Uh, uh, uh; not just yet." The sheriff grunted. "Do you solemnly swear to uphold the laws of our County, the State, and our Country and yada-yada — so help you God?"

"Sure," Gordan said and took the badge before Big John Schmidt actually gave it to him.

"I contacted an old friend last night, and he promised me that he could get a fire lit, get you someone from the FBI who gives a damn. I have a call in to an old boss to see if I could get some favors. I'll let you know when that happens. I may need to head out of state for a few days." Gordan took a breath.

"Sure." The sheriff was paying close attention.

"In the meantime, if you have a 'war room,' with a corkboard and the case files, I would like to start reviewing them. Maybe this afternoon I can get a ride up to the latest abduction scene with one of your deputies."

"Yeah, OK." The sheriff's forehead wrinkled. "I guess you thought a lot more about this than I did."

"I didn't want to come in dead weight," Gordan told him.

"I appreciate it," Schmidt said "We don't have a room set up. My office has been kind of ground zero." He pointed at several cardboard boxes on the floor.

"Do you have the space?" Gordan asked.

"Well, yeah. We have a conference room in the back." He headed down a hallway, Hudde in tow.

The sheriff stopped outside a door and then opened it, ushering in Gordan. He hit a switch just inside, and power flowed through the gaseous fluorescent tubes, creating light; Gordan looked at the long, narrow room.

"This will work great. Can it be secured?"

"Well, the door has a lock." The sheriff raised an eyebrow.

"How about a big corkboard?" Gordan began pulling folding chairs out from under the two tables set up end to end; he turned the tables on their side and folded the legs under. He kept several chairs out but folded the rest against one end of the wall.

The sheriff returned to the room rolling a big chalkboard. When he pushed it to the opposite end of the room, he spun it around, and a corkboard appeared.

What else? The sheriff was wondering.

"Do you have a large County map that would take up most of the middle of this board?" Gordan tapped the center of the corkboard several times to show him where he thought it should go.

"I don't know how this stuff works," Gordan said "but for me, I think I need to look at it from a distance first and then boil it down to individual facts. Second, maybe you have a statistic page for each victim, and we can place a pushpin into the map at the abduction site."

"The FBI says these are unrelated. Why would we put them together?" the sheriff pointed out.

"I know — and, generally, it would make sense that different ages and sexes would be different cases. But when was the last time two or three child abductors lived in the same area and carried out abductions near the same time, in the same place? I'm sorry, but I need to look at them somehow being related; I mean — what are the odds?" Gordan watched as the sheriff pushed pins into the map and then dug into the boxes for photos of the missing children.

The sheriff stopped what he was doing and turned to make eye contact with Hudde. "I know just about every full-time resident in the County. I would be shocked to find one of them behind this."

"Good. Then, maybe we *are* looking for a drifter." Gordan paused to walk up and look at the map pushpins and the dates and times of each child's abduction. He pulled down on his beard while he thought. "Nah. Not very likely a drifter. Just look at these dates." He continued to pull down on his beard. "Maybe a delivery driver or a traveling salesman. Do they still sell vacuums and things from the trunk of a car?"

"Damned if I know; I mean, we canvassed the areas near the homes; we are talking to the very few neighbors, but I don't think we ever asked that specific question." The Sheriff shrugged his shoulders. "This is very good. I'm glad you took me up on this."

"Well, let's stay open to every possible explanation at first. You and I — and anyone else you want involved — can evaluate the validity or possibility of each. We create our own think tank, so to speak, where nobody should feel insecure about posing questions or pointing out flaws in others' theories. It's going to take a team effort."

The sheriff nodded. "Yeah, sure. I don't mind the entire staff taking part."

"OK, but they should be sworn to secrecy regarding our work. It will all start as speculative, and you don't want anything floating out there until we want it to." Gordan said.

"Of course. Everything is run that way here." The sheriff was a bit taken back by Gordan's lack of trust in his department's ability to keep secrets, but he also was aware of how quickly he reacted to the suggestion. "You're right, though; this one has to be tight."

"Sorry I have to ask — " Gordan paused, looking intensely at Big John Schmidt, waiting for a response.

"What?" the sheriff asked.

"Anyone in your department extremely interested in these cases, volunteer to help specifically on those cases, or have any troubles in the past that were walked back due to their positions in the County?" Gordan never let his gaze leave the sheriff.

The sheriff stood to his full height and took a deep breath. "No, but it never really occurred to me." He walked to the side window and opened the blinds. "If it turns out that it *is* someone from these parts...." He stood silently for 20 seconds before he released the blinds and turned back to Gordan. "They most likely won't make it to any trial."

"Save everyone tax money, and I won't lose any sleep." Gordan turned back to the map. "A ten-year-old girl, a four-year-old boy, and then a three-year-old girl. There is nothing at all similar except that they all come from poor families in your County."

"That's right. Some sonofabitch is hurting kids, and I feel like we haven't gotten one thing to work off of."

"Tell me about the abduction sites, sheriff."

The sheriff came up and stood shoulder to shoulder with Gordan, joining him in staring at the info on the board. "Sarah

DeLucia, ten years old, blond hair, green eyes. Mother died of cancer, and then the father just about drank himself to death. But there is family, so when she went missing, they all showed up and searched the farm. If there was evidence, it was trampled, and we pretty much concluded that she'd been taken walking home after spending time with a friend after school about two miles away."

The sheriff reached out and touched the picture of Timothy Graham. "Timmy Graham, almost five years old. The kid is the kindest little boy, maybe a touch slow; we think he walked right up to a car and, poof! Gone. His mom's a "recovering addict," the sheriff said, making "air quotation mark" as he spoke. "She was full-on doped up the day he went missing; she woke up the next day and couldn't find him."

"Fuck," Gordan interrupted.

"Anyway," the sheriff continued, "this latest little girl is the cutest thing you'll ever see." He poked her photo and shook his head. "Anyway, she is four and was being baby-sat by her eight-year-old sister. We feel very confident that the perpetrator walked in the back door and took her. Of course, you met mom and dad at the Suites the other night. Deputy Bronson found a footprint near the road behind the house and near a back window. I'm confident it belongs to the shithead who's responsible." The sheriff raised up his right hand, flipping it palm up at shoulder level, in a 'That's it' motion, waiting for Gordan to come up with a question or statement; there was none.

"How about Bronson and me head up to the Tolbert house, and he can show me what he found?" Gordan started walking to the front of the building before the sheriff answered.

◆ ◆ ◆

Deputy Smith pulled the cruiser up to the area that they had identified as the possible location in which the perpetrator had parked. He flipped on the light bar and stepped out of the car, directing Gordan to the small red flags that the sheriff had left.

"Weeds growing so fast," the deputy noted, "but you could see the tire tracks through the young plants and then the treads in the mud." He looked at Gordan as Gordan looked over his shoulder.

"Sure, go on," Gordan encouraged him.

"From back here in the morning light, you could make out where the plants had been pushed, and then we found a shoeprint right here on the bank." "Bronson" pointed out the flag at that point. "If you step up here, you can see the Tolbert home, even through the woods."

"OK, let's go," Gordan said, and he followed the deputy to the back of the house.

At the house, the two men examined the footprint, still visible but slowly shrinking and fading from view. They entered the home from the back door and walked the entire house.

Gordan walked out the front door and headed over to the tire swing to the left as he looked from the front door. A car slowly went past the Tolbert driveway and then traveled down the driveway to the southeast, down to the trailer nestled in the woods there. Gordan walked to the road and observed a heavy-set, short female get out of the Ford. A young boy leapt off the stairs leading to the door of the trailer and took the woman's hand, leading her toward the back side of the trailer, where Gordan observed a wooden swing.

Gordan walked down the driveway toward the trailer. There was a beat-up and rusted pickup truck, an older model Chevy Cavalier, and a Ford Taurus that he walked past before he felt the need to wave when he was noticed. The woman smiled and waved back; the child paid him no attention. Gordan stopped and looked back toward the Tolbert home; only the northwest corner of the home and the swing could be seen.

"How ya doing this morning?" Gordan asked.

"Can I help you?" the woman asked in return.

"Well, I'm with the sheriff's department, and I was wondering if anyone has spoken to you."

"Why would they?" she asked.

"Well, did you know the Tolberts up there?" Gordan pointed back up the hill past the road.

"I've never seen anyone up there; I honestly didn't even know there was a family living in that house." She gazed up the hill for a moment before ducking her head to retrieve something from within the car. She stood back up and looked like she'd remembered something, saying "Oh, I guess I've seen the older girl out on the swing on occasion." The woman raised her eyebrows at him, as if she were asking if there was anything else.

A male yelling from within the trailer made Gordan forget whatever he was going to ask, and he headed for the screen door. He called out, "Sheriff's Department." before heading inside.

"Now, who the fuck are you?" A six-foot-tall white male with a ratty-looking light-blue dress shirt, sleeves cut off at the shoulder, was standing menacingly in the kitchen area. A white female was sitting at a small dinette table in a house dress, a cup of coffee in one hand, a lit cigarette in the other. She had one bony leg thrown over the other.

"Whoa — no need to get excited. I heard some yelling and thought I needed to check it out." Gordan had his right hand in the air, in the universal "stop" sign, and his left hand firmly on the grip of his handgun sticking out the back of his pants near his spine.

A voice from outside called out, "Everything alright in there, Hudde?" Gordan realized that 'Bronson' was a good partner.

The male was peeking out a stained curtain. "Oh, the sheriff's department. Well, then, fuck it. I gotta go to work, unless y'all came looking for me?" The man in the kitchen brushed past Hudde, saying "Hey" to Bronson as he went past. Jumping into the truck, he roared out, heading north.

"Don't mind him," the woman said. "He's half asshole, other half lazy; you want some coffee or something?" She stood and looked out the window, scratching her backside without any concern for Gordan.

Gordan introduced himself. The woman set down the smoke and offered her hand. "Sue Reynolds. And the jackass that ran outta here was my boyfriend Jack."

"Well, who's the woman outside?" Gordan asked.

"Forgot she was here for a moment. That's my case worker from the State." She made a face, rolling her eyes like she'd smelt something rotten. "She's making sure we taking care of my boy." She looked out the window again. "On the swing there, that's my boy from my first marriage, Luke; he's a good boy, he really is." Sue stood and looked at Gordan, waiting patiently for whatever was coming. She'd been in the system, and she knew not to give information without a question.

"I'm sorry; I was just wondering if you'd had the opportunity to talk to the Department about the Tolbert situation?" Gordan tried to be as neutral and calm as possible, trying to give off no vibe whatsoever.

"Yeah, the sheriff himself come by the other day. I can't say I got anything else to offer," Sue replied. "You don't look like you work for the Sheriff's Department, you know?" she asked Gordan, placing her hand at her throat. She was a tall woman, near six foot, at least as tall as Gordan. Her scraggly, shoulder-length, light-brown hair needed washing, and Gordan guessed she was much younger than she looked.

Gordan walked past her and looked out the window facing northwest; he couldn't see much of the house and couldn't see the police cruiser from this angle at all.

"I'm a consultant," he said carefully to her as he headed back to the door.

"Like a psychic or something?" Suddenly she was interested.

"Yeah, that's right," Gordan said. "Could you tell me anything about Kelly Tolbert or her husband?"

"I haven't seen the husband around here in a long time," Sue told him. "Kelly is a wonderful mom. I'm sure she is all torn up right about now. She really doted on those kids; she was always outside playing with them if she wasn't working. I honestly don't know where she got the energy." She took a drag on the almost-forgotten smoke. "I have always told them kids to come down here if they needed anything while Kelly was working."

"Have they ever come down?"

"Yeah. A couple times, I seen them outside playing with Luke; I don't let him cross the street, due to all the yahoos screaming around them corners too fast, but the one girl's older and she was OK to cross, I guess."

"Well, thank you," Gordan said, and he stepped back out into the light, heading back toward the woman and Luke.

"Hey, Luke. You ever play with the girls across the street?" Gordan knelt before the boy.

"I don't play with girls," Luke laughed. "I'm five!" he screamed out proudly.

"And you are?" Gordan looked at the dark-haired woman, closer to 53, maybe 55, he guessed.

"Sorry, Karen Barston. If we walk to my car, I can get you a business card. I'm from Georgia Child Protective Services, and you are...." She looked past Gordan to the deputy standing halfway up the driveway.

"Gordan Hudde, consultant to the Pine County Sheriff's Department." Gordan extended his hand.

She lost her hand in his oversized right hand. She looked at him questioningly. "What are you consulting on right now, Mr. Hudde?"

"The missing Tolbert girl," Gordan said. "Have you been here often?" he asked.

"A couple times a month lately, a little more often a few months back" She smiled at Gordan. "That's terrible to hear — the father?" she asked.

"Do you know something?" he asked.

"No, sir. Just playing the odds." She didn't seem overly concerned.

"If you think of anything you've seen while here, please leave a message at the Sheriff's Department. Gordan was heading back to meet with Bronson.

Something nagged at the back of his mind the entire trip back into town. Gordan eventually shook the cobwebs from his mind, knowing that if it was something legitimate, it would come back to him.

Chapter Sixteen

Rehan Tambe rose from the bathroom floor of his apartment in Syosset, New York. He looked for the time, forgetting that his wrist did not have a watch; the gift his father had purchased for graduating medical school had been sold weeks ago. He sat up to look into the living room for the clock and nearly had to vomit from changing position too fast. He fought that urge and made the struggle to his feet, walking out to the kitchen; he kicked the empty bourbon bottle by accident on the way.

The water felt cool on the back of his throat, and he stood on wobbly legs holding on to the sink, as if he were on a ship in rough waters. Tambe closed his eyes and took deep breaths until he knew the water would not come back. A slip of paper caught his eye, and he slowly slid to the floor to hold that small ticket in his hands and remember the dream that had died last night.

Everything he had left was in that ticket. A small school had somehow made it all the way to the Final Four, and the Big East powerhouse that faced them was giving up a dozen points! Tambe did the research. He saw that the center on the small Midwest team was a shoo-in for the pros; he knew the team shot an incredible 78% from the free-throw line. They played well as a team even against bigger and faster opponents, and somehow Tambe knew in his heart they would lose by only single digits! All of Tambe's money problems would be covered when the Big East team would not cover the spread! He pushed the ticket into his pocket.

Tambe had a future as a doctor, but this gambling — how it excited him; how he dreamed of winning big. His parents wouldn't understand, coming from India as they had. Tambe often told his friends that his parent were Vulcans. They had no time for frivolous activities; his parents did not waste any energy on anything that was not logically thought about and planned thoroughly. No one would understand the shame that they would feel once Tambe's situation was known.

If he had been lucky enough to be born Japanese, he could have helped his parents by performing *seppuku* and spilling his own entrails to return honor to his family name. But no, his Hinduism would suggest that he had destroyed Karma by separating his spirit from his body before it was destined, further shaming his parents.

And so, now Tambe sat here shaking from the DTs and fear from what would happen when the mobsters that he owed oh-so-much money to finally caught up to him.

A horrible sound broke his train of thought, splitting his head with pain — his own phone. He looked, and it was his fiancée, Sasha — well, she was only temporarily his fiancée. There was no way she would stand by him once his deceit and addiction came to light.

Another thing that he had once held dear to him had now also been ruined by his own stupidity. The moment the ticket became worthless last night reminded him of the one time that he had cheated with another woman. The moment, the exact moment that he had ejaculated, he was sorry, so horribly sorry. Before his semen had filled the receptacle at the end of the condom, he had wanted to flee and pretend that the sex had not happened. Like the used condom, the worthless ticket reminded him of his foolishness.

He ignored the call and put on his pants. Grabbing his empty wallet, he started down the steps to the street. He couldn't bear waiting for the inevitable call from the bookie he owed so much to. The cool gray sky slapped him in the face as he stepped out onto the sidewalk of the upscale town. He headed up toward the hospital where he currently was working emergency staff. He would shower there and stay away from the apartment while he tried to think.

A large black '70s Cadillac sedan crawled to a stop near Tambe as he walked. The car came to a complete stop yards ahead of Tambe, and the oversized driver got out and held the back door open.

"You have a meeting to attend, Mr. Tambe. Get in," the big man said.

At 5'5" and maybe 145 pounds, Tambe was not about to do anything crazy. He slid into the back seat and came face to face with one of the men he often saw hanging out at the bar above the bookie in the basement below.

"I really appreciate not having to run you down." Tambe only knew him as "Tock," as in "tick-tock," because that was what he was always telling the people who owed him money.

"I was going to come see Darcy. I was…" Tambe started.

"Oh, this is beyond Darcy. Darcy sold you out to the Russians, and so you've got somewhat of a different problem now," Tock told him with a slight grin. "You fucking smart-ass smart guys come in here thinking you will just run everything, but you don't know shit."

"I know," Tambe said dejectedly. *What reason would I have to argue anything now?* He was very interested in how calm he felt now, maybe like the state a deer falls into when a lion grabs him by the throat.

Tambe had no idea where they were when they stopped; he just got out and followed Tock into the old warehouse when he was shown the open door. Tambe saw that the mostly empty warehouse had a catwalk around the second floor and an office there. The lighting was sparse, but a voice called out from above.

"That's good right there. Get our guest a chair."

Tambe looked up right into a light fixture when he tried to see who was talking; he raised a hand to hold over his eyes and reduce the glare but still could see only the outline of a man on the catwalk.

Another man came out of the shadows with a folding chair. Unfolding it, he set it behind Tambe. He was grabbed roughly; his wallet, phone, and the last gambling ticket, that small piece of paper, the evidence of Tambe's weakness, were taken from him.

"Damn, boss, one more point, and Tambe would have had a good down payment for you," one of the men said while reading the losing wager.

"Yet here we are," the man above said.

The man to Tambe's right stepped around Tambe and struck him in the stomach with a right hand that doubled Tambe and dropped him to his knees. Tambe threw up the only thing he had left after last night — about 12 ounces of water — all over the shoes of the lackey.

"Motherfucker," the man yelled out, stepping backwards first to inspect his shoes and then forward again to kick Tambe in the face.

The voice from above saved him from more. "Stop right there, and help the man to the chair." Tambe was lifted by the front of his light jacket and dropped into the chair; the man then stepped back and looked up.

"Mr. Tambe, do you know what you owe my organization now?" There was some silence while Tambe attempted to re-member his name — let alone a dollar amount.

Tambe tried to speak but croaked out only something unrecognizable.

"Let me help you. It is now more than $350,000, and as you have nothing to offer, it will quickly rise to a much higher amount. Isn't that so, Mr. Tambe?" the faceless voice taunted him from on high.

Tambe sat lifeless, holding his stomach, trying to think. When he next raised his head, he noticed that there were now three men surrounding him.

"What, what do you want?" he screamed out the best he could.

"I want to be...compensated," the voice above said as it found the correct word.

"Hey, maybe he likes to suck cock," one of the men near him said.

Another said, "Yeah — hey, Tock! Show him your dick. Maybe he can suck half a million out of you!" The laughter echoed in the empty building; it would have hurt Tambe's head if he hadn't been so concerned with everything else.

Tock stepped up and got into Tambe's space now, shaking his hips in a threatening manner.

The voice above said, "No, I think I rather see that piece of ass he has at home suck some cock. Wouldn't you guys rather see Sasha here instead?" The man made Sasha's name sound like a stripper's name — *Saaashaaa*. It frightened Tambe more than anything else had to this point.

"No!" Tambe yelled out. "Anything but that!"

A man to Tambe's right slapped him hard in the face. "Shut the fuck up," he told him.

Tock looked down at Tambe and made a very sad face, "Hey, Tambe. How's a chick with a rack that size have no ass?" Tock tilted his head back and laughed; the others joined in. "Hey, I'm not joking, guys. You should see this tiny little chick with big tits and a flat ass — it's just not right!"

"Yeah, Tambe. Them tits is fake — right?" another said to him.

"Leave her alone!" Tambe screamed, spittle flying from his mouth.

The man upstairs called out, "Hey, Ritchie — drive over to the dental school there and pick up that sexy little *Saaashaaa*. Let's us all see for ourselves."

"No, no, no." Tambe was crying now thinking of his girl-friend in the clutches of these men. "Anything," he said to the floor.

"Well, back to cock sucking for you," Tock said. Unzipping his fly, he pulled out his member and shook it for Tambe to see.

The world began to get smaller, and Tambe felt the air leave the room. A stinging slap brought him back to reality as Tock was so close now that the weeping Tambe began to open his mouth, closing his eyes to the madness.

"Come on, Doc — open wide!" Tock was laughing as his penis just about touched Tambe's lips.

"Wait!" from above. "You just reminded me Tock — there is that one other thing. What do you say, Mr. Tambe — or, should I say Doctor — would you rather select what's behind door number three?" The shadowy figure began to move to the stairwell.

"Yes, yes — please! There must be something else." Tambe was afraid to feel any sense of relief.

Tock began to tuck his penis back into his pants. "I'm hoping you fuck this up because I'm gonna tear into that piece of ass you have at home, flat or not," he said to Tambe, leaning in close.

Alexei "The Beast" Orlov was suddenly standing nearby. Tambe would have found the nickname humorous and ironic if not for the circumstances, for "The Beast" was not a big man. He walked further into the warehouse. Tock pointed a thumb in his direction, and Tambe was forced to stand on shaky legs and began to follow. A drain crisscrossed the cement floor, with a metal grate across it so that you could step on it.

The drain went straight into the wall, and Tambe realized that this was a temporary wall.

Orlov stood at the door to this structure; he turned. "Some of our business operations have been thwarted by not having the right people in certain positions."

"What would you have me do?" Tambe was curious now.

"Would you be capable of stitching up one of my men if they needed it?" Orlov asked.

"Of course!" Tambe shifted his gaze from Orlov to several of his men, wondering if this was a trick question.

"Could you handle a bullet wound, then?"

"If I had everything I needed, I think yes, then." Tambe was a bit hopeful but did not want to appear so.

"It is decided then that you work for *me*, now, Tambe." Orlov then opened the door and stepped into a room that looked every bit like an offsite surgical facility.

Tambe walked around, opening the counters and drawers. "Yes, you have everything one would need here." He looked down at the cement floor. "But I suspect your ability to ward off infection would be compromised, with the current floor and walls; it would be tough to sterilize your instruments.

"Look at that — already a productive member of our team; we are open to suggestions. Meanwhile, here is a pager. If this goes off and you are not here in 20 minutes, well, let's just say we will be inspecting your *Saaashaaa* very, very thoroughly." Orlov looked down at the little Indian doctor. "No offense, Doc, but the boys have piqued my interest, and we can always find another doctor to take over."

"No — please, no. I will take care of your medical needs; whatever it is you need, I will not fail this."

Rehan Tambe had no idea how badly he would later wish that they had just killed him instead.

Chapter Seventeen

Gordan spent the better part of the next day taking the drive to Virginia and was currently driving up Dolley Madison Boulevard, getting ready to make the turn into "The Farm," the common nickname for CIA headquarters.

After the appropriate amount of time, he was allowed to pass the security barricades and enter the halls he used to roam freely, without the babysitter who was currently walking approximately five feet in front of him.

The uniformed guard stopped outside a door, knocked once, turned, and waited. A secretary Gordan did not recognize opened the door and looked at Gordan questionably; unscheduled visits were something that wasn't done during her time stationed here.

The guard turned brusquely and marched back the way they had come, while the young redhead ushered Gordan to an inner set of doors and opened them, allowing Gordan to enter first.

"Gordan! You tired of civilian life by now?" John Stevens, the director and Gordan's former boss, stood up from behind the heavy desk. The office was well lit from natural sunlight, as the third floor office faced the morning sun. The white blinds were turned at about 60 degrees. The two men exchanged a handshake; the big black man's hand was nearly the same size as Gordan's. Hudde stepped to the window and looked out at the beautifully manicured lawn.

"Good to see you, boss, but I'm afraid I have just gotten started being a civilian."

Stevens pointed at a chair. "You need coffee or anything?" Gordan shook his head negative. Stevens said to him as he sat down, "You look like you could get back to work right away."

"You look like you've put on a few since getting the "big chair," although: 300 or 310 lbs. — what's the difference?" Gordan smiled and patted his own stomach a few times.

"Fuck you, kid. Come visit me when you're in your fifties." But the big man was smiling. His big right hand reached out and wrapped around an oversized coffee mug.

"You look more and more like a shaved grizzly bear every time I see you — do you know that?" Gordan said.

"As much as I miss you insulting me and generally being a pain in my ass, I still do a little work around here. If you're not crawling back begging for a job, why the need to drive all the way from Podunk, Georgia?" He accentuated this with a smile.

"Nice to know you're keeping tabs on me, but no; I'm here to beg for a favor. You could find a glass to break, make me crawl for some entertainment." Gordan reached up and made a fist around his chin hair pulling on his beard while he waited.

"Oh, shit — what country do you want to invade now?" Stevens looked stern over the top of the mug while he sipped.

Gordan raised his hands and shook his head "No." "Nothing like that." He shifted in his seat and pulled something from his pocket, throwing it onto the desk in front of Stevens.

Stevens picked up the badge and looked it over. "What the fuck have you gotten yourself into now? You working for Andy in Mayberry? Fuck, son — you must be beyond bored."

"Long story short, this town I'm currently building a home in has had several kids abducted over the course of the last 27 or 28 months — three kids, to be exact." Gordan shifted in his seat, sitting up straighter.

"What the hell does this have to do with you or me?" Now Stevens was getting serious. "This sounds like strictly an FBI issue."

"I know. I called in a few favors. Someone is probably there now, taking an additional look…"

"And?" The big man was now leaning over his desk; his face showed that he was working on how this problem was somehow coming into his lap.

"Seriously, boss — nothing major. I just thought I might be able to help a little if I could borrow 'The Kid' for a few hours." Gordan leaned into the desk, on the front-right corner.

Stevens leaned back into his chair, started to say something, and then stopped himself. After a brief pause, he shook his head. "I don't want to know anything else. I have to say this, Gordan: If you're going to play civilian now, then be a civilian; play by the rules, and live a quiet life" He stood up and towered over his former agent "But if you want to get back out there, making a difference and playing in the fast lane" — he paused but got no response — "I'll call down to the dungeon."

"Thank you, sir." Gordan showed respect for the man going out of his way when he certainly did not have to.

"Thank me by not starting another congressional hearing." He showed him to the door. "Hudde?"

Gordan stopped and turned in the hallway, looking back.

"I don't think the country is done with you yet," Stevens said and then turned back to his cage.

Gordan walked the hall to the elevators, where another uniformed guard was waiting for him.

They stepped into the elevator and then turned back to the door; the guard took out a key and placed it into the lit board before him.

"Lingerie, please," Gordan quipped.

The guard did not respond at all, and when the elevator stopped in the sub-basement, he stepped aside and allowed Gordan to walk past. Gordan said, "Thanks" as he walked past and headed in a familiar direction. Gordan stopped at the proper door and pressed the button, looking up at the camera above him.

"Mr. Hudde — come in. It's been a long time." A 5'7", approximately 27-year-old male with sandy-colored, shoulder-length hair opened the door.

"Cut the 'Mr.' Crap, kid," Gordan said as he walked past. "I'm not that much older than you."

"Then quit calling me 'kid,'" the man shot back.

"It's a compliment, like you're the "Billy the Kid" of technology — get it? You should be proud all the rest of us call you something honorable. Besides, most of us can't pronounce that Slavic name anyhow." Gordan hit him in the shoulder as the "kid" caught up and ushered Gordan into a room dominated by a computer chair surrounded by an array of six 30-inch monitors, with another dozen across the top of the wall.

"What the hell is so difficult about 'Mykhaylychenko'?" he said, standing with his hands on his hips in front of Gordan.

Gordan raised his eyebrows and said, "Really?" He walked over to the plush chair and said, "If you let us just call you Ivan, it would be easier."

"What favor am I doing you today?" The Kid plopped down into the plush oversized chair and spun around to the keyboard. Flexing his fingers, he said, "Give me something challenging — come on."

Gordan gave him a quick rundown of what was happening in Pine County and stood waiting for The Kid to come up with something.

"I was thinking maybe some satellite surveillance?" Gordan threw out.

"Oh, I'm not moving anything, but hold on..." The Kid's hands flew over the keys; screens flashed and were gone, replaced by others, and it almost made Hudde dizzy.

"The FBI currently has a satellite positioned to keep an eye on a Muslim group in South Georgia. I can't reposition it, but I could change resolution to include your neck of the woods." The Kid looked up at Gordan questioningly.

"That sounds good for starters," Gordan said.

"I can start conducting Internet searches for tags regarding anything that could reference child abduction, sex rings, perverts — maybe see what I can find on the Dark Web."

"What the fuck is the 'Dark Web'?" Gordan looked down and shook his head.

"For laymen, I would call it an 'unsearchable Internet.' It's a place people go to ensure that prying eyes don't find them easily. If one shares an Internet address with only people they trust, then it's close to impossible for anyone to stumble onto the site accidently. It's one of the largest sale stores for drugs and guns in the world. I don't know why that wouldn't include perverts and predator rings." Ivan turned and looked up at Gordan.

"Stevens will have my ass if I pull you from anything important, but I appreciate anything you can do to help, Mykhaylychenko." Gordan pronounced his name perfectly. Gordan patted his shoulder and headed to the door.

"Hey, Gordan," Ivan called out.

Gordan turned and looked back. "Yeah?"

"When I find something — and I will — how do I get ahold of you. Do you own a phone?"

"Send it to the sheriff of Pine County, Georgia — John Schmidt — OK?" Gordan waited for the positive response and headed back out to the elevator. When it arrived, the doors opened to another uniformed officer.

Chapter Eighteen

"Look, Agent Andrews. I'm happy to help out, but could you wait for the sheriff? He'll be here any minute. I'm sorry, but I don't think you should be back here." Deputy Goodwin was obviously unhappy with having to try to rein in the FBI agent.

Agent Andrews was staring at the evidence board that the sheriff and Hudde had put together in the back conference room. Dressed in a black jacket, white dress shirt, and black slacks, she looked every bit the cookie-cutter FBI agent stereotype. However, she was somewhat above average in looks, as she was the same height as Goodwin, and her long blond hair was pulled up into a tight bun, so tight it looked like it hurt. Her eyes were bright blue, and the tight "uniform" gave away a few secrets: She was into fitness, and she carried a full-sized .45.

Andrews turned and looked into Goodwin's eyes. "Look, deputy. I don't know him, but a guy named Hudde called in a favor, and here I am. Now I take it that your filing system here consists of these boxes?"

"Yeah, but…"

Andrews interrupted: "And the other agent sent here concluded that these possible abductions were all unrelated?"

"Well, he dealt only with the sheriff, but I think so."
Goodwin started to leave, giving up on his opposition to her
presence back here.

"Goodwin," she called out to him.

He turned at the door and called back: "Agent?"

"You guys wouldn't happen to have tea, would you?" She
didn't bother to look back at him.

He shook his head, unhappy with this turn of events. "I'll
check." He exited the room.

Agent Andrews stood before the corkboard, looking at the
pins, the sites, the town, and the roads. She pulled out her
phone and pulled up a Georgia road map to see where the
routes left the County and where they continued to.

She slipped off her black jacket and dropped it onto the
chair; then she bent and looked at the labels on the boxes. She
walked over to a table folded against the wall and dragged it
out to the center of the floor. Unfolding the legs, she stood it
up and began to get to work.

Deputy Goodwin came in with a steaming cup of water
and a box of assorted tea bags. "I didn't know what you would
want." He left it and started to walk out.

"Goodwin," she called out again.

In his head, he thought, *Now what?* But he stopped and
turned to make eye contact with her "Yeah?" He raised his
eyebrows.

"Thank you."

The steam left his bruised ego a little. "You're welcome"
he said as he exited.

Goodwin walked to the front desk and was about to let Sharon at dispatch know he was heading out when the sheriff came into the building.

"Where is she?" The big man went past Goodwin and Sharon without slowing down.

"Well, she's made herself at home in the conference room." Goodwin was a little nervous that he had made the call to complain now.

The sheriff would have slammed the door if it didn't close on pneumatic hinges. "Can you tell me what the hell you're doing here?" He walked directly up to the FBI agent, now sitting at the table.

"Trying to help you solve some cases, maybe save your ass come next election." Andrews stood and turned to face the big man. "Maybe you can step back and just say 'Thank you'?"

Schmidt just then noticed the paperwork spread across the table and everything rearranged on the corkboard "What the fuck! You can't just walk in here and start pulling apart everything we have tried to do here."

"Listen, sheriff. I've got my own cases to be working; I didn't ask to come here and babysit you backwoods, fax-using sons of bitches, so why don't you back the fuck up and start over again!" She accentuated the last point by driving a forefinger into his chest.

The sheriff was thinking about what he would do to her if she were a man when Gordan Hudde came into the door.

"Whoa — I could hear you guys a block away. This is entirely my fault; I'm the guy who made the call that caused you to be here, agent. Agent...?"

She looked past the sheriff and said, "Andrews."

"Agent Andrews." Gordan paused. "If I made a call that you're upset with and now you're here, please blame me, but we could sure use the help." Gordan threw his hands into the air in submission. "Sorry, sheriff. I thought I could make it here first."

"That would have been nice," the sheriff said.

"Why did you ask for me? I don't know who you are," Andrews said to Gordan.

"I'm sorry — Gordan Hudde," he said and extended his hand. As she took it to shake, he said, "I don't know who you are. I didn't ask for you." She lost her hand in his and shook.

"Well, why the fuck am I here and not working my own cases, then?" She was steaming.

"Because I foolishly asked for the best, I guess." Hudde began unconsciously rubbing an old wound above his left eye.

"Well...now I feel stupid." She looked at the floor. "Tell me, Mr. Hudde: How do you make a call and get me reassigned?"

He smiled at her and noticed that the sheriff was looking at him, with his hands on his hips, probably thinking the exact same question.

"Ah, what difference does it make? I did favors for someone; then they return them — right? That is how I see the world working." He looked back and forth at both of them.

"Tell me — now that were all friends — what have you found so far?"

She shook her head and ran her hand up to the top of the blond bun on top, exhaling out all the tension as she did so. "I've only just gotten started, but I can't believe this all is unrelated."

"That's exactly what agent Sanders has told me during his brief stay here."

"That's it? Didn't he offer anything else?" Andrews asked.

The sheriff, now completely calm, lost all the hostility from the moments just before. "Nah. He gave me all kind of stats on abductions *versus* all other scenarios, he offered help with some of the evidence analysis, and he gave me two more names to locate and interview."

"Anything?" She looked at him, her deep blue's burning briefly into his brain. He noticed that they looked bluer due to the whiteness of her unblemished skin; suddenly, he felt hot again.

"Well, I've located only one of them so far; neither of them reported as authorized." He suddenly felt ashamed not to have anything more.

"Well, they both have already violated conditions, so I say we find them and put the screws to them." She was taking charge, but she suddenly stopped and looked at Hudde. "Just what is it you're doing here?"

Gordan shrugged his shoulders. "Absolutely anything I can to help the sheriff stop this from happening and stop a bad guy or guys." He placed his right hand on the sheriff's left shoulder.

The sheriff nodded. "He must have some other, hidden talents — other than being handy in parking-lot scenarios," he added.

Andrews looked a bit confused but turned to Hudde and asked, "Any past law-enforcement experience that will come in handy?" She looked at Hudde with the same steely gaze that had begun to wilt the sheriff.

"Nope." Hudde stood still, staring back, both hands on his hips, and smiling. "I'm what they call... a *con-sul-tant*." He accentuated each syllable and showed her the badge.

She wasn't amused. "Then you don't need to go with us."

"I'm a lot handier than I look; after all, I got you here." Gordan followed after the two as they headed for the door. He stood momentarily watching as she got into her vehicle and the sheriff took shotgun. He thought a moment about following in his truck but gave up and jumped into the back seat behind Andrews. He hoped she would sit a little closer to the steering wheel to afford him some leg room, and, as an added plus, he wasn't sitting behind a cage as he would have been if the sheriff had been driving.

"Right," the sheriff directed Andrews' driving. "Then head north at the 20. We'll head up into the mountains, and you'll have to move slowly. Between the trucks and the ruts, it can be dangerous."

"OK" she acknowledged. "Read me the rundown on this guy." She looked over at the sheriff, and her sedan drifted across the middle lane. Jerking the wheel, she righted it. "Sorry."

"You miss the driving portion at Quantico?" Hudde asked from the back seat, having a difficult time not being in control.

The sheriff started reading out loud: "Freeling, Zach: white male, 37 years old. Kidnapping and rape pled down to lesser charge of unlawful imprisonment and sexual misconduct of thirteen-year-old female neighbor. Did his three years in Florida State Correctional and moved to Atlanta. Last checked in with Sheriff's Department there just more than a year ago, so he is in violation of yearly updates and home-address-change compliance." He looked up and turned back to look at Gordan, feeling that he would not know this info; Gordan nodded.

Andrews slowed to make the turn north and then hammered the gas to get back to speed.

The sheriff continued. "Your fellow agent had a report that Freeling is working at a logging operation about 10 more miles from here. I called ahead and spoke to the shift manager — um…a guy named 'Don.' We've had some issues there before, and he'll get Freeling out for us to talk to beyond the rest of the guys on crew there."

They drove in some silence until the sheriff warned Andrews of the turn to a dirt road just ahead.

Andrews acknowledged but failed to slow much as she rocketed off road and started up the first slight elevation change to an ever-steeper one. They hit a slight swale across the road that caused the big sedan to bottom out. The vibration hurt as it traveled up Gordan's spine.

"What part of 'slow down' didn't you get?" Gordan asked.

"Maybe we should have taken Gordan's truck," the sheriff added.

"Maybe I should get rid of all this excess weight," Andrews said, adding "Whiners."

Gordan noticed that she'd slowed considerably, though, and it was an opportune time, as she was almost forced off the dirt road by a tree-trunk-laden tractor-trailer coming fast in the opposite direction. Dirt and other debris showered the car as it zoomed past.

Gordan glanced up into the rearview mirror, where he could see Andrews' eyes focused and narrowed, looking ahead. "Hey, Sébastien Loeb — I've got a lot to live for."

"Fuck you." She glanced up into the mirror and saw him looking over her shoulder. "I don't know who that is, anyway."

"He's a champion rally car racer; you are not." Gordan really hated not being in control.

"You're going to live. Sit back and relax, you big baby. I can hear you breathing." She smiled for the first time since they'd had met, though.

Suddenly, the road leveled and opened up from the heavy trees of the woods they had been traveling through. Big rigs, bulldozers, and a backhoe lay dormant at the moment, standing near a trailer and a half dozen trucks and cars.

Andrews slid her sedan close to the trailer.

"Cops and agents always parking in the handicap spot," Gordan noted.

"I'm guessing you don't have many friends," Andrews noted.

"Hey, am I wrong?" Hudde stretched out his arms and took in a deep breath. You could smell the cut wood and wet earth; he liked it.

Two men turned and started walking in their direction. One was short and heavy set, wearing a bright hunter-orange hard hat. His crisp blue-denim work shirt, unblemished by work, proved him to be the supervisor. Following was an average-height white male that fit the description the sheriff had read on the way up the mountain.

"You Mr. Freeling?" Andrews stepped forward and extended her hand.

"Who are you?" Freeling said, looking out from under a grey hard hat, a long blond ponytail hanging out the back.

"I'm FBI agent Andrews, and that there is the sheriff of Pine County, "Big John" Schmidt, and friend. Seems the sheriff didn't know you'd been living in his County and was a bit upset. I thought I should supervise this visit."

Freeling took his hardhat off and hooked it under the crook of his right arm. "That ain't no FBI concern. What are you doing here? Sorry, sheriff. I've been living outta my broke-down car over there." He pointed at an old, beat-up Chevy Impala. "I'm waiting to get a paycheck to get into town and come see you." Freeling turned to the sheriff.

"How long you been up here?" Andrews asked.

"Sheriff, I ain't done nothing wrong for you to come looking for me, and I certainly done nothing to get no FBI agent to come talk to me." He jerked a thumb back at Andrews. "So tell me what this here visit is about. You probably gonna get me fired." He scratched his left eyebrow with his left thumb.

Andrews asked again from behind Freeling: "How long you been living here, Freeling?"

Freeling didn't turn to look at Andrews; he looked down at his beaten, steel-toed work boots and dragged a heel in the mud before looking up at Schmidt. "Sheriff?"

"Big" John Schmidt looked down at the felon. He'd dealt with all kinds, being a sheriff in a rural area; he certainly wasn't about to take any bait from this guy. "Son, why don't you just answer the agent's question?"

"We're missing a little girl?" Andrews pointed out.

Freeling felt a nerve being touched. He wheeled around, finally making eye contact with Andrews. "Great — you can read my jacket. Listen — that little girl was thirteen going on thirty. That girl teased me that entire summer, hanging around in them tight things, and ya know? I'd get you confused for a teenager before that shapely little thing. She was spilling out all over — not a skinny little bitch like you." Freeling was now nose to nose with Andrews.

"Sheriff, I apologize for not reporting to you, but go check out my car. I couldn't get there. I been here a week. Go check with the supervisor — and I ain't got no taste for little girls. I don't know what you all are looking for." He continued standing eye to eye with Andrews while addressing the sheriff.

"Anybody attest to you staying in your vehicle?" the sheriff asked.

"Everybody knows I'm staying here. Once they all leave, I can't go anywhere less it's in a 'dozer," Freeling said, matter-of-factly.

"Alright." Gordan stepped forward, finally making his presence known. "You've had your fun with the agent. Why don't you back the fuck up?"

Andrews obviously wasn't backing up and wasn't going to complain, but it was making Gordan nervous.

"Now just who the fuck do you think you are? You're not wearing a uniform or any fancy duds." Freeling stepped toward Hudde.

"This is, technically, your parking lot, isn't it?" the sheriff asked now from behind Freeling.

"I'm the department psychic," Gordan smiled.

"What the fuck you been telling them about me!" Freeling said, walking at Gordan.

"I wouldn't do that," the sheriff said, almost under his breath, while he placed a hand on Andrews' shoulder suggesting she wait.

"I told them there was a rodent under distress up here living in some guy's rectum, and look — here you is." Gordan's smiled went unchanged.

"Fuck you!" Freeling threw a giant right hook swing at Hudde, who ducked under and grasped Freeling's wrist as it went overhead. Hudde turned it over and down, pulling Freeling forward and forcing his arm to lock, elbow out.

Gordan was still smiling as he pulled down hard on Freeling's wrist with his right hand and started pushing down on Freeling's right elbow with his left. Freeling had a choice: Fall forward on his face, or lose his elbow.

His face in the dirt, mud, and gravel, Gordan dragged him a few feet before letting up. Keeping the pressure on his arm, he leaned in. "You better not be leaving anything out, or I'll be back after dark," he whispered into the man's ear.

"Alright, Gordan. Mr. Freeling got the point, I'm sure he'll communicate anything if he remembers." Gordan felt the sheriff's hand on his shoulder, and he stood up, releasing his grip on Freeling.

Freeling stood, pulled some mud from under his lip, and spit. "Fuck all you," he said, as he stooped to pick up his hard hat and then walked away.

"For the record, I don't need any help," Andrews said to both men.

"For the record," Gordan started, "I did that for me and that thirteen-year-old. You can come back and kick his ass to prove a point later if you want; I'm hungry." Gordan walked to the sedan and slid into the back seat, slamming the door closed behind him.

Andrews looked up at the sheriff. "Did you buy that?"

"Yeah, I think I did. His story sounded right, and he hasn't been seen around here till just lately."

"What's with the 'parking-lot' thing?" She nodded at the direction of her car.

"Not sure yet. I just know I would wait until I'm inside before I disagree with the man, is all." He slipped his Stetson off and headed over to the front passenger side, chuckling to himself the whole way.

She didn't get the joke but shrugged her shoulders and headed back to the car as well.

When she was strapped in behind the wheel and heading in the right direction, she said, "I don't know what you said to the man back there, but you could have seriously hurt him and hurt any case we may have needed to make in the process."

"Listen, 'Agent Uptight': You just said, 'I don't know what you said.' So I was wishing him the best in his new home. Maybe I was asking him out on a date. Maybe I was apologizing for tripping him up. The key is you don't know, so relax." Gordan tried to sit back and relax himself, but her driving wouldn't allow for it. "Besides, he isn't your guy," he said, matter-of-factly.

"How do you know?" She looked at him through the mirror.

"I just do."

The sheriff added, "As much as I enjoyed watching that" — he licked his lips and paused — "I have to admit that Andrews here is correct: From a law-enforcement angle, this needs to be done by the book so that we can get convictions in court." He turned as much as he could to make eye contact with Hudde. "That would stand up back there because he took a swipe at you first. But — just for future contacts — you need to be extra careful; many of these criminals have a better understanding of our rules than we do, and they will goad you into making a mistake."

"I hear you, sheriff."

Chapter Nineteen

Gary Reavers flipped up his laptop and turned it on. He looked at the envelope that he had written the web address on and allowed the page to load. His lips moved silently as he read. "Huh?" he said to himself as he turned off the laptop.

He walked over to his couch and turned on the TV and PlayStation, using the remotes. He'd found his friends and sent a message. Now it was a waiting game.

Reavers went outside to smoke and enjoy the late evening. He told himself that this was a pretty good gig and he hoped he could make enough money for later; it made sense that he could save, without the drugs causing him to waste money and make poor decisions. Sometimes his thoughts went to wondering what happened to the kids he was delivering, but that was counterproductive to him moving up in the organization. He was sure they would use him for more in the future, and that would bring him the money he felt he deserved.

Chapter Twenty

The sheriff, FBI agent, and Hudde sat drinking some coffee in the conference room at the back of the sheriff's office, looking up at the corkboard.

"The other non-compliant sex offender Agent Sanders told us about has been working at a farm west of here, but, according to my deputy, nobody up there has seen him for a few days. I assume your folks searched SSN trying to locate him. If he is getting paid under the table and using an alias, we won't find him anytime soon." He looked at Andrews.

"If he's doing all that, there must be a reason, and I mean nefarious," Gordan said.

"I agree." Andrews traded eye contact with both men. "How about your list or sex-offender registry?" she said to Schmidt.

"Well, they haven't been a problem for years." He waved around several sheets of information. "And this group has been here for quite a few years now; I wouldn't suspect any of them at the moment. We can run around for the next two days finding them out-and-about or wait for tomorrow afternoon, when we can find them all in one place."

"What?" Gordan stood up. "These creeps hold meetings or something?"

"Where have you been, son? Haven't you heard of NAMBLA?" The sheriff was a bit dismissive.

"Wait a minute!" Gordan was obviously shocked. "These lunatics hold a meeting out in the woods or something? Is this known by the people in the community?"

The sheriff stood, running a hand through the thinning hair on the top of his head. He was tired. "Yes, Gordan. They hold a meeting." He held up a hand to stop a Hudde protestation. "It's all legal, and they have lawyers standing by, salivating, and waiting for us to violate their 'rights.'"

Gordan tapped the map on the corkboard. "You've got this horror happening in the County, and these sick fucks are holding a meeting." He was exasperated.

"Well, I'm second guessing bringing you with me." Schmidt sat back down hard on the little metal chair, causing a shriek from the tile floor.

Andrews stood up and met Gordan at the corkboard. "No. You guys go. I want to visit each crime scene and see how many of the families I can meet."

Gordan sighed very loud and deeply and raised his right hand. "I promise to be on my best behavior."

"OK. Then I'll meet you tomorrow at the library, Gordan, and then all three of us can meet at Teddy's for early dinner — maybe sit out back and kick around what we have?"

"OK," Gordan replied

"That works for me, sheriff. I just need some addresses for my GPS," Andrews said.

"If you're going now, I would like to see how you work," Gordan said to her.

Andrews shrugged her shoulders as if she didn't care. "I'll pick you up at the inn, in about ten."

Gordan stood still for a moment too long.

"It's the only place to stay. I need to check in."

"Of course," Gordan said and turned, heading out to his truck.

◆　◆　◆

Gordan was a little more comfortable sitting in the front seat in Andrews's dark government-issue sedan. He sat quietly as she navigated the country roads. Telephone poles whizzed by on Gordan's right in staccato fashion, occasionally branching off into different directions or heading up what appeared to be a remote location up a dirt road.

Light played tricks as it flashed between trees, first dark and then bright, making Gordan feel sleepy. It was hypnotizing.

Andrews' GPS suggested a turn ahead, and she slowed the sedan. A large iron gate just off the road was attached to four strands of never-ending barbed wire that ran from post to post to the next tree line.

Gordan noticed that many of the fence posts were made from what appeared to be knotty pine branches; they certainly were not store bought.

A twisting, winding dirt road appeared in an opening in the trees; the fence turned at a right angle, heading farther away from the road. Two horses were chasing each other up and down a field, and, then, on the right, a large area opened up, holding a 1920s-looking farmhouse and several other bare wood buildings, a barn or two, and possibly a chicken coop or something, Gordan guessed.

They got out of the car and were immediately hit by the scent of a working farm, Gordan had been on many, from his youth working on dairy farms in America, to sheep herders in Western Europe, to goat herders and poppy farmers in Afghanistan; he liked it.

Andrews held her forefinger under her nose, crinkling it up, obviously not liking this at all. She looked down at her feet, making sure that nothing was messing up her boots. She looked up and caught Gordan smiling at her.

"What?" she asked.

"Nothing yet," Gordan said, still amused.

"The daughter would have been taken from the road around there." She pointed out into the distance, where you could see the road across a field and between the trees. "Her friend lived about two miles northeast of here."

Gordan followed her gaze. "She would most likely cross the open field instead of walking the road all the way to the driveway, unless she was worried about her shoes." He looked at Andrews, who was still making a "stink face."

"I'm not kidding," Gordan added. "I grew up around dairy fields, and, unless it was nice and dry, I doubt I would take a shortcut and ruin her Chuck Converses."

"Oh, OK, then; let's see if we can find the father."

"Can I help you folks!" a voice called out from the house.

A thin, frail-looking man came down the steps to the old home; his hair once was dark, but, now, it was greyer and cut close to the scalp. Gordan thought the man looked to be in his early seventies, even while he knew from reading the reports that he should be approximately fifty-two.

"Sir, my name is Susan Andrews. I'm with the FBI, and this gentleman is Gordan Hudde. He's currently working with your County Sheriff's Department." Andrews extended her right hand. Gordan noticed that Andrews was an inch taller than Anthony DeLucia. He nodded his head at the man's eye contact.

Mr. DeLucia stood still, waiting for something from the two of them.

Gordan couldn't help himself and asked, "Italians in this area seems a bit odd. When did your family migrate here?"

"Maybe you watch too much TV. My great-grandpapa and his brothers moved to New York just before the turn of the 19th century. They were supposed to make some money in America and then go back to Sicily and grow the family farm, but the story is that they came here to make something of their own." He paused. "Would you like to come in and sit down? My legs aren't what they used to be."

"Where is the rest of the family?" Andrews asked.

"They all live in towns now. Didn't like farm life as kids, so now they are raising their own closer to civilization — some in Atlanta, too." DeLucia rubbed his grey head and looked about as they ascended the four front steps.

"It's beautiful here," Gordan said.

This was the first time that DeLucia had smiled. "Yes, sir — it is, isn't it." And he nodded somewhat solemnly at Gordan.

"What exactly can I do for you two?" DeLucia said as he took a seat on an old wooden rocker on the front porch.

Gordan tested the railing before placing a haunch on it and adding weight onto it.

Andrews sat on the only other chair. "Sir, I don't know if you are aware, but there have been two other missing children since your Sarah went missing."

"'Taken,'" DeLucia interrupted.

"Sorry, sir — 'taken,' I meant to say."

"Nah, you didn't. That's what all you folks like to do — speak in ways that don't mean anything specific. *Missing!*" He spit out the word. "Like she got lost or something walking the same street or woods she walked many, many times."

Andrews regained her composure. "Sir, we would like to revisit your daughter's abduction and try to see if anything was missed before."

"Go on." He waited for something of value.

"Was there anything going on here back then that you've thought about over the last two years, that maybe you should have mentioned it?" Andrews pulled out her phone to record the conversation.

"Her mama died; anything like that happen to you as a child? Hell, it tore me up so much I slipped into drinking more and more every night; I didn't know what was going on. But I tell you this: I made sure the work got done and food was on the table every night! Nobody can tell you otherwise." He looked defiantly at the two.

"Nobody has said such a thing," Andrews assured him.

"Well, I woke up about 2:30 in the morning, and I hadn't heard her come in. So I went upstairs, and her bed wasn't slept in." He looked back and forth at the two. "I looked. I grabbed a lantern, walked around the farm, looked down in the well, and checked in the horse barn, but I couldn't find her. I walked all the way to her friend's house to check the sides of the road and all." He looked down, shaking his head. "But, nothing; we never saw her again."

"The sheriff come out?" Gordan asked.

"Sure, you can't say anything bad about Schmidt; they called in all my family, got me sobered up the best they could, and formed search parties. But, nothing." He licked his lips like he was tasting an invisible drink. "Makes me want to drink, it does. Then I get mad at myself all over again before I reach for a bottle. And I keep one right in there over the sink — tease myself, test myself." He nodded at Gordan.

"I understand, but there was nothing you could do that night. The most alert person would have been powerless; I've been there," Gordan said.

"Knowing all that help you, son?" DeLucia asked.

"Just enough to keep me right," Gordan told him.

DeLucia looked hard at Gordan. "I guess I can see that."

"What can you tell me about that night?" Andrews asked. Then she added, "Was it raining? Did your daughter take anything or leave anything that she normally would?"

DeLucia sat forward on the rocker, looked down, and rubbed his scalp, thinking. "It was later in the summer; wouldn't get dark-dark until near 8 pm, and it was nice out. I don't remember anything out of the ordinary, but I know I told the sheriff everything; honestly, it's a blurry nightmare for me now. My wife got taken from me, and then my daughter. I know life's not fair, but sometimes you wonder."

"Did your daughter walk to or from her friend's home often?" Andrews continued.

"A little less during school months but all the time during the warm summer months; I mean almost every day. Aw, hell — the way I was back then, it probably *was* every day." He looked beaten by life.

Andrews sat forward, getting into the old man's space. "Mr. DeLucia, I have to ask this: Did you ever harm your wife or daughter? Did you ever harm them during a fight or during your drinking binges?"

It didn't go as Gordan expected.

"It's a reasonable question," DeLucia said very calmly. "I didn't ever harm either of them, and I didn't start drinking until the wife was taken from me. Trust me. The sheriff asked, but even the Rodgers girl will tell you — hell, she's getting near a teenager now— that my Sarah never said nothing like that."

An old yellow Lab plodded up the staircase; it curled its greying muzzle and growled at Andrews as it went by, finally stopping and plopping down near DeLucia's feet.

"Even animals don't like the FBI." Hudde surprised himself by saying it out loud.

DeLucia made a crooked little smile while reaching down to rub behind the dog's ear.

"Where you been?" he asked the dog, who refused to answer.

"Do you mind if we keep the car here while we walk the route your daughter would have taken?" Gordan asked.

Andrews shot him a look.

"No, I don't mind, but don't hold out any hope you'll find anything. And be careful of the way people drive these roads. You'd be surprised."

Andrews stood and offered her hand again to DeLucia. "Thank you for your time, sir. We didn't mean to bring up bad memories."

Andrews and Hudde started down the dirt driveway, and Gordan heard DeLucia say, "But that's all I got."

"These boots aren't all that bad, but I didn't intend to walk four or five miles," Andrews said as the two walked past her vehicle.

"You look like some kind of 'spinner' hard-ass, so quit complaining."

"You have been staring at my ass, Gordan?" Andrews said playfully.

"I haven't. That's not what I meant, but now that you mention it, why don't you walk in front of me?" he joked back.

"I am proud of my workouts, but now I find you a bit creepy." She looked at him out of the corner of her eyes.

"Relax," he said, "You aren't really my type, so don't worry about it." Gordan began walking with longer strides.

Andrews, nearly as tall as Gordan, easily kept up.

There were two homes on the right side of the road about a half mile apart before they walked up to the Rodgers home on the same side of the road as the DeLucia home, now about two miles southwest.

Gordan stood in the yard and looked back the way they had come. "It would be so easy if you knew she was coming. If you were expecting her, there are many places to stage the abduction."

Andrews glanced up at the home. "DeLucia is right: The friend said nothing like a good reason to run away was ever offered by Sarah."

"Yeah, but..." Gordan looked 360 degrees around. "Who else would know that Sarah was going to be out walking that evening?"

A pickup truck rocketed past about 20 miles over the posted speed limit, straddling the solid yellow lines at the center of the road. They were just off the edge of the road, and yet the slipstream created by the truck still made Andrews' sport jacket ruffle in the breeze.

"A hit and run, maybe," she said out loud before she added, "No — the Sheriff's Department and the search parties would have found the body," answering her own question.

Gordan plopped down into the grass and said, "There is so much information. I feel like I should know something by now, like a pattern should be seen." He looked up at Andrews. "Why don't you go get the car and I'll sit here and think."

"If I make it to the car alone, I will end up at the Mountains Inn alone."

"Jeezus — be that way." Gordan got up and started back.

They walked the road, and darkness fell, Andrews kept her flashlight out, turning it on whenever a vehicle neared. Except for the traffic, the road seemed the only safe place from the deep, dark woods and brush that seemed to encroach on each side.

Gordan returned to his military roots and walked point. The wind began to pick up, causing the fresh leaves to rustle and shake. Evil had traveled these same roads at one time, and both Hudde and Andrews were deep in thought, trying desperately to figure out who that evil was and how they could stop it.

When they hit the DeLucia driveway, they both stopped and stood silently, waiting — waiting for something positive to come from their time spent there today.

Gordan broke the silence. "Have you ever saved any children during these cases?"

Andrews shook her head "No." Gordan felt her head shake more than he saw it. She said, "Well, I have been involved in getting a couple of kids back from a relative abduction, but never on anything like this. We found the suspects and the victims' bodies, and our investigations led to successfully prosecuted cases, but I can't offer these families any real hope."

"And what happens to most of them — the suspects?"

"Fuck, Hudde. We catch them. We don't...I don't have anything to do with the prosecution." She turned up the driveway, heading for her car. "I'm not responsible for that; when we're lucky; some crazy felon in prison fixes it for us."

Hudde slid into the front seat. The dome light did not come on automatically, which Gordan appreciated. "So that's where we are now, rooting for jailhouse justice?"

"I don't know what you've been doing your whole life, but law enforcement is all about working within the law, and we do pretty well, in my opinion." She turned over the vehicle and drove farther up the drive, where it opened enough for her to turn around.

"Do you ever get disgusted with the system?" Gordan sat back, waiting for an answer.

"I'm hungry" was her reply.

"Oh, I have a treat for you: The barbeque place we're meeting the sheriff at tomorrow..."

She interrupted: "I don't really do barbeque; do they have salad?"

Gordan frowned. "Potato, I think."

"Please." She turned to look at him as they cut through the ribbon of pavement that kept them safe from the advance of nature ever creeping, ever trying to return civilization back to the savage land it once was.

◆ ◆ ◆

The dark sedan slipped into the parking spot directly across from Hudde's room at the Mountain Suites. Andrews barely touched the gas getting up into the "H"-shaped parking lot.

Andrews slammed the lever into park and slid out into a perfect 72-degree night. She looked at Hudde over the roof. "How about something from the diner we passed back there?" She paused and then added, "I'll buy if you fly."

Gordan laughed out loud. "I haven't heard that since my Army days. OK, I'll go.... What is it you want?"

"I want a fucking salad, with dressing on the side, maybe Caesar? Yeah, that sounds good. Make that chicken Caesar salad. Don't fuck it up, Army." She dug out a twenty and handed it over the roof.

Hudde looked quizzically at her. "And for me?"

"How the fuck are you in such good shape? You're a human garbage can." She dug out another twenty and handed it over.

"Thanks, mom," Gordan said and headed to his truck. He turned it over, backed up, and headed back the way they had just come.

Gordan cruised up and turned left into the parking lot at "Gabes Diner," a place he had only come in for breakfast so far in his stay in Otter. He took the last well-lit parking spot right in front of the diner, where his truck would be easily visible from inside and from all the booths across the front of the dining area.

The bell above the door clanged several times as he opened and then allowed it to close behind him. He scanned the establishment, as he always did, and felt secure. He smiled at the man behind the grill, and he took a spot at the counter.

Gabby "Gabes" Tucker was immediately standing before Gordan; her dark-brown and pink-polka-dotted dress was covered by a yellow smock. Her dark hair was piled high on her head. Every time Gordan saw her, he felt he had somehow walked back into the 1950s.

"Hey there, Ms. Tucker." Gordan smiled up at her. She was easily 50 pounds overweight, but she had a beautiful face and wore it all well. At what Gordan guessed to be about 48 to 50 years old, she also was the most energetic and lively person in every room she ever entered. It was tough not to be pleased to see her.

"Oh, Honey." She placed a hand on Gordan's forearm "You better call me 'Gabes,' or people will talk." She made a look like it was already true and placed her hand near her chin.

She stood back and looked down at Gordan. She knew the room was paying attention "Now, I told Teddy that Mr. Hudde would grow tired of the barbeque and need a good ole-fashioned meal sooner or later."

She then leaned in very closely, like they were alone in the room. "What can Gabby do for you?" Then she stood back and winked, but she pulled out her check pad and waited for an order.

Gordan couldn't help his mind running away with some X-rated imagery of Gabby in garters and hose, spilling out from the top of a corset.

Gordan looked back up at Gabby a bit flushed. Her evil grin wasn't helping. He picked up a dinner menu and said, "Oh, I'll need a chicken Caesar salad and…"

"What size would that be?" Gabby asked.

"What?" Gordan's mind was running away "...Oh, a large, I guess." Gordan scanned the menu a little and said, "Maybe a meatloaf sandwich and some seasoned fries — to go that is."

"You hiding someone in those Suites, Sugar? The town gossips would want to know." She allowed one hip to drop lower than the other, waiting for a response.

"Oh, no, it's for a coworker. Thank you, Gabby."

"You betcha, Honey. Just sit tight." She only had to make a quarter turn to place the slip of paper onto the chrome-plated wheel that spun so that the grill master could get the order.

Gordan turned to scan the room. He saw the Tolbert woman working the floor, waiting on tables around the side of the room; they exchanged a glance before she went back to work. Another younger, skinny blonde girl, probably in her late teens, worked the front of the business, maybe five people working the place altogether.

Gordan sat facing the windows looking at nothing in particular, running his right hand down his beard, thinking. It seemed that just a few moments had gone by when Gabby tapped his shoulder and led him over to the register near the door. One large Styrofoam hot container, one large clear one with green leafy things, and several bags of dressing were sitting on the top.

"Thank the Lord you have the dressing on the side. She never would let me hear the end of it." Gordan said out loud.

"I guess there goes my offer for bringing dessert later." Gabby smiled at him as she bagged the items.

"You better be careful, young lady. One day a guy like me might just take you up on it," Gordan warned her.

"Stop teasing," she said, pushing his shoulder as he left.

Before the bell stopped dinging, and before he could set the food down on the floor of the passenger side of his truck, Gordan heard his name.

"Mr. Hudde"

Standing in the open passenger side to his truck, Gordan saw Kelly Tolbert walking across the parking lot, smoking a cigarette and waving at him.

"Yes, ma'am?" Gordan stood still.

"I'm sorry to interrupt you, but I haven't heard anything from the sheriff, and every moment seems excruciatingly long. I just had to know."

Gordan turned and offered his hand to shake; she took it and held on.

"Mrs. Tolbert, I'm really not the guy to ask, but we have gotten some additional FBI help, and I think she wants to talk to you tomorrow and then go by your place; in fact, she is next door to you at the Inn." Gordan felt a bit uncomfortable but didn't take his hand back.

She pulled his hand and placed it onto her chest, now holding his wrist tightly. "Please, please, ya'll have to promise me that you will do anything to get my Debbie back. Will you do that?"

"Of course," Gordan said.

"Do you have any children, Mr. Hudde?" She looked down at his hand, fingers sprawled across her chest. "I don't see a ring."

"Almost once, but, no, ma'am — no wife, no children."

She stepped closer to him, looking up into his eyes. She was crying without any sobs. "Promise me."

Gordan moved his hand and took her by the shoulders. "Kelly — may I call you 'Kelly'?"

"Yes, sir," she said quietly.

"Then call me Gordan, please. Kelly, I will do anything it takes to bring your Debbie home. Nothing could, no one could stop me if they would try." He was looking into her eyes; he wanted her to know it was true.

She now cried out loud and hid her head into his deep chest.

Neither Gordan nor Kelly Tolbert saw Russell Tolbert as he allowed his truck to idle past the diner. Russell's hands tightened on the steering wheel, and his knuckles turned white as he watched his ex-wife hugging that other guy in the parking lot. "You think I'm some kind of moron?" he muttered to himself as he hit the gas and reached for his cell phone.

Chapter Twenty-One

Gordan allowed his truck to idle to a stop in front of his room. Across the small parking lot, FBI agent Andrews's room light was on, probably waiting impatiently for her salad. Gordan slid out and walked around the front of his truck, intending to retrieve both meals to see if Andrews wanted company while eating.

Lights played across the two buildings as someone pulled into the parking lot. Gordan was unable to ignore it, as he was always looking at movement and noise — the curse of a hunter.

Russell Tolbert was driving into the Mountain Suites Inn, looking for the dark-blue Toyota that he knew that Hudde drove. He saw it without seeing Gordan standing behind the passenger side. Russell drove past and turned around in the back of the lot and placed it into park just as his phone rang. He picked it up and said, "Where are you?"

He looked up while talking and saw the guy just standing there, not running or hiding as he should be. Russell listened for a few moments and then said "Yup." He listened for another moment and said, "Because I can see him, that's how." He set the phone down and turned his truck off.

He climbed out and stood before his truck.

"Nice evening, isn't it, Russell." Gordan called out to him. Gordan saw no weapons except a bottle. The belt knife there, as always, though.

"You shouldn't mess with another man's wife." Russell said without real feeling.

"Well your ex-wife seems to be a very nice person, but I just don't know her all that well," Gordan noted. "Just what do I owe this meeting to?" Gordan heard an engine roaring in the background but made nothing of it.

"You sure look like you were getting to know her pretty good back at the diner short time ago." Russell tipped his head, hearing the engine getting closer; it seemed to give him strength; he took a step away from his truck and took a swig from the bottle of Jack as he did.

Gordan opened his truck and removed the bag of food; he began to walk across the small lot to the room directly across from him. Andrews opened the door and looked out. "Everything alright?" she asked, a bit concerned.

"Yeah. Someone's a bit confused." He handed her the bag and said, "Go ahead. I'll be right with you."

Gordan was about to ask Russell what he was planning when the roar of the engine seamed to reach maximum volume from out on the street, and he figured he would wait. Gordan turned to see a burnt-orange '69 Camaro roar into the parking lot, sparks flying from the front bumper as they took the rise into the parking lot too fast.

Obviously seeing Russell in the parking lot, the person driving slammed on the brakes, leaving a warm rubber smell permeating the air. The driver jumped out before the echo of the commotion had left the enclosed space between the buildings.

Gordan would have been happy to applaud the entrance except the driver was carrying an aluminum baseball bat, tapping the barrel in his palm as he said, "Hey, brother."

Charlie Watson climbed out of the passenger side of the Camaro, not as sure of himself as the Tolbert brothers, but much better than the last time Gordan had seen him.

"Listen, Russell. I know what that could have looked like back there, but I was merely picking up some dinner, and your wife was asking about the investigation." Gordan was trying hard to throw cold water on this. He walked out to confront all this head on.

"Is this the guy?" The brother was looking back and forth between Charlie and Russell. "He don't look like much — maybe a bit like somebody shaved a gorilla." He flipped the bat over to Russell, who threw the Jack bottle over to him.

Watson, now behind Gordan, called out, "This is him, Donnie — some kind of psychic working for the Sheriff's Department."

Gordan stole a glance over his shoulder at Watson, making sure he wasn't holding a weapon. Gordan took some deep and measured breaths, readying himself for a surge of activity and acquiring the extra oxygen that his body would need.

"My name is Gordan Hudde." He held out his hand to the brother. "Donnie?" Donnie took a swig from the bottle but didn't extend his hand.

"Your brother is mistaken, Donnie. What he saw was his Ex-wife upset and looking for a little condolence is all. She knows I'm working with the Sheriff's Department and she asked me; that's all." He flashed his hands palms up as if to show "Nothing to hide here." Gordan felt he was really going out of his way to "play nice" and was proud of himself.

"Having your hands all over her is that what *con-do-len-ces* means now?" Russell called out to him.

"Listen here, mister," Donnie said. "My brother is gonna kick your ass, and we're just here to make sure you don't run away." He turned and smiled at his brother. "Maybe join in if we have to."

"Well, if that's what has to be done," Gordan said to them. "I just would like to be on record saying that I got no bone to pick with you, Donnie, except what you've done to that '69 Camaro. Anyone who puts an air scoop and big slicks on an old classic like that deserves to have their ass beat.

"And, Watson, you should know better. You should have run the moment you guys pulled in here." Gordan finished, walking directly between them, the brothers to his front, Watson behind him. He flexed at his knees, pulling up on the thighs of his jeans to get a bit more room. Gordan shrugged his thick shoulders and turned his neck, stopping to look down at his black Nike combat boots, feeling in control of his body from his toes to the tips of his fingers.

"Come on, Bruce Lee — what have you got?" Donnie laughed and started to take another swig from the large glass bottle. "Go on, Russell. Kick his ass." Donnie started to tip the bottle up and lean his head back.

Gordan dipped his shoulders and transferred his weight forward while taking a half step backwards, throwing a wheel kick at Watson behind him.

Watson never saw it coming and began to fall the moment Gordan's size 13 touched his chin.

Gordan continued the momentum, spinning forward, striking Donnie across his right cheek with his own left foot.

The bottle fell and struck the ground at just about the same time as Donnie's head.

Gordan looked at the light-brown liquid pouring out onto the pavement and said to Russell, "Now that's a shame."

Russell, holding the bat much like a sword, began pushing it toward Gordan's midsection, yelling, "Stay away from me!"

Gordan grabbed the barrel of the bat and began pushing it toward Russell's stomach. Russell had to use both hands and began backing up until he backed into one of the support beams holding up the overhang to the hotel.

Having Russell's hands both tied up with holding the bat, Gordan's left hand was free; he used it to throw one, two, and then three jabs at Russell's nose. Blood flowed out over his lips, and the third strike sent Russell's head back into the beam. His knees went weak, and he dropped down. He maybe would have fallen on his face except that, after throwing the bat away, Gordan snatched him by the throat and dragged him back to his feet.

Gordan leaned in close, gritting his teeth while he spoke — in nearly a whisper — into Russell's ear.

"Listen, you stupid motherfucker. I don't like people hunting me. It makes me nervous; it makes me think I have a problem. I don't like problems; I'm a guy that gets paid to get rid of them. Are you listening to me, Russell?" He squeezed a bit harder.

Russell nodded slightly; Gordan's oversized hand was restricting nearly all the oxygen and blood flow to Russell's head.

"I know you did prison time. I know you *think* you know hard people. Hell, you may think *you're* hard. Let me tell you: I'm off-your-charts mean. I'll leave this town without any living relatives of anyone named Tolbert if I even get a whiff of Tolbert DNA anywhere near me. Do you understand me, Russell?" Gordan shook him like a rag doll. Gordan released his grip a bit, and Russell gasped for air, nodding his head in the affirmative.

Gordan was not done. "If your grandmother looks at me wrong on the streets of Otter, I'll hunt you all down. History will not know you. You got that?" Gordan released his grip totally, and Russell dropped to one knee.

Russell coughed out a "Yes."

"Get out of here before I change my mind," Gordan said, standing dangerously over him.

Russell started to walk over to his brother, and Gordan yelled "Hey!"

Russell flinched and turned to look at Gordan.

"I didn't say nothing about helping your brother or Charlie, did I?" Gordan stood with his hands on his hips.

Russell shook his head "No" and turned, walking back to his truck. It fired up and gingerly left the parking lot leaving two unconscious men, a baseball bat, and an almost-empty bottle of whisky behind.

Hudde noticed Andrews standing in the door, looking at him.

"What?" he said as he walked toward her. "I'm hungry. You didn't touch mine, did you?"

"What the fuck just happened out there" She glanced out the blinds to see if there really were two men on the ground.

"Well, that's what I am going to refer to as the 'final warning.' I hope they were listening." Gordan pulled up a chair at the small table and opened his sandwich. "Oh, good — it's still warm." He took a large bite and chewed while closing his eyes. He made some growling noises to acknowledge his enjoyment.

When he opened his eyes, Andrews was still standing over him. "You kind of come off...I don't know...maybe a little "goody-goody," but you're a crazy, mean son-of-a-bitch, aren't you?" she asked.

Gordan shrugged his shoulders "I don't like being threatened." He took another bite and pushed a couple of fries in, too. He pointed at her salad and grunted.

Andrews shook her head. "I'm not sure it's a fair fight with your background."

Gordan sipped his coffee while trying to swallow a mouthful. "First of all, there isn't a military guy worth a shit planning on a "fair" fight, and, second, you did notice they had three guys?" When she didn't answer, he just shrugged his shoulders and dug back into the meal like it might be his last.

She pulled up a chair and slowly prepared her salad, looking at Gordan from the corner of her eyes.

They heard the engine roar; the walls shook, and then it got slowly quieter as the Camaro put distance between it and the Mountain Suites.

Chapter Twenty-Two

Gordan set the coffees down on the front of the sheriff's car early the next morning. Parked in front of the library, he carried a box of pastries under the other arm.

"How aren't you 300 pounds?" the sheriff said, peeking into the pink box.

"I'm a freak of nature," Gordan replied just before stuffing an entire doughnut into his mouth. "Just wait until barbeque this afternoon." How any noise came out around the doughnut, the sheriff was not sure.

"Want to tell me about your run-in with the Tolbert brothers last night?"

"What the fuck? Doesn't anyone keep their mouths shut around here?" He shook his head "No. I've got nothing to say, but I will tell you this though: The next confrontation ends in some hospital time." Gordan took a sip from the Styrofoam cup.

The sheriff looked at him and then reached for his own coffee. "Wait until you reach 50 — it's all downhill from there."

"I see that," Gordan said, very flatly, and, when he looked up at the sheriff, he was staring a hole in him. Gordan nearly spit out his coffee. "Just messing with you, sheriff. "Come on, now. Tell me where we find these shitheels holding their child-molester meeting."

"Let's go" the sheriff said, reaching over and fixing his Stetson. He leaned into the car and set his coffee into the cup holder.

Gordan rounded the car and opened the passenger door.

"Where you going?" the sheriff asked.

Gordan stopped and looked over the roof. "What, do you want me to drive?"

"No, this is it."

"What? Come on. I thought we'd be tromping through the brush sneaking up on some cabin or something." Gordan was confused.

"Welcome to the twenty-first century and threatened law-suits from the ACLU; it's in the library."

"I ain't saying anything," Gordan said, throwing up his hands in disbelief and falling into step with the sheriff.

Gordan followed the bigger man into the quiet halls and down the steps to the musky cellar that held the paper books and magazines that Gordan loved so much as a child. He couldn't believe that some sick group was now holding a meeting in the center of such a good town. It made no sense whatsoever.

The sheriff walked through the library, tipping his hat at the woman behind the counter. He stopped at a door and took a deep breath, stretching out to his full height; the leather gunbelt creaked as he reached out for the door lever.

Three men all looked up with surprise; one shut a laptop. Gordan was not surprised but somewhat disappointed that these men were not evil looking or grotesque. They looked like every day, ordinary guys sitting around discussing the upcoming baseball season, not possibly dangerous people who shouldn't be allowed outside, let alone in a town's library.

"Sheriff," the leader said. "Is there a reason you've invaded our scheduled time here?"

"Yes Stephen. I need all of you to come down at your convenience and give us some statements at HQ sometime this week."

Stephen looked down his nose. "Should we bring attorneys?"

"If you didn't know, our town is missing some children. Guys like you are the second place to look; so I'm looking."

"I don't plan on helping you with anything if there isn't a warrant or an arrest associated with it," Stephen said. The other two looked about a bit nervously, not as sure they wanted to agitate the local sheriff as their fearless leader was.

The sheriff cleared his throat and stepped further into the room. "I'm asking because I need to clear each and every one of you before I move the investigation forward. If I had any notion it was any of you, this is not the way it would happen."

Stephen pulled out his chair and stood, making it obvious that he was making a phone call.

The sheriff addressed the other two still seated. "I don't have the manpower to chase you guys around. I never hassle you guys about anything, but this is different. Get down to see me."

"This group is about love, sheriff. We don't have any reason to come talk to you," one of the seated men stated.

"Well, then, it will be real quick, and I can focus on more important things." The sheriff spun around and started out. Gordan followed. When they'd made it into the stairwell, the sheriff stood and repeated the deep-breath routine.

"Does that help?" Gordan asked.

"Not one bit." The sheriff strode quickly up and out into the fresh air. Turning to Gordan, he said, "I could kill that mouthy one with my bare hands." He clenched his fists into the air. "I guarantee that I'll get a letter from his attorney by the end of the week."

"That's funny. When the guy told you 'It's about love,' I wanted to push past you and kick him in the face." Gordan looked up at Schmidt, waiting for a response. There was none coming. The sheriff set his jaw, and they got back into the car, heading toward the center of town.

"Sheriff" came over the radio.

"Go," he said.

"I need you to head south on Weaver for about 10 miles." It was Deputy Goodwin.

"What do you have?" The sheriff sounded a bit impatient.

"I think I found the vehicle of the other guy you were looking for."

The sheriff glanced over at Gordan and said, "The other guy the FBI told us was living here and never reported?" Then he grabbed the radio and announced "Fifteen mikes." And he switched on the lights.

Gordan called Agent Andrews and let her know where they were headed. She informed him that she had interviewed Kelly Tolbert and had looked over the crime scene with deputy "Bronson." They were incoming as well.

♦ ♦ ♦

Goodwin was standing on the small patch of green between the pavement and the overgrowth off the pavement, his vehicle's light bar switching between red and white strobes right behind him. Sheriff Schmidt pulled right in behind the other vehicle, and, before Hudde had exited the squad car, Andrews's vehicle slammed to a halt in front of Goodwin's vehicle, sliding a few feet before coming to a full stop.

Gordan suddenly felt happy that he had gone with the sheriff to the pervert meeting.

There wasn't much room on the side of the road for three official vehicles, but with three sets of lights warning traffic, you'd have to be really distracted to hit any of them, even with a third of each sticking out onto the pavement.

Goodwin led them all a couple of car lengths in front of agent Andrews's vehicle.

Goodwin cleared his throat. "I was coming up north and caught a flash of something. Turns out it was reflection." He pointed down at the ground.

Everyone noticed the tracks leading into the heavy undergrowth, and every head turned, looking into the dark woods at the same time.

Goodwin continued, "Follow me, and you will see where I caught the reflection. It's got to be a million to one. I had to be driving then; the sun had to be perfect in the sky."

The overgrowth was all brush and smaller plants. Gordan could see the plant life that hadn't sprung back from a vehicle driving over them. The larger trees were all at least 10 feet away, showing that, at one time, this path was used to move vehicles, tractors, or something. Gordan saw the vehicle and guessed that they were about a half block from the road.

"Nobody touch it," Andrews called out. She looked at Goodwin. "You haven't already, right?"

He shook his head "No." "As soon as I got the plate, I called it in. This is the closest I've been to it."

"OK, good." Andrews leaned in to the driver's side back window to try to see anything of importance. "Just a bunch of empty beer cans."

Gordan, looking in from the opposite side, called out, "I've got an envelope on the passenger floor."

Andrews pulled rubber gloves from her pocket and began pulling them on as she headed around the car, a dark-brown, ancient K-car. She slowly pushed in the button with her thumb, and the door clicked open. She glanced briefly about the interior of the vehicle before grabbing the envelope and standing up out of the car.

It was not sealed, and she flipped it open, carefully removing a triple-folded piece of copy paper.

She read from it: "I can't make it stop. I've tried, and I don't want to anymore. I got nothing to leave anyone. Ed Bain."

Andrews turned to the sheriff. "That's your missing perv — right?"

The sheriff nodded his head "Yes" and then said "Yup." He began looking around.

Gordan began walking forward. A large tree had fallen 15 feet before the vehicle; he stepped over it and continued on. The land rose to the north and seemed to get thicker with old growth, but it appeared lighter ahead.

Gordan called out to the others, "It looks like an old barn just ahead."

They all walked carefully as if they had descended into one of those Hollywood movies where the cannibals would attack at any moment.

A small, shiplap barn, worn from many years in the humid temperatures and southern sun, stood leaning lazily inside a meadow the size of a football field. The grey old wood may never have had been painted; the barn leaned slightly to the north but didn't look dangerously close to falling...yet.

Gordan strode up to the barn door. The rollers looked like they may have moved, but the lean of the barn caused the right side to dig into the earth. This was no way in.

"Over here!" Bronson called out.

A man-sized door on the correct side more than likely meant that they could gain entry.

Andrews pulled both her service weapon and a flashlight, prepared for the darkness inside.

"I can smell it," Gordan said as they staggered at the door without anyone giving orders. The FBI agent went in first, followed by the sheriff and then both deputies; Gordan stood in the sunlight.

They came out each reacting to the stench of death differently; Bronson just nodded at Hudde when he came squinting back out into the light.

Andrews holstered her weapon as she hit the fresh air; Gordan reached over and took her flashlight, heading into the barn.

Gordan closed his eyes once inside and took very shallow breaths through his mouth to do the best he could to combat the stench. He opened his eyes and took in the barren floor and several old moldy bales of straw left behind by someone long ago.

A body was hanging down from the main support beam. Blue jeans and a dark sweatshirt seemed to indicate it was a male at one time. Gordan noticed that one shoe was missing and saw that it was about four feet away from the overturned tree stumps. Gordan guessed that the dead guy had stacked the stumps together and maybe the shoe was lost when he began to struggle because death didn't come fast enough.

He grabbed the shoe-clad foot and pushed just a bit. The body was very stiff, and blowflies suddenly flew from the face in numbers. His eyes were missing, probably taken by a bird in the first 24 hours it had hung there. Gordan had seen enough, and he exited into the daylight.

"Been there a while, maybe four days to a week?" he handed the flashlight back to Andrews. "I think there are maggots in the facial wounds."

"Yeah. I've got a call in to Atlanta; see if some of our tech boys can process the crime scene."

Gordan glanced at Schmidt.

"Yes, the sheriff is OK with that." Andrews shot him a look.

"We've got to search this area, right?" Gordan looked at the surrounding country-side and scratched his head. *Who knows what that sick fuck did before he punched out?*

"Bronson! Get those Union County search and rescue guys on the horn; we need them and a cadaver dog if they got one," the sheriff yelled out when he really didn't have to.

"Yes, sir." Bronson took out his phone and walked a safe distance to have a conversation.

It took the FBI only about nine hours to get a Tech RV up there; they shut down all traffic about a half mile north and about a mile south, where detours would effectively allow locals access to their homes.

The FBI teams didn't sleep. They just set up large stadium lights and got right to work. The sheriff and his people, along with Hudde and Andrews, began a systematic search around the old barn, looking for anything that would lead them to believe that, before he hung himself, Bain had brought any of the local children to this site.

Bronson placed stakes into the area directly around the barn, marking the area that their small team had searched. Nothing had been found, but this would keep a bigger group from being in the way of the FBI team moving around the barn like ants on a drop of sugar.

When it became too dark for them to continue, the sheriff's team broke for the evening and Gordan, Andrews, and the sheriff stopped in to Teddy's for a dinner outside under the sky on the old wooden picnic table.

The team ate the food they had selected and carried outside in silence. Gordan was the first to offer a thought.

"It has to be, right? I mean, what are the odds that some pervert offed himself in the woods right here where several little kids are missing?"

Andrews wanted to speak but had her mouth full. Schmidt started. "I never take anything for granted in this job, but you are right — it looks very suspicious."

Andrews nodded in agreement before swallowing and offering, "I agree, but why would he kill himself if he was still interested in the children?"

Gordan stood up to stretch and look at the sky, now dark enough for stars to be visible. "That's just it. He couldn't stop himself; he said so himself. So he finished himself off, did us all a favor."

"If that's true," Schmidt paused to sip an iced tea, "and I hope I'm wrong, he could have had the kids somewhere else and did this away from that unknown location." He pulled a toothpick from his top pocket and went to work on something between his teeth.

Andrews nodded in agreement again. "If you get that search team up in the woods tomorrow, we can focus on homes in the area; see if anyone has seen anything, or even find the place he must have been using as home base."

Schmidt climbed out of the table and stood, allowing food to get to the bottom. He watched Gordan walking around, running his hand over his beard.

"You don't sit still all that much, do you son." He didn't mean it as a question.

"Hey, sheriff. I've got some heavy equipment and my trailer showing up tomorrow morning at the home site. I may head out there first and make sure everything is running on all cylinders before meeting you guys."

"Sure, Gordan. I appreciate everything you've done so far. If you need time, you're not punching a clock — hell, we're not even paying you. Just do what you have to. You sure don't owe me any explanation." He patted Gordan on the back as he lumbered by.

"I sure hope our boys find something," Andrews said to Gordan after the sheriff drove off.

Gordan turned to look at her just as she released the bun of golden hair on the top of her head, shaking it free of whatever forces had been holding it in place. It poured off her head and splashed over her jacket past her shoulders to the middle of her back.

She caught him looking. "It's like wearing a fucking helmet." And she smiled.

Gordan thought he may have underestimated her in the looks department, maybe because of the "I'm as tough as you are attitude" that she gave off.

"Quit staring at me." She got up and took her paper product to the garbage.

"Don't flatter yourself; I just hadn't figured you had that much hair. You really aren't my type, so relax," Gordan said.

"Funny how that changes sometimes," she said to him and started to walk to her vehicle.

Gordan jumped up into his truck and headed to the Inn; in the parking lot, he said goodnight to Andrews and headed into his room. Flicking on the TV, he caught a big breaking news story that the US government was bragging about the reduced violence on Americans at the southern border; it also seemed that fewer drug interdictions had occurred. The anchor speculated that our enforcement policies were working.

"You're welcome," he said out loud to the happy news anchor.

Chapter Twenty-Three

Sarah DeLucia sat on the beach, staring out at the slight waves and the sky that came together as one off in the distance. When her rapist was not on the island, they had come to let her roam free; it wasn't as if she could go anywhere. This place was beautiful, she had to admit. She collected shells and played wherever she wanted, as long as she never tried to enter the adult side of the island. She wondered where "here" was, anyway. She started to wonder what her friends were doing. They would be entering junior high school, maybe playing volleyball or even going to a dance or two. Then she thought of boys, and her mood darkened, because she knew what boys did when they grew up.

Boys grew up to be men, and men touched girls where they should not be touched. She had seen her parents together once when she was little. They were all naked and acting like they were having fun in the bathroom. Her mom had a talk with her about love and men and making babies; she said that they would have a talk when she was a little older, but she didn't need a talk anymore. Her mom had lied, because HE told her it was love that they shared, but it hurt — it hurt badly, and he did it anyway.

But he wasn't here now. No need to cry any more. It never helped anyhow.

Her stomach growled, and she threw a handful of sand at the water and walked inside to see the cook.

As she entered the large sitting area and bar, she came across Abrahim. He wasn't bad, but she hated Malik, who was never far behind. He looked evil, like someone out of a movie.

"Ah, the little princess." He placed his hands palms up at hip height, taking in her visage. "Tell me, is today the day you swim to freedom?" He smiled and took her chin in his hand, lifting it, forcing her to look at him. "Another young child is coming today. Maybe she is your replacement — I don't know — but maybe you could soothe her and keep her company."

"If I have to." She pulled her face away and went up to the barstool to ask for a sandwich.

"She is much younger than when you came here. I am sure she will need a friend." And Abrahim walked away to do whatever he did as warden to this beautiful prison.

Sarah could remember when she had first arrived, ten years old, drugged for days and feeling so alone. She remembered feeling like she could roll into a ball and disappear. But she couldn't, no matter how hard she tried, and now she dreamed of becoming someone who could get away from this place — Wonder Woman or Lara Croft, maybe. Her hatred for the people who'd done this to her simmered just under the surface.

Chapter Twenty-Four

The Union County search team fanned out for a second day while the FBI team packed up and began to move out. A light morning rain had left the lush green landscape completely sopped, and anyone tramping through the brush was, too. The sky was beginning to break up, and maybe the sun would be out soon — as if that could brighten the mood.

The dogs brought in with the search team were barking off in the distance, and the sound made Gordan feel both encouraged and frightened at the same time. He did not want any of the children found here, buried in some rich-earth shallow grave or stuffed into a hollow under an old, rotted, fallen tree root.

Gordan walked in the direction of the sheriff, continually looking into every dark place. John Schmidt saw him coming and held up a few moments, allowing him to catch up.

"I just don't see him putting a huge effort into hiding bodies if he was thinking about suicide," Gordan said.

"I know." Schmidt took off his hat and wiped his forehead with his forearm. "I keep praying we don't find anything."

"I've been thinking the same thing for the last two days, allows me to keep hope."

Schmidt's radio crackled, and he was requested to come back to the road by Goodwin. Gordan followed. They remained silent and vigilant the entire one-mile walk back to the pavement.

Before Gordan broke through the heavy brush near the road, he heard some yelling. As he bent and pushed through the final overhead branches, he stood straight and observed Kelly Tolbert in the street.

"Is it my Debbie? Did they find my baby?" She was hysterical, shrugging off Goodwin, who was trying to calm her.

Goodwin turned to the sheriff and said, "I tried to tell her, but..."

Tolbert wailed — that was the only way Gordan could describe it — and fell to her knees.

The sheriff helped her to her feet and took her to the rear seat of his cruiser.

"Kelly, we haven't found anything but an adult male."

She interrupted any further thought from Schmidt. "Not here. In North Carolina. I saw it on the news they pulled a little girl from a river."

"I didn't hear, Kelly. We've been up here the better part of the last three days. Let me make some calls, and I'll let you know." He lumbered off a safe distance and began making some calls.

It felt like an eternity for Gordan, waiting for the sheriff to return. He did not have the words to comfort Mrs. Tolbert, and he watched her sitting in the sheriff's car in obvious torment. He could feel the sadness emanate from her, the defeated mother who had lost a child. Not having children, Gordan could not put himself in her shoes. But standing here, watching, he felt he could break down in tears himself. He'd vowed to her before that he would help find the culprit(s) who'd done this, but now he vowed to himself that he would one day remove this scum from the face of the earth.

The sheriff lumbered back and placed his hand on her shoulder, "No, Kelly. They think it was a little girl taken from Tennessee."

Kelly began sobbing, saying, "Thank God," and then she seemed to correct herself. "Oh, no — I don't want it to be anyone's child!" and she dropped her head into her hands.

The sheriff leaned down. "We understand," he said, as he continued to pat her shoulder.

Gordan saw her body language change, and she suddenly stood up. "I'm sorry, sheriff; you have plenty to do other than console me. Please forgive me." She started walking back to her car.

The sheriff tuned and walked back to where Gordan was standing. Gordan didn't make eye contact with him, but he spoke quietly and simply. "If we find this phantom, if I am able to touch him, I will save your taxpayers money."

"That's not the right attitude, son. We follow the law, and we give a suspect all the rights that you fought for. Otherwise, where does it stop?" He patted Gordan on the shoulder as he walked away. "Doesn't mean I don't enjoy knowing it *might* happen."

Gordan walked around and got into the sheriff's vehicle, Schmidt turned to him. "I want to go back and look at some maps."

"I wish I had something else I could offer." Gordan didn't like to feel like he wasn't helpful. Even worse was that here, he felt completely helpless.

"Maybe you should just go check on the progress at your place. Could be the best thing right now."

The sheriff dropped Gordan off at his truck. Gordan went and checked out of the Mountain Inn Suites; he knocked on the door to Andrews's room. She opened the door and walked back to her almost-packed bags.

"Is that it, then? Gordan asked.

"I can't be any more help for you here. If the Tech guys can get anything, maybe I can help further." She went back to hanging a few things into a garment bag attached to the top of the bathroom door.

"Did you hear about a little girl found in North Carolina? I guess they pulled the body from a river."

She stopped and turned. "No, I hadn't heard. I'll find out and stop in on my way to Maryland; I'll let you know."

"OK. That would be good, I guess."

"You going to miss me?" she smiled as she zipped up the bag and threw it on the bed next to a matching, heavy duffle-like bag.

"It's not the way I saw this playing out — you leaving and the area still has no answers." He walked over and grabbed the duffle. Lifting it like a dumbbell, he added "Heavy."

"Extra ammo." She grinned at him. "No, just some manuals I've been looking at. I'm disappointed as well, but there seems to be so little to go on." She threw the garment back over her shoulder and followed Gordan out to the parking lot. "Look, you have my info now. If you or the Sheriff's Department find anything new, please call me. I want to help."

"Sure." Gordan threw the bag into the back seat when she opened the car door for him.

"Alright, then." Gordan shook hands with her and drove off to his new trailer.

The bulldozer had finished what would one day be the switchback driveway, now muddy and slick. The dozer stood about five stories higher up from the trailer, the steep property keeping it safe. Gordan appreciated the dozer maintaining the high ground; he looked forward to one day looking down from there from a living-room window.

Whatever activities had been going on here were now finished, and the lack of human noises was soothing to Gordan.

He looked over the new trailer, now perched upon a slab of concrete that was nearly three times the size of the trailer itself. Gordan had asked for the larger slab, because he felt that the location would be good for a barn or metal shed.

He stepped up and stomped his feet to lose any mud hanging on between the treads of his boots. He climbed the steps to the trailer and then took his boots off before entering. A linoleum floor near the door allowed Gordan to set down the boots without soiling a rug. He walked around in his socks, looking over the fixtures; it was more than satisfactory. He figured that, when the power got run from the road, he could stay in the trailer easily for three to four months, if needed. But, for now, it was dark and the well was not hooked up, so he was going to need to get water from the store.

Gordan sat in a chair and closed his eyes. He was so disappointed in this feeling of failure, and he kept seeing Kelly Tolbert racked with pain. Gordan fell asleep, but restless and uncomfortable dreams wrestled him awake.

Lights played across the windows of the small kitchen, and Gordan leapt to his feet, peeking out. A sheriff's vehicle stopped outside and Bronson hopped out; his flashlight played across the door to the trailer. Gordan slid his boots on and stumbled out the door just as Bronson stepped up onto the oversized concrete pad.

"What's up?"

"Sorry to bug you, but the sheriff thought you may want to know."

"What?"

"Another kid is missing."

Chapter Twenty-Five

Gary Reavers strummed his fingers across the steering wheel. He wasn't happy about the extra driving he was going to be doing. He wasn't happy about the location he had just used again. This meant no more from there for a least a year, maybe two — well, it better be more like three. But, he was going to be paid double for this one, and that was well worth everything else.

Reavers mind was working overtime while he headed up to Greenville, South Carolina, to catch the I-85. He thought about his other "finders." *They better start helping me out, or my pay could be really hurt.* He knew it was unwise for him to look for targets by simply trolling, and that's why they had set this up the way they had. Whoever "they" were, it was working. *What I should do is find some other good locations like this Georgia one had been. Maybe a little closer to home. This driving-the-entire-east-coast thing would get old. That last one, though, was perfect. I didn't have to do any legwork myself. Finding someone in child welfare was a real goldmine. Maybe I could get her transferred.*

Reavers drove the speed limit or very close to it. He came to complete stops. He made sure his trip was completely without incident. Visiting Bayonne, New Jersey, brought back memories. Driving near the docks and shipping yards, he remembered some days when he believed he would not live to see another. He followed the directions given to him, and, during the first moments of daylight, he pulled into what appeared to be an abandoned building. His engine slowly cooled in the sea air as he pounded on the thick wood-and-steel door.

It cracked open, and a large, bearded man was standing in the morning sun. *"Da?"*

"Um, ah, I got a special delivery for Mr. O — "

He was cut off. *"Da. bring it in."* The big man stepped aside.

This kid was a bit older and heavier than anyone Reavers had collected before; Reavers struggled but got him in the door and dropped him gently.

The obviously Russian man flipped the blanket off the kid's head and checked for a pulse.

Reavers offered the kneeling man a bottle and a new syringe still encased in plastic and said, "About 15cc's of this every two to three hours keeps him out — keeps him out, out."

"Good," the man said with a heavy accent. He turned over a thick manila envelope, which Reavers had the good sense to place firmly under his arm and head out to his car. He wondered what they were going to do with a retard, but, once safely inside his car, he peeked in to see the cash bundled with rubber bands. *What do I care?* He slid the envelope under his seat and then began the long trip back to South Carolina.

◆ ◆ ◆

As soon as the pager started buzzing, Rehan Tambe began feeling ill, but he got out of bed and dressed. He stole a glance at his slumbering, dark beauty of a fiancée and prayed that this would one day go away.

Following directions, he entered the driveway of the old warehouse, located in New Jersey, at the docks. There was a moment where he tried to feel that this would be like training for him, as if he were practicing in an emergency room. Would he have a bullet wound or broken limb to try to fix? *Yes, yes — this will be just like training. See — it won't be so bad.*

Tambe was given a chance to scrub up in a sink and put on hospital scrubs; one of Orlov's men mimicked his every move and nodded at him when he was fully dressed in scrubs, too.

He was ushered back into the room that he recognized from before. The AC was on high, and a sheet was covering a form on the operating table at the center of the room. Large lights had been installed to ensure that lighting was not an issue. He was confused: There was no anesthesia, and the sheet completely covered the small form.

"What problem do we have here? Is this a corpse?" Tambe asked as he pulled the sheet down. This was no gangster injured in a shootout or beaten in a turf dispute. This was a Down Syndrome child, maybe eight to ten years old — very much alive. Tambe looked over the body and found no obvious injuries.

"What is happening here? Why is this child here, and what can I do for him?" Tambe's fear was percolating as stomach acid began burning the back of his throat.

The other man spoke through the cloth mask as he pushed a tray of surgical tools toward Tambe. "We have orders for heart, lungs, liver, kidneys, and maybe eyes as well. We will be notified later."

"This child is fine!" Tambe stepped back. The breakfast he'd had on the way over was beginning to feel as if it would come up.

"What the fuck! I can't do this! I've taken an oath!" He looked frantically around the room. It spun from his fear, and Tambe almost lost consciousness.

"Orlov said this would happen," the other man said and pointed at a TV hanging from the wall. It came on, and Tambe watched as his precious Sasha was seen from across the street of their apartment, crossing from the living-room window to the kitchen. The camera panned down to the street, and there, sitting on the steps to the complex, was Tock. He waved.

"Choices, doc. Let's get to work." The man placed a gloved hand on his shoulder.

"I'm not a murderer," Tambe said.

"You are today, one way or the other, doc; you choose this 'tard or your girl."

Tambe couldn't see the grin through the surgical mask.

Tambe watched as a shaking hand snaked out from somewhere under his head and grasped a scalpel.

Chapter Twenty-Six

Gordan stood in the side yard of the Williams family house. It was on the north side of the road, and Gordan could see three other homes, all on the south side of the street. He could see an old pickup on blocks and a dirt bike lying on the side of one of the homes. No vehicles and no lights at the second home. A dark Ford Taurus and a little Honda at the third home. A porch light was on. He was thinking about walking down to assist Deputy Goodwin with the canvassing when Schmidt approached him.

Andrews drove up and parked in the street. She joined Gordan and Schmidt, looking for an update.

"Welcome back," Gordan said to her; she just nodded in return.

The sheriff cleared his throat. "Peter Williams is nine years old, about 5'2" tall. He has Down Syndrome. He roams these woods near his house all the time looking for animals. His mom loses track of him about two times a year, and we've all been here before, so I'm not panicking yet, but..."

"You can't wait half a day to see if we find him nearby," Gordan finished for him.

"Exactly."

"Has the kid wandered far before?" Andrews asked.

"No, not really. He just doesn't think anything of lying down and sleeping or following a dog or deer if he sees one." The sheriff placed his hands on his hips and looked down at the ground. "Jesus, if he's gone..."

Andrews looked about at the woods. "You get those Union County boys over here to help?"

"Yeah. They're on the way," Schmidt said.

"I'll head over to see what your deputy is finding at the neighbors'," Andrews said, and she started walking down the street.

"I've got something I'd like to check out. I may be gone for a day or two," Gordan said to Schmidt.

"Really? Right now?" Schmidt took his hat off. Gordan thought he looked ill.

"I don't want to get any hopes up, and it's probably illegal, so you never heard anything, but we can hope." Gordan placed his oversized hand on Schmidt's shoulder. "Don't worry. This is going to get solved."

"I wish I could be as positive," Schmidt said to him.

"Well...fake it for a bit longer." Gordan took off to his truck.

◆　◆　◆

Gordan drove through the late-night and early-morning hours. Beating rush-hour traffic, he pulled into the park at Langley and caught a few hours of sleep in the cab of his truck.

He walked through headquarters and followed another armed guard into the familiar elevator to the dungeon.

The guard stopped before the door and slid in a keycard. A loud *Click!* followed, and Gordan said "Thanks" to the guard before pushing into the room. The hum of electronics and the feel of charged air filled the room; Mykhaylychenko pushed back in the oversized desk chair and looked over the magnifying glasses that he wore down on the end of his nose.

"Gordan!"

"Hey, Kid." Gordan strode over to the console, always impressed with the array of equipment and the ease with which The Kid operated everything at once. "A little young to be going blind, or have you turned off the porn blockers?"

"Funny, man. But I started running the satellite imaging as soon as I saw you come into the lobby. What date do you want to look at?"

"What? Are you fucking psychic as well?" He didn't wait for an answer. "Yesterday, 1500hrs until about 2000 hrs."

The Russian's hands flew over the keys, and, without looking up, he said, "Big screen."

Gordan looked up and observed the lush landscape of most of Georgia from a geosynchronous orbit nearly 22,000 miles above the earth.

"Impressive, but is there any way ..."

The image tightened up to just Pine County before Gordan could finish and then tightened again to take in the town of Otter. The image began updating every minute, moving the image time forward at 10-minute intervals. Vehicles came and went from the two homes across the street. Gordan observed the dark sedan come in near 1530hrs. Gordan observed a light sedan at approximately 1740hrs at night on a road maybe a quarter mile northeast of the Williams residence. It was not moving for one sequence of photos, meaning that it was parked for 10 to 19 minutes.

The two men watched the entire stream of photos until Gordan observed the sheriff pull into the Williams driveway.

"Back to 1740hrs, Kid. That light sedan had to be it." Gordan stepped up until he was standing nearly under the large, 72-inch screen. "OK, there it is. How long can we follow it?"

"Well, I can only keep pulling back the image, and the entire time, we lose some resolution, but until or if he leaves the state." The Kid took off the glasses and focused on the screen, his fingers never sitting still on the keys. "Looks like its headed east and north."

They watched as each time the screen updated, the vehicle moved further toward the edge of the screen. "I'm going to lose it now," the Russian said, and he looked up at Gordan.

"Where is that?"

Plastic clicked and clacked, and a roadmap-overlay image dropped onto the current image. "It looks like it's on Interstate 85, heading to Greenville,"

His fingers flying, he began to narrate: "South Carolina uses highway cameras to monitor traffic. I can check into..."

he looked up at an image of live traffic and leaned forward in his chair. "They look to be about 12 minutes off from actual time, so I'll check back at this time last night and scan forward, to see if that vehicle continued forward without getting off the Interstate…"

The two men watched in silence for the next 15 minutes. Gordan was starting to get nervous. "Guy must be driving slow. There it is," The Kid pointed out.

"Any way to get a plate?" Gordan went from possible disappointment to excited.

"No, the resolution sucks on these cameras, but if we can monitor this vehicle, maybe we get lucky and he takes an off ramp."

"Don't lose him, Kid." Gordan stepped closer to the big screen.

"And there you have it," The Kid called out. "Shell station at the corner of 28th Street and Tavern Avenue at about 2012hrs!" His fingers continued flying about the keys. "I can't find an online CCTV system." Keys pounded out more; Gordan stood still, not wanting to disrupt even the air.

"It's only a year-old station, and the plans on file at the town hall show that they have a dozen cameras." The Kid looked up at Gordan.

"Nice work, Kid!" Gordan reached out and grabbed a memory stick before he started moving.

Ivan Mykhaylychenko called after him: "Don't forget to check on current date time before you start searching."

Gordan waved over his shoulder. The elevator did not move fast enough, and Gordan raised more than a few eyebrows as he hurried through the building in his civilian garb and excited attitude.

7.5 hours back to Greenville, South Carolina.

Chapter Twenty-Seven

Susan Andrews was exhausted; she had gone from a relentless two-day search near the suicide barn to the current search near the Williams home. She knew that the sheriff had confirmed in his own mind that the boy had been taken. There was absolutely no evidence yet, but she knew from his attitude, the way his shoulders had been slumping and his head hanging as he crashed the same wet woods.

Her phone rang, and she got news from the CSI boys in Atlanta.

She dropped the phone back into her pocket and turned to look for the tired big man; he was right behind her.

"News?" he asked.

"They haven't found anything belonging to anyone else, no fingerprints, no hair; the hanging will be recorded as a suicide. I'm sorry, John." She pursed her lips and looked into his face. As if on cue, the rain started falling hard again.

Schmidt looked about at the men and women from two counties stomping through the brush and saturated ground, looking at this point for a body, hoping not to find one.

"One more day, and then I'm calling this search. I'm sure this is the work of whoever..."

"I don't think you should do that, sheriff" Andrews offered. "The Williams family deserves a few more days, I think. I'll stay a few more to help in any way I can."

The sheriff looked down at her. When his hat tilted forward, extra water ran off the front brim. "OK. You're right. Thank you." He sighed deeply. "It's going to be an awful night."

◆ ◆ ◆

Gordan's truck slid sideways as he screamed into the parking lot in Greenville, South Carolina. He looked at his watch — just over six hours. He slid out of the seat and looked over the gas station. It seemed to be the standard now, several dozen pumps surrounding a small quick-mart style store, coffee, pizza, and everything twice as expensive as it should be.

The double doors slid open two seconds after Gordan got to them. In his impatience he almost kicked them in, but they finally moved, and he stormed into the foyer.

At 2100hrs, the rush of workers heading home was over, and, as it was a week night, there seemed to be little other traffic. Gordan rushed the teenage clerk behind the counter, reaching into his coat pocket as he took big strides.

The clerk shrunk back, his eyes getting big and round as a heavy-set bearded man had parked directly in front of the store and was now rushing the cash register — his worst nightmare.

Gordan flashed the Pine County badge and looked at the young man's name badge. "Ryan, I need to speak to the manager ASAP!"

Ryan's knees grew weak as the adrenaline pumped and he realized he was safe. "Holy shit, officer!"

"Son, I'm in a hurry," Gordan stated, matter-of-factly.

"Sharon called in. I'm the only one here until midnight," the kid said.

Now Gordan was taken aback. "What? Isn't that unsafe?" He shook his head at the stupidity. "I need to see your CCTV system."

Ryan began walking Gordan back into an office area and then stopped and turned. "Wait. I think I have to get a warrant or something." He looked at Gordan as if he was going to confirm the thought.

"Ryan, a child has been abducted; it may well be a life-or-death situation." Gordan placed a thick, oversized hand upon the shoulder of the younger man. "You can let them know that it was this, or I shut this place down for a day or two."

"Ah, hell," Ryan said. "They'd throw a shit fit if we closed this place for five minutes." He opened the door, and Gordan stepped into a small office with a desk, a 30-inch monitor, and a black computer rack, with the components of the CCTV system taking up three spaces on it.

"You know how to use this, kid?" Gordan looked at and then moved the mouse; a control screen popped up on the monitor.

The kid pushed Gordan's hand aside and said, "No, we're not allowed to be in here or use the camera system." He smiled slyly at Hudde. "What are you looking for?"

Gordan looked at his watch. The time on the system was only one minute off. "Yesterday evening, say...start at 2000 hrs. and go forward."

"When?"

"Eight pm and go forward." Gordan stood back, and, suddenly, 20 individual small screens began popping up onto the monitor.

Ryan looked up at Gordan. "There are about four more cameras in the back room and behind the store, but you would need to pull them up separately."

"No, this is good." The small screens did not play continuous video but appeared to update, like someone slowly flipping through still photos. When the internal clock showed 8:13 pm, a light-blue Chrysler pulled up to a pump.

"There it is. Can we blow this one up and back it up a little?" Gordan patted Ryan on the shoulder. "Good job."

The full 30 inches of screen now showed pump #8 as a very light blue; it almost looked white in certain light. The Chrysler pulled into view. And finally, maybe a break for the good guys, as a small, white male, thin build, dark goatee, and jet-black hair stood up and began to walk into the store.

"Remember this guy?"

"I wasn't working last night."

"Too bad. Follow him." Gordan looked at the screen, which changed over to above and behind the female cashier.

The male stepped up and paid cash. "Can you save this to a memory stick?"

"No, you need a password; I can play everything you need, though."

A customer came through the doors, and a bell rang. "I gotta go"

Gordan walked out to his truck and found his current burner phone. He dialed Mykhaylychenko, who not only answered at this later hour but said, "What, Gordan?"

"I just opened this phone yesterday?" He shook his head. "Never mind. I got this kid pulling the video, but he can't download it for me."

"Does the unit have a phone jack in the back?"

Gordan walked back into the small office, where Ryan was back at the controls.

"Ryan, see if you can find a plate number." Gordan squeezed his head behind the computer rack. He spoke into the phone, "Yeah, it looks like there's a phone jack back here."

"OK, Gordan," Mykhaylychenko said. "Disconnect the office phone, and plug the phone jack into the back of the main unit. Tell the kid to stop working on it; I've got it from here."

Just then Ryan leaned back and said, "Here ya go, officer." He had a big grin on his face, as a South Carolina plate number was visible.

Gordan jotted it down on an office pad, tore it off, and crammed it into his pocket.

The big monitor suddenly froze. Then it flashed and went to black before a green screen came up. Over the phone,

Gordan could hear the plastic keys being punished. A series of numbers and emblems flashed across the screen. It would flash to another and then another screen, playing out several times until the power appeared to turn off on the entire system.

The monitor went completely dark, and a small red light came on, just under the manufacturer's nifty identifying mark.

"Did you just break it?" Gordan asked into the phone.

"Oh, I'm so *fired!*" Ryan said.

And then green lights came on where red ones once shone. After a reboot, the Russian said, "It's mine."

Mykhaylychenko reassured Gordan: "You can leave, and I'll forward the video…" There was a pause. "Your phone's a piece of shit. I'll forward it to the FBI agent you've been working with."

"OK. Tell her not to open it until I get there in about two hours." Gordan patted Ryan on the shoulder. "Nice work, kid," he said as he flipped him a hundred and told him to keep the change after he'd topped off his tank.

Chapter Twenty-Eight

Sasha rubbed Rehan Tambe's back as he seemed to try to throw up his entire intestinal tract. He was beginning to shake, and she went to the medicine cabinet to get the thermometer. She walked back and placed the small rubber tip into his ear as he lay across the toilet.

"It's just over 100, honey." She walked to the kitchen and came back with a glass of water and some dry white crackers.

"I'll be OK. I think it was something I ate," Tambe offered. He climbed into bed. "I just need to sleep some more...you know that I love you — right, my Sasha?"

"Of course, my poor little man. Sleep now, and get better. I need to get to work."

Tambe reached out and gripped her wrist, a little too hard, and she spun back around as Tambe said, "Be careful out there. Please do not talk to strangers." He looked at her, and she could see the fear. "Promise me!" Tambe was frantic; she was worried that the fever was worse.

"Maybe you need to go to the hospital?" She put her hand on his forehead, as if her hand would be more accurate than the device.

"I would never do anything to harm you — I mean, not on purpose," Tambe said weakly before falling to sleep.

Sasha refilled his water glass and left it on the nightstand before heading out of the small flat.

◆ ◆ ◆

Gary Reavers awoke from a coma-like state just after the sun came up. He rolled his neck and wondered why his body ached so much from just driving — although sleeping on this couch probably hadn't helped much, either.

He picked up the beer bottle and turned on the laptop at the same time. By the time the computer re-booted, he would be done in the kitchen and bathroom. The manila envelope packed with bills was the only reminder of the last couple of days. Reavers thought he may take the next couple of weeks off, even if something came up, he felt so wiped out.

He wrapped the brick of bills with aluminum foil and placed it into the freezer with the others; he honestly did not know what he had in the "bank" now.

He walked into the bathroom, scratching his ass as he pissed into the bowl; he flushed with his foot.

For breakfast, he grabbed another beer, plodded over to the couch, and plopped down to see what was happening on the computer. He looked at the wooden table where he had scratched the info he needed to type into the address bar.

He had a message.

Oh, man — just when I thought I could take a break!

He stared at the icon, thinking that, if he didn't click on it, then they would think he hadn't seen it.

He took a sip from the bottle and then set it down on the table. *Well, maybe it will be an easy one, or just a short drive.* He positioned the arrow over the icon and clicked.

"Stop all. Plate run in GA. Go to work."

These few words struck Reavers in the gut like a sledge-hammer. He leapt to his feet and punched the air.

"No way! I didn't do anything wrong!" he screamed into the ceiling. He finished his beer and then went to shower. He'd never been to work in the three years that he had been doing this. He would need to find the address that had been given to him.

As the water cascaded over his head, he knew that this would be temporary and he would be back at it soon. That's right — no need to worry.

Chapter Twenty-Nine

Gordan pulled into the Suites thinking that Andrews would be in her room studying the info that the Russian had sent her. Her car was not there. He knocked anyway because maybe she had left her vehicle somewhere and then had been dropped off by the Sheriff's Department. But there was no one there.

He walked across the wet parking lot and was just starting to unlock the door when lights flooded the area, and he turned to see the FBI vehicle turn in at her door.

Gordan walked across the lot and opened her car door before the engine turned off; it startled her. She was a wet mess after another day out in the woods searching for a child that Gordan felt sure was no longer even in the state.

"Fuck, Hudde. Can't you wear a bell or something?" She twisted in her seat and swung her muddy boots out to the pavement.

"Sorry I just think I've gotten something; I can't wait to look it over," he said.

She rose up out of the car seat like someone near death. "Is that what that email is? I followed directions to download, but I haven't looked yet." Her dark jacket was saturated, and the bright FBI on the back stood out even more, shining in the sparse light of the parking lot. She had a watch cap over her bun of hair that Gordan knew to be tightly wound, kind of like she was, under the hat.

It started to rain again. Cold rain in the darkness, added to the low-60s temperature, was enough to sap the strength from anyone.

"Fuck" she said and started toward her room. Gordan thought she seemed to be defeated. "Grab the bag." She didn't turn around when she said it.

An obvious bottle of something was in a brown bag on the passenger side; Gordan reached in and grabbed the neck. Taking it with him, he closed the door hard, and the security system on the car honked the horn when she hit the button in her jacket pocket.

She stepped into the room and sat hard on the small desk chair near the door; in slow motion, she began to untie her boots and take them off, rolling the socks down and off.

Gordan stepped into the room. "Make yourself useful and pour a couple of fingers — for you, too," she said to him as she inspected her feet.

He walked into the bathroom and found a couple of plastic cups, pouring about two inches of the Jack Daniels into each; he brought them out and handed her one.

"Here's to whatever you got." She downed the liquid, and he watched as she reacted to it. "Another," she announced.

After she had downed the second, she slid the wet jacket onto the floor and leaned back in the chair, taking a deep breath.

"You know, I'm thinking about quitting. I'm so sick of this day after day, week after week. Seeing the gut-wrenching pain of parents and never being able to offer them anything; I just don't think I can make a career of that."

She held up her empty cup.

Gordan finished his first and then poured them both another.

"Well, it's not your fault, especially after seeing a meeting of perverts a few days ago. Our society grows softer and softer, and if you take direct, decisive action, you'd probably end up in prison."

"Right?" she said to him, nodding and now just sipping at the whisky.

"You know, I just wanted to make a difference, and the hassle that I've gotten just to be here — you wouldn't believe it. And now, I'm seriously thinking of quitting." She closed her eyes and allowed her head to tilt back, taking deep, slow breaths. "I've been thinking about this whiskey and a hot shower and at least six hours of sleep all day, I think. I think *we* haven't slept in almost three days."

Gordan looked at her and knew that they all needed to take a break and get some sleep before they made a drastic mistake or crashed a car. "Here, send this plate number to the sheriff; tell him we'll talk about it tomorrow at 0700hrs."

She fired up her phone and tapped out the message, glancing briefly at the wadded-up paper Gordan had given her.

"You know, I'm not gay," she said to him, getting up from the chair and walking into the bathroom, slugging down the last of her cup.

The shower started, and she came out and looked at Gordan.

"I never said that," Gordan offered.

"Everyone thinks it because of the way I act and because I don't do much makeup or wear skirts."

Gordan stood a bit uneasy near the door, which was still open slightly; he couldn't tell the difference between the water running from the roof and the water from the shower.

"You like women, don't you Gordan?"

"Yes, of course. It's just that my last relationship..."

"She's an idiot if she left you."

"She was killed right in front of me."

"Oh, I'm sorry." She looked at him for a few moments before continuing. "Time for you to move on, Gordan, I need to be wanted and maybe even held for a while, and you need to get beyond your past. You can't be celibate for the rest of your life."

She turned away from Gordan. A full-length mirror in front of her allowed her to keep looking at him.

"I've worked hard to look good, but if I wear anything a little tight, revealing — hell, even a skirt — some of my co-workers get offended or believe I didn't earn my position. Are you offended, Gordan?"

She undid her slacks and shifted her weight side to side as she slid the tight slacks down her legs, finally stepping out of them altogether. Her legs were long and muscular; definition showed at her calves and thighs; they were milky white and flawless. They led up to an incredibly compact behind covered by some lacy "boy" shorts that made it appear that somebody had shoved a volleyball with a crease in it into them. He watched a bit mesmerized as she shifted her weight, and he could see the muscles flex and then relax, stretching the fabric dangerously. Then she giggled a bit when she leaned the other way.

She tilted her head back and repeated the act she'd performed at Teddy's of unleashing the long, golden locks on the top of her head that were wound so tight, like the rest of her. She reached up under the locks and massaged her scalp, making the hair dance across her backside. She turned her head left and right, and then she started unbuttoning her dress shirt.

"Right now, I'm your type, Gordan," she said to him, looking at him through the mirror. "Tell me."

Gordan could feel the blood coursing through his veins; his breathing had become deeper, and he felt an overwhelming desire to crush her in his arms. Gordan turned to close and lock the door.

"You look like some Norse goddess sculptured in marble." He strode forcefully across the room.

♦ ♦ ♦

Reginald Lenard checked on the four children currently being held captive. He was not concerned with anything beyond their physical well-being, and, in that regard, everything was going fine. He managed this facility without ever losing a single child. He was very well compensated for this, and it was much better than being involved with illegal activities of his past.

In the beginning, he'd had some reservations, but with the six-figure pay, the total lack of potential injury or violence to him, and the promises of good things to come in the future, he had gotten over them. The "packages" came and went, being delivered to places that, for all he knew, were better circumstances than where these urchins came from in the first place.

He knew of western European wealth that looked to adopt children in good health from America. He knew that some children might have been destined to land in the sex trade. He also was well aware that some wealthy pedophiles did not like to travel to Third World hellholes to satisfy their sexual appetites. All these things were true, yet Lenard was able to look past them in order to make the living he thought he deserved.

A buzzer brought Reginald from his thoughts, and he strode to the monitor to observe the refrigerated truck that had backed up near the roll-up door. The driver(s) never left the cab of the trucks; they merely drove and therefore would be unable to assist in any significant way with a police investigation.

He hit the red button near the screen, and the large metal door began heading into the cylinder which hung above and accepted the door as it coiled itself inside.

The box truck with the bright vegetable paintings and the saying "Farm Fresh" painted across the side backed into the barn.

Reginald hit the green button, and the door started down. Reginald went to the back of the truck and unlatched the roll-up door. Pushing the spring-loaded door up, it finished itself, stopping fully open. Reginald grabbed the ramp and lifted and pulled it out to the ground. He walked to the front of the cool box and slid over a hidden panel. There was a padded floor and foam-lined sides. It looked pretty comfortable to Reggie.

He walked down and slid open the slide lock to one of his cells. Walking in, Reggie found a sleeping little boy around six years old on the simple cot there. The boy's eyelids could barely open, the drugs he had ingested with his dinner keeping him unconscious.

Reginald scooped him up and carried him up and into the hidden compartment in the truck.

Reggie repeated this with a small girl who'd also been sleeping throughout the entire move. He slid back the panel and flipped the small latch, making it impossible for the children to get out without assistance.

He closed the door of the truck and slid the walkway back into the bumper. Banging on the passenger door as he passed, Reginald pushed the red button near the barn door and watched the delivery truck pass into the night. Where it would go, where the children ended up, was none of his concern. Now he had just two left to babysit until the next delivery.

Back in the office, he checked for messages on the computer. There was one for him which said to immediately head to secondary location and to make sure the packages remained intact.

◆ ◆ ◆

No light was yet sneaking into the hotel room from outside, but Susan Andrews lay awake. Her head was under Gordan's right arm, and, lying on his chest, her head rose and fell with his shallow breathing. His strong heart beat loud in her left ear. She traced the bullet hole scars around Gordan's chest down to a nasty, jagged scar across his hip that had to be part of a terrible story.

"I can't feel that," Gordan said quietly, as if anyone else could hear. "Too much nerve damage."

"Let's pretend a little longer," she asked.

"OK"

"Tell me something about your childhood that you've never told anyone else."

He reached around her with his left hand and pulled her hair away from his nose and mouth; it tickled.

"I was scared all the time," he said.

"The big bad CIA agent?" She turned into him and lay completely over his chest. She began to trace the scar over his left eye down to his hairline, near his ear. "Somebody did a fabulous job here."

"I do not know how I survived that one beyond saying it was the grace of God."

"So what about the scared little boy?" She gathered her hair and began to tickle his neck with it like a feather duster.

"My parents died before I really remember. My only surviving family member, Uncle Conner, took care of me for the next several years." He paused, thinking.

"Was he mean?" she asked, stopping her playful tickling and looking into his green eyes.

"Oh, hell yeah — just not to me. I would have given anything to stay with him."

"What happened?"

"A few fights he had in town, topped off with an argument with some jackass in elementary school, and suddenly he was found unfit by the state. I was thrown into child protective services." He spit out his obvious distaste for that.

His breathing began to quicken just thinking about this.

She felt it. "I'm sorry. You don't have to continue. I don't mean to upset you."

"No, it's alright. Maybe it will explain to you why I want to help these kids we're looking for. The foster parents were short tempered and did hit us. The kids in the new school system liked to tease me. I was a runt back then. I didn't — I couldn't defend myself. I hated every minute of those days. I seemed to be afraid of everything, everywhere."

"What happened?" She laid her head onto his chest and listened, her small breasts pushed against his skin. He thought he could feel those hard, dark nipples pressing into his chest.

He ran his hand over her head, feeling the softness of her hair and the softness of the skin on her back.

"I got my ass kicked coming home from school one day right in back of a gym, and it was owned by this hard-as-nails "old school" master sergeant who just happened to be out back throwing out some trash. He bandaged me up and suggested I start coming to his gym."

"That's it? That how you became the man you are today?"

"It's funny. He was a little guy, too. I mean short but very muscular. I saw that and thought, 'Well, he's short but tough; I can be that, too.' I just started out by mimicking what I saw people doing there, and then I became a fixture, like the gym mascot or something."

After a slight pause, Gordan continued. "He got me going to one of his friends' Dojos learning Judo and some other things. I wanted to emulate the guy. He had helped me so much — so that's why the Army."

"Did you get beat up anymore?"

"Oh, quite a few times. I could really take an ass-kicking." He laughed.

She leaned back up on her elbows and slapped him on the shoulder. "This is a horrible story. I'm so sorry for you."

"I'm just relaying what happened. I gave up crying about it long ago." He smiled, showing no signs that this might still be affecting him.

She said, "OK, then. Go on."

"I had a late growth spurt, finally caught up to most kids my age, and started putting on weight. I returned the favor a few times — no more ass kickings. Now when something goes bump in the night, I sneak out and 'bump' right back."

Gordan put his hands in her hair and mussed it up more than it already was. "Old Master Sergeant Darby helped me join the Army before I was old enough," he chuckled. "That guy was awesome! See? Happy ending. Now I can't wait to see what we can do with the sheriff today."

She said, "Maybe someday we can do this again, but, for now, why you don't go get cleaned up, and I'll meet you at the office."

"Roger that," he said. "Next time, you can tell me how you became an FBI agent."

His massive shoulders flexed as he slid on the t-shirt. She watched with pleasure as the striations in the muscle tissue rolled and flexed. He had to work to pull the shirt over his extra-wide upper back, and then it unraveled and slid the rest of the way over his thinner, taut midsection on its own.

"Oh, that's boring" she replied. "I think some stories about how those scars came about might be better."

"Classified," he said, as he slid out the hotel door.

Chapter Thirty

Reavers took the phone from a young woman in her early twenties. "Yes, yes" he said into the receiver.

A strong male voice, someone who believed in himself, said, "Mr. Reavers, you are a dedicated and loyal employee, so make sure everyone there can identify you from a picture lineup. Do you understand?"

"Yes. I didn't do anything to get identified, I tell you..." Reavers started to argue his case.

"We can't take any chances now, can we? So to ensure our future success, fit in until we find out just why your plates got picked out. Maybe it was something simple like an intersection red-light camera."

Reavers made a face, as if the person on the other end could see it. "Out in the sticks? The boonies don't got no stoplight cameras, cameras." He shook his head, very unsatisfied with this explanation.

The voice was calm. "Regardless; for now, you need to fit in. Good day, Mr. Reavers."

Reavers hung up the phone and backed away into the kitchen. The people here all seemed to know exactly what they were doing. He walked out through the dining area and into the warehouse that was full of the homeless putting away their things and folding up the cots that had been their beds the night before.

Reavers was disgusted, as he never had taken charity when he was even at his worst; better to steal something fair and square than take charity. The cheerful, happy attitude of many of those "working" at this place disgusted him just as much. *Why not put your efforts into something that would help you help yourself?*

His eyes never stopped moving. He never stopped looking for a way to take advantage of someone else or to protect himself. He was a street animal, and, while his current real job had been protecting him from the reality of the rest of the world, this job put him front and center with people he used to come into contact with all the time.

For fun, he began to identify the people who were active users and what were they addicted to.

His "game" was temporarily interrupted by some greasy-looking, college-aged kid. "Hey, man. You're working today — right?"

Reavers understood what the kid was doing — trying to pressure him into some action.

"I work for the big guys in procurement; do you know what that is, is?" He accentuated it with a sneer.

The kid backed away. He was a bit uneasy running into someone not so easily intimidated by a simple question.

"I've got much more to do than slop food for some losers, so run along, along." Reavers felt the cool grip of the knife in his pocket. He pictured sticking this kid in the neck and then watching everyone else running from the bloody visage he would become as he stumbled back into the kitchen.

"What are you looking at? Run along. You want to get fired, fired?" Reavers thought the kid smelled of eggs, coffee, and grease as he got into his personal space.

The young man stepped back and laughed. "Fired! You're funny, man — I'm not a paid employee." And he stomped away.

Reavers found some stairs and walked up them. Finding an unoccupied office, he sat down and began to play a game on his phone.

◆ ◆ ◆

Nearly 350 miles to the north, Reginald Theodore Lenard looked about the barn that had held so many captive over the years he had worked for the "co-opt," as he called it. He knew that someone was scared if he was being ordered to abandon this place.

Then he had to wonder what the fear stemmed from: Had one of the men who delivered the children to him gotten caught? Was the FBI right now gathering forces in a field nearby, waiting for a judge to sign a warrant? Would he drive down the street in a few moments directly into a roadblock?

He shook his head. *No time, and not the time to worry about this; stiff upper lip and all.* He finished unhooking the computer equipment and slid his laptop into a shoulder bag to travel. He stopped at the door and looked back into the concrete-and steel structure, pulling the main breaker. The lights went off, and he slid into his car, heading west to the secondary location.

Chapter Thirty-One

Gordan showed up at the sheriff's office well before Andrews and just after John Schmidt.

They walked together back to the "war room," discussing how six hours of sleep just wasn't enough to make up for the previous three and a half days.

The sheriff put a hand on Gordan's shoulder ushering him into the room first. "How do you believe that this plate number has anything to do with the missing boy?"

Gordan walked to the corkboard, setting his coffee cup on the table corner. "John, you asked me to help, and I want to. I just can't tell you how I know what I know."

He looked closely at the newly placed pushpin at the Williams residence. "If the car I say was observed…right here just a quarter mile behind the Williams home" — Gordan pushed a new pin at that location — "and it was sitting there for somewhere near 20 minutes, would you want to speak to that person?"

"Damn straight." The sheriff looked deadly serious.

"Let me add that, other than cars in and out of the homes on the street, no other traffic was observed for a two-hour period other than our mystery car." Gordan turned and looked past the sheriff as Andrews came into the door.

Gordan couldn't help but notice now how femininely she moved and he hadn't noticed before. Now he envisioned those dancers' legs, hidden by the black slacks, instead of paying attention to her rough attitude.

"Tell me you got something good, sheriff," she said as she strode to that end of the room.

Schmidt cleared his throat and started pulling information out of a large manila envelope. "Gary Reavers; 42 years old, 5'9" tall. Here is a photo from the South Carolina DMV, and here is a photo from the New York State Department of Corrections, where he spent four years being rehabilitated." He pinned the photos to the top left of the corkboard.

When he finished, he turned, placing his left hand on his hip and his right on the butt of his handgun. "I was just getting the old 'Need to Know' lecture from your pal here, but we will need something more to get an arrest, and I can't really just go talk to him in another state based on..." — he shared a glance back and forth between Hudde and Andrews — "... nothing I can offer a judge."

Andrews nodded, "Sure, but I can go talk to him without any reason, to see what kind of excuse he had for being in your neighborhood here."

"I'm coming." Gordan stood up.

"No, I got this," Andrews said. "I've got a call into South Carolina Branch, to see if they have anything, and they will meet me there. I don't need you to beat a confession out of anyone."

Gordan shrugged his shoulders. "I've got a foundation getting poured, and I can sit and go through the case files looking for something someone missed. I actually keep getting that nagging feeling that something is staring me right in the face, but I can't grasp it."

"Everything is appreciated — anything you both can do. Thank you." The sheriff patted them both on the back as he walked back to the door. "In the meantime, I've got to let the mayor know we're all working as hard as we can." He turned and walked out the door.

When the door closed, Gordan turned to Andrews. "I do a lot more than beating information out of suspects. So, you want to rethink my offer?" He put on a big, fake smile.

"I don't think I like your choice in music. So, no — I'm just fine alone." She walked out without any fanfare or mention of the night before.

Gordan turned his right hand palm up so that he could look at his watch; he had nearly two hours to look at the paperwork before he would go meet the architect and contractor up at his home site.

Placing the four boxes before him left to right, oldest case to the most current one, Gordan began to empty the boxes and reading the files along with all the statements made by everyone ever interviewed by the Sheriff's Department.

It was like finding concealment in the brush and then waiting for your enemy to move first so that they would give their position away. Gordan felt like he could will the correct information to the surface if he concentrated hard enough. Gordan took a moment to glance at his wrist and found that he needed to be home in five minutes. He rubbed his eyes and knocked on the sheriff's office window. As he went by, he held up two fingers so that Schmidt would know he intended to be back in two hours.

Gordan slid up into his truck and wondered how Andrews was doing in the Palmetto State.

◆ ◆ ◆

Andrews' vehicle slowly stopped in what served as a driveway at the home address of Gary Reavers, just outside Columbia South Carolina. It was made up of two lanes of worn dirt obviously pounded out from years of vehicle traffic. She slid out of the car, which she had parked perfectly to see into the back yard and the front at the same time. There was no other vehicle there, and she walked a complete circle around its perimeter before heading to the door, expecting no one to be home.

Andrews paused on the front steps, looking about to see if her local counterpart would make it. She heard no oncoming traffic, so she turned back toward the front door, first loosening the pistol several times in its holster on her right hip, under her light jacket, before ringing the doorbell. It ended up being a loud and annoying buzzer that sounded as long as you depressed the button; she held it down longer than she needed to.

Nobody home.

She looked into any window that was available to her; she saw nothing out of the ordinary. She walked the grounds again, looking for any fresh digging or other oddities; she found nothing.

She was peeking into the small wooden shed when another FBI vehicle pulled into the driveway and parked behind hers. She walked over, happy to see a coworker who, hopefully, had some additional information for her.

A thin black man stood up and out of the vehicle. He was wearing the standard black suit of FBI agents everywhere, and he extended his hand. "Jones, Denny Jones." He was as young as she was.

"Andrews." She smiled a little as she always thought of *"Bond, James Bond,"* whenever anyone introduced themselves that way.

Jones ignored it if he'd noticed it. "I've got that info you were looking for; the guy works for a charity nearby, something like *The National Foundation for the Indigent and Poor.*"

"I'll follow you. Nobody is home," she said, heading to her car.

She followed, not paying enough attention to the direction, but she knew that, with an address, she would be fine later. They came up on what appeared to be an old church with a two-floor warehouse next door. Pulling in, they parked side by side. There were several shopping carts with an assortment of useless materials inside. They entered the old church first and found an earnest young man who was giving instructions to others, cleaning pots and pans in the church kitchen.

Andrews threw a thumb at her chest and said "Andrews" and then used the same thumb to point over her shoulder. "Jones," she said, and then she flashed the badge. "FBI; do you have an employee here by the name of Reavers?"

The young man pointed to the second floor next door but said nothing.

"Has he worked here long?" Andrews asked.

"Not for the church. I guess for the non-profit, but you'll have to ask him." The young man did not seem to be happy about something; Andrews chose to believe it had nothing to do with the FBI asking questions.

"Thank you," she said, and they headed across the church parking lot, looking for the entrance for the building next door. When they entered, Andrews was hit by both a musky and disinfectant odor all at once; her eyes watered.

People were stacking folded cots on the side of the wall, and someone was mopping the concrete floor.

Jones held up the driver's license photo of Reavers to the older male handling the mop, who just shrugged his shoulders without really looking at the photo.

"We're not getting anything from these people. It's a tight-knit, closed-mouth group," Jones noted.

They walked the entire first floor, poking their heads into every room and closet. A loading dock area in the back had been turned into a makeshift shower room with hoses and tarps hanging from strings as partitions.

There was a sign on the stairwell doors, saying, "Off Limits," and tape was across the railings. Andrews stepped over the tape, and Jones followed. The noise and activities of the down-stairs area fell away as they opened the door to the open floor plan of the upstairs area.

They walked quietly across the floor toward the only of-fice visible; Jones peeked into the glass and nodded, pointing inside. Andrews opened the door with her right hand on the grip of her weapon.

"FBI," she called out as she opened the door. Jones mim-icked her to the side of the small window of the office, watch-ing for any sudden movement by whoever was inside.

"What the fuck!" Reavers leapt to his feet, obviously star-tled by the intrusion. The chair he had been sleeping in fell behind him.

"Sorry, sir. Are you Gary Reavers?" Andrews stepped in and flashed her ID. "This is Agent Jones."

Jones stepped in and nodded.

"Motherfuckers nearly gave me a heart attack, attack." Reavers tried to shake the sleep from his head.

"Mr. Reavers, we have been looking for you to ask a few questions." Andrews looked over the bare room with just the one chair and a simple folding table. Somebody was obvi-ously hiding out from the activities downstairs. "We thought the upstairs was off limits. We didn't expect to see anyone up here."

"Just the homeless bastards, bastards." Reaver, now awake, was looking intensely at both agents. "Just what can I do for you, you?"

"Have you always stuttered?" Andrews asked.

Reavers folded his arms and just stood waiting.

"Are you on a break or something?" Jones asked.

"Yeah — 'or something.' Is that it, it?" Reavers walked out of the smaller office to the open warehouse floor.

"Mr. Reavers, have you been out of South Carolina recently?" Andrews stepped in front of the suspect while Jones stood off to his right.

"What is this about, about?" Reavers asked.

"Sir, I need to know if you've driven out of state over the last few weeks." Andrews was looking for body language, but a guy with the nervous ticks of this suspect sure made things difficult.

"Look, we have someone who got a partial plate and a description of a large sedan. Can you tell me the make, model, and color of your vehicle?" Andrews was lying about the plate.

"I stutter, but I'm not stupid. You already know all that shit if you're here talking to me, so what is this about, about?" Reavers looked back and forth between the two agents. Neither said anything, so he turned his back on them "See you later; I got to get back to work, work." Reavers started to walk away.

Andrews called out after him. "Have you been to Georgia lately, Mr. Reavers?"

Reavers stopped and took a deep breath while he thought. *Partial plate* stuck in his mind. "No agent, I haven't been to Georgia for a long time. Now if you have any further questions, I suggest you pick me up and then wait for my at-at-attorney." He turned and walked toward the double doors of a large freight elevator.

"Come on," Andrews said to Jones, and they walked quickly toward the back side stairwell and went through the door. They hit the door, and then Andrews started running. When they burst out into the sunlight of the access street behind the warehouse, they immediately observed the light-blue Chrysler. Andrews took a couple of pictures of the vehicle as they approached and then two close-ups of a tire. A back door opened, and Reavers started approaching them.

"Thanks, Mr. Reavers. Talk to you soon." Andrews waved over her shoulder as they walked away.

◆ ◆ ◆

Normally when Gordan was deep in thought, he would wrap his hand around his beard and pull down slightly as if he were trying to straighten it. Currently he was holding his forehead in his hands, eyes closed, trying desperately to ignite some kind of second sight. He wanted so badly to help his adopted town find their missing children. After meeting with the foreman at his home, he hurried back to continue researching.

He didn't want to mess up the documentation from each box, so he had each case spread out on the desk before him, the corresponding evidence box directly under them on the floor.

There were the initial-contact reports and then the pictures from each location; he was familiar with the Tolbert, DeLucia, and now the Williams homes and surrounding countryside. He thought maybe he should take a break from looking at documents for information he wasn't even sure was there and go look at that residence.

There was a racket coming from the front desk, and Gordan strode out to see what was happening.

Dan and Leslie Williams, the parents of missing Pete, were arguing with Mary, who was currently the secretary/dispatcher for the small office.

"I assure you the sheriff knows you are here, and he asked me if he could meet you later at your home." Mary sounded flustered and most likely had repeated this before.

Leslie Williams was a sturdy-looking woman of approximately 38 years; she wore denim bib overalls with a flannel shirt underneath; at 5'6" and about 160 lbs., she looked capable of injuring Mary if she desired. Her husband Dan was only an inch or two taller and most likely of similar weight; he was standing a bit nervously to the side.

"I understand Peter is the fourth child stolen, and I demand to know what is being done." Leslie pointed over the desk at Mary, who was nodding her head furiously in agreement.

"What's that big oaf doing — planting yard signs for his next election?" Leslie pointed at the ceiling; her husband placed a hand on her shoulder, and she shrugged it off. "Get off me!" Dan shrunk from her righteous anger.

"Honey, let's go wait at home," Dan said a bit sheepishly, taking a step toward the doors.

"I don't know if you remember me. Gordan Hudde; you're the Williamses, Leslie and Dan." Gordan extended his right hand; only Dan took it. "Listen, I'm only a consultant brought in by the sheriff, but if I could help you in any way, well, maybe we can go back to the office area."

Leslie studied Gordan. "You sure don't look like any lawman I've ever seen, why — aren't you the psychic?" She closed her eyes and took a deep breath, looking for composure.

"If that were the case, I'd have met you at the door; now, isn't that right, Dan?" Gordan said.

Dan said, "I reckon so."

Gordan continued by leaning in as if Mary couldn't hear. Both Dan and Leslie unconsciously leaned in similarly. "If you come with me, I'll take you to our command center, and I don't think you all should be in there, but maybe we can talk."

The two followed Gordan down the hall and then across the back of the building to the first of two doors leading into the conference room. He turned to them and swore them to staying at the far end of the room and to keep anything learned here strictly confidential. After all, other family information was kept inside. They both nodded their heads in agreement and followed Gordan inside. Out in the front of the building, Mary craned her neck to watch the three turn the corner, and then she sat back down and took a deep breath.

Gordan allowed the Williamses to take in the corkboard filled with the map and the photos, and then the table full of glossy photos that Gordan had just been reviewing along with many of the other documents.

"First, I'm a consultant the sheriff hired. I have some background with many other government agencies, and the sheriff thought that I may be able to get everyone working on the same page. Remember, I'm not sure I should be telling you this information."

Leslie Williams put her hand on Gordan's bicep. "Please — we will keep it a secret; our boy...." She shrugged her shoulders and closed her eyes, unable to continue.

"It's OK, Mrs. Williams; I just need you to know that we are doing everything we can to find your boy." Gordan placed his hand on her shoulder and made eye contact with Dan. "I cannot promise you anything — understand that. But we think we have a lead. We have been working almost non-stop for the last four days, but we are as desperate as you to find out what has happened here and to bring justice; I can and will promise you that."

Mrs. Williams started crying, clasping her hand to her mouth as if she could make it stop. "I'm sorry. I'm sorry. I've been selfish, but what about the other children?"

Gordan shook his head. "We just don't know if all these disappearances are related. It's my guess that they are, but right now the FBI says, "No.'"

"Tell the sheriff I'm sorry for taking up any of his time. Please find my boy. Find our children; please go back to work." Leslie grabbed Dan by the arm and pulled him out of the room and headed toward the front door. Mary stood as she saw the Williamses heading up the hallway, thinking that there would be more of an outburst, but they strode past silently. Leslie stopped at the door and turned to address Mary; she apologized, asking that Mary tell the sheriff not to go out to the house unless there was some additional new information.

Gordan dropped down into the chair he had been occupying for several hours. This was the second woman, the second mother, to whom he had made promises; he hoped the Graham woman would be different, and he walked out to his truck, just in time to see the sheriff pull into the parking lot.

Chapter Thirty-Two

"What have you heard from South Carolina?" Schmidt asked as soon as he was out of the vehicle. He didn't bother to put on his Stetson as he headed toward the front door of his office. He put a hand on Gordan's shoulder as he walked past him, pulling him along.

"I haven't heard anything. I was hoping you had." Gordan turned and followed the sheriff.

The sheriff walked straight back to the coffee, filling a black mug with a sheriff's star emblem; he slid it to Gordan without asking and then filled his own "world's best sheriff" oversized mug. Then he walked into the conference room, turning on the lights and stepping aside to allow Gordan in before closing the door.

Schmidt looked over the paperwork and photos spread over the table. "Find anything interesting?"

Gordan walked back over to the table full of documents he had been studying for the better part of the day. "I want to say, 'Yes.' I know that there is something in this pile…" — he knocked the table with his knuckles to emphasize the point — "…I know I've probably looked at it but I can't see it yet." He shook his head, upset that he had not found what he was looking for.

Schmidt took a sip of coffee, pulled the phone from the wall, and pulled on the cord from the back, seeing if it would reach the table. It did, so he hit "Speaker" and started dialing.

Gordan reached over into the neatest pile of documents and pulled them toward him. He hadn't looked at the Williams case yet because — well, because he had been there from the first night. What could he possibly find out?

The phone was ringing. It stopped when he heard "Andrews."

"Andrews, its sheriff Schmidt with Hudde here. We both were wondering if you found anything." He began to pace back and forth before the phone, making eye contact when he would turn and come back toward where Hudde was sitting.

"I was just going to call you. Glad you are both there. I'm sitting at this Reavers guy's house right now. I'm going to hit him up one more time tonight when he gets home."

"What did you get today?" Gordan asked.

"Get this: I fed him some bull about someone getting a partial plate in Georgia, and he took it. Said he hadn't been to Georgia in a long time." Andrews's voice had some excitement in it.

"Why is that significant?" Schmidt looked at Gordan with his brows furrowed.

Andrews cleared her throat on the other end. "Well, if the guy was legitimately on business and I told him about the plate, I would expect him to confirm he was there and explain his business in the area. Even if he was just joy riding, I would expect the same, but this guy denied it, and we know he was there: Why lie? This is confirmation to me that this guy has involvement."

"Makes sense," Schmidt confirmed. "Now what?"

"Now I think I'll rattle his cage a bit when he gets home from work before I head out of here, ask him about all his charitable work."

Gordan stopped leafing through the paperwork to look up at Schmidt with his own brows furrowed.

"Wait — where are you going?" Schmidt asked her.

"I've been called in on a case in West Virginia. Not sure how long I'll be, but I will be back. I think we are on to something here."

Schmidt was a bit agitated about this. "Can't they get somebody else? This info may be the break we are looking for, I mean. And shouldn't you just take this suspect in and see what he knows, anyway?"

"Sheriff, what do we have on this guy that would allow me to pick him up?"

"At a minimum, he lied to you. That is still a crime, isn't it?" Schmidt stopped pacing.

"It is — a very weak one, but how do we prove it anyway, with Hudde refusing to share." Andrews's voice trailed off a bit. "Anyway, he already threatened to lawyer up if we bring him in, so I don't think it would work."

Gordan sat up straighter and cleared his throat. "Hey, Andrews?"

"I'm here"

"Did you make contact with a female Georgia representative of child welfare when you canvassed the area near the

Williams house?" Gordan pulled a page from the documents he was looking at and slid it over to the sheriff.

"Yeah. Shorter, heavy-set woman. Gave off a very defeated, burned-out feeling...Boston, Bison..." Andrews searched her memory for a name.

"Karen Barston," Gordan helped.

"Yes, that's her. Why?"

"What did she offer you about the people across the street, the Williamses?" Gordan now stood up.

"She didn't think she had ever seen anyone across the street, so she couldn't help us. Why, Gordan?"

Gordan grabbed a few pushpins on the corner of the map that had no reason for being. "Andrews, I know you can't see this, but you made contact with this Barston at the Williams residence." He pushed a pin on the map. "And I made contact with her across the street, the only home visible from the Tolbert residence." He pushed another pin on the map and then turned back and began pushing papers around.

"Ah, here it is: The Department has a State report about the living conditions at the Graham home, and guess who signed it?"

"No shit?" Andrews' voice rang out.

"That's three out of four." He pushed a pin at the Graham residence.

"I don't remember anyone from the state at the DeLucia home. They were actually a good family," Schmidt offered.

"Remember the route you and I walked back and forth from the DeLucia home, Andrews?" Gordan asked.

She replied, "Sure, there were only two homes where Sarah would have been seen coming or going."

"Oh, shit!" Schmidt grabbed a push pin from Hudde and placed it onto the map approximately where those two homes sat between the DeLucia home and the girl's girlfriends. "The Department was called out many times to that home before they up and moved."

"Four for four — this can't be a coincidence!" Gordan added, "And this is what has been bugging me for the last few days: When I first came across her, she told me she had never seen anyone at the Tolbert home, but then she said she did see the "older daughter," so she knew there were two girls there; she was lying."

Andrews interrupted. "Here comes my suspect. I'll give you guys a call late tomorrow."

"Now what?" the sheriff turned to Gordan. He rubbed the back of his neck and let out a deep sigh.

"What if you call her to see if she could bring in anything about the Graham family she has on file. You could tell her you're grasping at straws and need any help she could provide. Once she's in here act like she is helping and slowly turn the screws, see how she behaves." Gordan finished his mug of coffee.

"I like it," Schmidt said about the plan and then added, "Right here under our noses." He shook his head in sadness as he continued to study the map.

◆ ◆ ◆

Karen Barston stood at the reception desk with a large book bag over her shoulder. The dispatcher held up one finger and then hit an intercom button. "Sheriff, a Ms. Barston is here to see you."

Karen Barston started to walk over to one of the modern-looking plastic chairs to take a seat when the sheriff opened the inner door.

"Ms. Barston, thank you so much for coming in. You don't know how much I appreciate it." He ushered her into the conference room and repeated the secrecy oath that Gordan had given the Williamses yesterday.

"Of course, sheriff. If I can help, that's all I'm here for." Barston walked under the much taller man's arm and into the room.

Gordan Hudde stepped away from the ever-growing pile of paperwork on the table near the corkboard in the back of the room and shook her hand. "Remember me? Gordan Hudde." He walked over and flipped another table upright, pulling out the legs so that Barston would have a clear place to set herself up at.

"Coffee, tea, or something?" the sheriff offered.

"Why yes — some coffee with a little sugar would be nice," she replied.

Gordan went back to sitting behind the mound of documents and continued to read, ignoring Barston, who sat taking in everything she could see.

"Are you getting anywhere? With the investigation, I mean," she asked Gordan.

Gordan just nodded at the door as the sheriff reentered.

"Here you go." The sheriff set the Styrofoam cup down in front of Barston. "Now ya see, what we're trying to do here is revisit everything we already have done and try to see if we missed anything," he said to her.

"What can I do to help you?" she asked.

"Well without reading those reports, just tell me what you were doing at the Graham household — what you tried to do or did do before little Timmy there went missing." The sheriff nodded encouragement to her and walked around to look at the map while she began to speak from memory.

"Well, the State got some calls of concern, from the school I think, because the mom didn't come pick Timmy up, or she looked under the influence when she did."

Barston bit her lip a little, thinking. "I went to the home found it in terrible filth — no real food, and the boy was just the nicest little boy; it broke your heart."

"What did you do?" the sheriff asked.

"Well, first I tried to get mom enrolled in some programs, go see a therapist, and get into AA, but she didn't want to, and I started the paperwork to have Timmy removed."

The sheriff began to walk around to the other end of the room and looked out the window to the outside. "Always in the best interest of the child, isn't that right?"

She had to turn one quarter in her chair to look over at the sheriff. "That's right; I can't be concerned with the parents' needs or desires when it comes to the welfare of the child."

Gordan then stood near the map. "Ms. Barston, do you know what these blue push-pins signify on this map?"

She turned and squinted, putting her glasses on, but before she could say anything, the sheriff spoke, and she turned back to him.

"Those blue pins are the locations of the abducted children over the last three and a half years, Ms. Barston."

Gordan asked, "Do you know what the yellow pins stands for, Ms. Barston?"

She turned back and studied Gordan.

"These pins represent you, Ms. Barston, and the locations where you were actively working cases for the State," Gordan said.

Gordan pushed the pin in his hand into the map at the Graham home, stating the name; he then repeated it three more times with each of the other children's names.

Karen Barston began putting items back into the shoulder bag she was carrying. "I don't know what's going on here."

The sheriff asked, "Did you know that you were near all those crime scenes?"

Gordan watched as panic set into Barston; a red flush traveled up her neck around her ears and cheeks.

Gordan stepped in close to Barston. "Just how would you contact the people who are abducting these children?"

She looked like she was about to pass out. Barston dropped a paper, and, when she bent to pick it up, her glasses fell off her face and slid across the floor toward the sheriff.

He bent and picked them up. When he approached Barston, she asked, "Are you going to arrest me?"

"Tell me, Ms. Barston — should we?" the sheriff asked.

Gordan stepped back into her line of sight and knocked on the table. "You're scared out of your mind — either of being arrested or out of fear that the people you've been helping out will find out you have talked to us."

"I, I don't know what you want," she said, looking over her shoulder for the sheriff.

"Ms. Barston, we want the truth. It's that simple."

The flush running up had now taken over her entire visible flesh, like sunburn on a pasty-white individual.

"I'm going now." She stood and slowly approached the door as if either man would stop her before she managed to get outside.

Gordan couldn't help himself. "When this comes crumbling down, and we are close, you can be near the rubble or under it."

The sheriff followed her to the front door. "Don't leave the state, Ms. Barston."

She looked back once as she got to her car and then sped out of the parking lot when she realized that she was not going to be detained.

"You really need to pick her up and search her home before any and all evidence gets destroyed," Gordan said as they watched her car speed away.

"Based on what evidence?" the sheriff stated, more than asked.

"You know there has to be something at her home," Gordan said. "I have to guess she's somehow working with this Reavers guy, but to what ends? Do you think they are a couple of serial killers who met on line?"

"No judge is going to give me a warrant based on what we have."

"You could let me go get the info we need — no need for a judge." Gordan was thinking out loud, knowing that this is exactly what he would do.

Schmidt turned to Gordan and stuck his finger in his chest. "Listen up, son. I agree with you on everything, but we've got to do this right and legal if we want it to hold up in court. I'm the top lawman here. I can't be beating statements out of women no matter what we think they've done."

"Listen, sheriff. I understand, but after what you just witnessed, do you have any doubt about Barston's involvement?" Gordan lightly pushed Schmidt's finger down and away from his chest. "I wouldn't need to beat her. She just about shit herself in the conference room back there; you hurt my one feeling, sheriff."

Schmidt placed his hand on Gordan's shoulder. "Look, Gordan. This County needs to have a trial and see justice get done. I just can't have this all thrown out and have it blamed on my incompetence for failing to rein in my people."

Gordan nodded his head and then ran his hand down his beard. "I understand but don't you feel the clocks ticking on this John, maybe if we hurry we could save a life."

Schmidt looked at the floor and then shook his head "no" saying "I'm sworn to uphold the law, Gordan, and now so are you. We can't just go off half-cocked on a guess and then lose the entire thing in the process. Let's give it some time and find out what Andrews has later. I understand the passion, son, but this is the thinking that gets you standing on the wrong side of the judge." He walked past Gordan and into his office, closing the door on this conversation.

Gordan gave up the battle but not the war. He was OK with waiting to hear from Andrews and maybe something that she could help them move forward with, but he wasn't going to wait indefinitely. He walked to his truck and headed up the street for dinner.

Teddy and his family were a pleasant sight to see, a close-knit group working together, at least outwardly happy to work, and doing a fine job of it, too. Gordan said hello and grabbed his favorites, heading outside to a table to eat slowly and enjoy the evening air.

It was amazing to watch the casual activities of the small community forever moving forward, doing business as usual, not slowing down or seeming to notice the loss of a few of the smallest residents. Of course, it was necessary to move forward, but, like with the war, it was strange to know what was happening and observe others moving about without seeming to have a care.

On the other hand, what should anyone be doing, he thought. *Hiding behind closed doors or running screaming through the streets?*

"How's the barbeque there, Gordan?" Teddy pulled him out of his deep thought.

"You know it's the best thing I've ever had." Gordan just couldn't muster any real enthusiasm.

Teddy put a haunch on the corner of the table. "All right. What's going on? If my food doesn't bring a smile to your face, I've got to know what's so bad."

"Teddy, watching your family working and getting along inside brought a smile to my face and made me feel good; I was just lost in some thoughts about the missing kids just now." Gordan licked his fingers and then wiped them with a napkin. "Hey, got any of that moonshine out back here?" Gordan cleaned off the table and took the plastic and paper over to the trash.

"Ah, medicine for the soul!" Teddy waved Gordan over to the smoking shed; the long, thin spring slammed the rickety screen door behind them.

Teddy scratched the back of his head while he looked over a shelf of condiments and large cans of spices. "This will heal what's ailing you, Gordan." He reached up high and pulled down a mason jar. Teddy twisted the top off and handed it off to Gordan.

Gordan took it and took a bit too much. He tried to fight the coughing fit that followed but failed. When he stopped, he looked up at Teddy with tears in his eyes. "Wrong hole," he said, and then he whistled.

"Small sips there, son — you don't try guzzling this stuff!" Teddy took the jar away from him and took his own sip; then he handed it back.

Gordan did it right and then handed the jar back. The two headed back out to the table, and they took opposite corners to sit on.

"Thanks, Teddy — that hit the spot," Gordan said, not looking over at him.

"Whenever something ails you, come on over, and the doctor will fix you up." They sat in silence for a few minutes. "We all have been saying prayers that this missing-kid thing will work out somehow." He shook his head sadly. "The entire community is behind you and the sheriff solving this."

"Thanks," Gordan said. "Sometimes I wonder if the law isn't really just hindering getting it solved."

"Somebody mess with one of me or my kin, and, I'll tell you — there'd be no need for the law." Teddy nodded once in Gordan's direction.

"Right?" Gordan agreed.

"Well, God forgive me for even thinking that...but that is what I think."

Gordan got up and slapped Teddy on the shoulder. "Thanks, man. That's exactly what I needed right now."

"Oh, yeah. I actually helped?" Teddy smiled

Gordan nodded. "Damn straight. I'm gonna go home and get some good sleep and see what tomorrow brings, hope for something positive."

"Man, and my wife nowhere around to see this," Teddy said, heading into the back of his establishment.

Gordan started back to his property. Although it was very dark, he found the driveway because they had cleaned it up, and the heavy equipment made it more obvious. Gordan thought maybe he would install a gas light out here to mark his driveway entrance. He rolled across the meadow and headed up the slight hill to where his trailer was parked.

He slid out of the big bucket seat and looked around. It was such a satisfying feeling that this was getting done. *This is exactly*, he thought, *how others in town can forget the terror of child abductions: They just go on with their own lives if it doesn't affect them.* He stole a glance skyward and could see the silhouette of his home growing up and out of the ground above him. He unlocked his trailer and turned on the TV for a little light. He kicked off his boots and set his holster, complete with the Wilson .45 inside, down on the floor near his head on the sofa.

Chapter Thirty-Three

Sarah DeLucia hadn't seen her owner — her "benefactor," they had called him — in some time. Even at her young age, she'd managed to separate the beautiful surroundings from the evil being done to her. Two years now, she had been held here far from the Georgia country roads and occasional snow that came with it. She remembered the childish girl who arrived here and how she and her friends before had had crushes on boys, some young singers, or movie and TV stars, but this was something she knew nothing of before.

She looked at the sand and the ocean. Sometimes she dreamed of getting in the water and swimming away, but she knew this was suicide, and it was always quickly forgotten. She needed to survive and beat these people somehow. She didn't yet know how. She just knew she would, and, for now, they wanted her to talk to the new little girl who had arrived, so that was what she was going to focus on.

The darker of the Arabs, Malik, reached into his pocket and pulled out his keys, which jingled as he opened the door for her to enter.

The wail that came from the smallest child here on the island could have broken glass. Sarah covered her ears as the door closed behind her.

Debbie Tolbert stood up from the corner she had been cowering in. She took a deep breath, readying herself for yet another record-breaking scream. The sight of another young girl gave her pause.

Sarah sat on the bed. "Please don't scream anymore. I'm sorry that you are here, but nobody is going to hear you; OK?"

"Yes, they will. My mommy will hear me" little Debbie said, a bit defiantly.

Through all her sadness, Sarah managed a smile for the cute little blonde, "I don't belong here, either, but nobody has come for me yet. Let me ask you, did you live near the ocean?"

"I don't think so"

"Well, you do now, so I wouldn't plan on anyone hearing you. Maybe we can be friends. Would that be OK with you?" Sarah reached out with her hand to see if Debbie would take it.

She did reach out, and Sarah pulled her up so that they sat together. "Why don't you tell me your name."

"Debbie." Her tears had washed clean paths down her dirty cheeks.

"Ok, Debbie, my name is Sarah, and it is nice to meet you"

Debbie looked up at Sarah. "Why don't you think my mommy will find me?"

"Well, I think that they took you and me far, far away from where we lived," Sarah said to her.

"Like a fairy tale?" Debbie asked.

"Yes, I think you are right. It is like a fairy tale, and we have to stick together so one day we can beat the evil prince."

"Oh, no!" the little one screamed out.

"Wait! He pretends that he is nice, but you and I know he is bad. We have to keep this a secret, OK?" Sarah held those little hands in hers.

"OK. I can keep secrets," Debbie assured her.

"Then it is a deal. We will stay close until we plan our next step, and we will keep the secret and tell no one else."

"Deal," little Debbie agreed. "But what are they going to do to us?"

"I do not know for sure; lots of kids have come and gone from here before, but remember that we can always talk to each other, no matter what happens, OK?"

"OK." Debbie wasn't sure that this was OK; however, she was happy to have some company even if it was from a big girl and not another kid that she could play with.

◆ ◆ ◆

Gordan stood outside the growing structure that would one day be his home. The extra-thick slab had been poured, and it appeared to be a misshapen boomerang with one fat end that would soon be a garage.

The foreman came out and shook Gordan's hand. "Morning, Mr. Hudde. What do you think so far?" he said, as he turned to look at the activities with him.

"I'm so excited to get it done; I can't wait to see the finished product," Gordan noted.

"Well, this is a first for me — I can tell you that. 'An above-ground bunker' was what the architect said, and, well, I'll be if it ain't. The cement trucks are really struggling to make that driveway. I'd stay well away from them, but these three-and-a-half-foot-thick steel-reinforced walls will be a thing of beauty!"

"I'll bring up a half keg to celebrate when it's finished, and we all can share a beer," Gordan promised.

"Sounds good to me." He slapped Gordan on the shoulder and said, "Have a good day!" He walked toward the next mixer that was backing up to one of the forms that needed to be filled to build a wall.

Gordan walked back down to his pickup and drove out to the road, turning to head into the town. He was hoping that the sheriff had heard something from Andrews. He was really chomping at the bit to get someone talking.

He yanked he current temporary cell phone out and looked at it. Maybe it was time he got a real one; he dialed the Russian at CIA headquarters.

"Yeah, Gordan."

"You know, if you were a chick, I'd really dig that accent"

Ivan cleared his throat and made sure his voice was an octave lower. "You field agents are all freaks."

"Aw, poor Ivan, show me where they have touched you," Gordan laughed "Seriously, Kid: What have you come up with on the Reavers and Barston connection?"

"Sorry, Gordan. Nothing."

"What? You're shitting me. There has to be phone calls or emails, texts — something."

Ivan shook his head even though Gordan couldn't see him. "Sorry, Gordan. I can't find anything, nothing via texting, email, snapchat, twitter — I mean no form of communication history that would identify them as being acquainted. Sure, they have both done some work for the charities, but their tax forms were filed in different states, so I doubt it."

"Fuck." There was a pause. "Don't give up, Ivan. They know about each other somehow; maybe it is through the charity work."

"Well, I tried to take a look at that, but it would take a team of forensic auditors and platoon of investigators a year before you could make anything of it."

"What?" He had lost Gordan.

"These charities all share money. So, if a large donor helps one charity, the funds may end up at another, and so on, and so on."

"Ok, I'm with you." Gordan was concentrating hard.

"So once the funds comingle, how do you know who or from what organization the funds came?" Ivan stopped for a moment, and, when Gordan offered nothing, he continued. "Imagine a beach ball covered in the names of charities and big individual donors."

"Go on," Gordan whispered.

"Now picture an imaginary line that connected every charity or name with funds going back and forth between these entities all the time." Ivan paused for a breath. "Tell me where a single dollar started and where it ended."

"It's really that bad?"

"Maybe worse. I mean every big-name charity you can think of has given to the charity, from the Red Cross to The Perkins Foundation for Exploited and Homeless Children."

"Seriously? Some groups could be funneling money or laundering it through charitable organizations?" Gordan was surprised.

"Yes, Gordan. It's probably happening right now. In fact, I guarantee it." Ivan couldn't believe how unknowledgeable Gordan seemed to be on this.

"Well what if you could get into the financial files for something like the Perkins Foundation? Would that help you to understand how funds were being distributed? Or, wait: Maybe the FBI is onto some of these groups right now; we could see if that charity Reavers works for is dirty."

"First, sure, but nobody is going to give me that access, and I told you it would take a team. I searched some FBI databases, and it doesn't appear they are working any of these types of cases…"

"Don't sell yourself short, Kid. We always have an 'in' on old politicians, and I bet somebody could get former Vice President Perkins to give us access."

"I won't stop digging, Gordan, for another connection between Reavers and Barston, but there are simple ways, like the mail or private servers, or just a drop. If it's electronic, I'll find you something, Gordan. Don't worry."

"Thanks, Kid. I'll call the boss and see if I can get a meeting with Perkins."

Ivan chimed in. "On the boss front, Gordan — he's getting a bit perturbed with the time I'm giving your investigation."

"Thanks for the warning." Gordan hung up just as he drove into the Sheriff's Department parking lot.

Gordan re-dialed and hit the proper numbers until he was speaking to Stevens. His old boss sounded tired. Gordan tried to keep it light.

"Hey, boss. Thanks for allowing The Kid to help out this small county here. I'm sure his involvement is going to crack this thing."

"I'm going to have to pull the plug on it soon, Gordan." Stevens's voice was like slowing down a recording of a grizzly bear growling.

"I understand. Hey, listen: What do you know about former VP Albert Perkins?"

"He is the republican establishment, neo-con, family values, as blue as a blue blood gets. Nobody on either side of the aisle will say a bad word about the guy, and he's been out of the game for eight years now."

"Do you know him; get me in to meet him?" Gordan was hopeful.

"Your missing kids' case can't have anything to do with Perkins; what are you going to talk to him about?"

"There is some question about how charities work, and Ivan thought that if we could look at his books for the Perkins Foundation, we could gain some insight into the flow of finances within the charity game." Gordan paused, listening to Stevens' breathing for a moment. "No accusations of any wrongdoing by his organization — just looking for background."

"Yeah. OK. I'll see if I can do anything for you there, but Gordan?"

"Yeah, boss."

"The man has a lot of friends. Please play nice."

"Sure, John — on my best behavior. Thank you." Gordan hung up.

Gordan looked up just in time to see the sheriff pull up and get out of his vehicle. The big man looked as if he had aged several years in just the few weeks Gordan had known him, as he walked, a bit stooped over, into the building. Gordan felt the need to be a bit more cheerful and slapped the sheriff on the back when he met him at the coffee table.

"Come on, John. Something good has to happen soon. Have you gotten that call from Andrews yet?" Gordan filled his cup with black coffee and then turned and leaned against the counter, waiting for a response.

"Nothing, Gordan. I've got families, the Mayor, and the town all looking for something, and I can't share what little I have." He looked at the floor and shook his head. "I can hardly stand looking at myself to shave."

"Something good is going to break for us soon. I can feel it," Gordan said, with a forced smile. "Let's go call Andrews, see if her boys have come up with anything in South Carolina."

The sheriff sat hard behind his desk and hit the speaker button. Looking at her card, he dialed the number; one ring and it went to voice mail. The sheriff asked her to get back, saying he needed some good news — that this investigation was going somewhere — to tell the families.

"She'll call back with something, and then you call me — OK, John? I would like something positive to happen, too." Gordan got up and walked back to the conference room to look over the documents some more.

John Schmidt knew what Gordan really wanted to do, and he had to stop thinking about it or he may tell him to go ahead.

Chapter Thirty-Four

Gordan headed north to the mountain retreat in West Virginia owned by the former Vice President, Perkins. He knew this was grasping at straws, but at least he was moving forward. He was a big believer in continuing to advance and never taking a defensive position. If this took a day, at least it would be a day that he was not sitting looking at John Schmidt, thinking that the law was stopping them from helping some children out there.

It was not the longest of drives, maybe near 400 miles, but it was a twisting and curving rout, making Gordan concentrate more than he was sometimes known to do on long drives.

He found the small street in the town of Fayetteville, West Virginia, and then the gate to the estate of the former Vice President. He hit the button and identified himself at an unmanned gate. Someone acknowledged him, and the big Iron Gate slowly swung open, splitting the iron "A" and "P" that met in the middle perfectly. Gordan eased his big blue pickup thru the gate and drove slowly up the hill toward a giant log-cabin mansion that appeared through the trees. The circular drive had one other vehicle in it, a big Cadillac Escalade, which seemed to be the vehicle of choice for the important and self-important, who required drivers.

Gordan slid out and whistled as he took in the home and the surrounding grounds. He reached into the cab and pulled out the closest thing he had to a suit jacket, a suede one. One of the Secret Service men, in traditional black and white, met Gordan as he stood looking at the view.

"Mr. Hudde?"

"Oh, yea. Sorry. This is breathtaking." Gordan followed the man toward the front doors.

The man nodded at Gordan and spoke into his lapel. "At the front door now," he said, and then he turned and walked back toward the Cadillac.

Gordan returned his attention to the door as he heard locks turning and he stepped up to the door ready to gain entry.

"Jeezus, where did they find you?" Gordan said to the big man who opened the door.

"Right this way, sir." The man motioned with his left arm, and he led Gordan into a study, complete with 12-foot-high walls filled with book after book. A ladder fashioned after those in bookstores and libraries was attached to the wall and rails so that it could be slid from side to side.

"Six-foot-seven and three hundred and five, if you're still wondering," the big agent said to Gordan.

"Play some football or basketball?" Gordan asked.

"Some football. I ran the forty in 4.7 my senior year."

"Holy shit! Why are you a Secret Service agent?" Gordan asked the obvious question.

"I had a 'temperament problem' — didn't like authority." He smiled a big, toothy smile.

"And the Secret Service took you in?" Gordan was a bit taken back.

"No, this is a private firm, mostly ex-military, but they couldn't pass me up. I guess they needed help keeping the military pussies in line." He nodded in the affirmative at his own observation and smiled broadly.

Gordan had a sense of humor. "You should have gotten into the service. They always like to work with bad attitudes."

"Yeah. I hear you were a war hero. I thought about it, but I really don't appreciate people, especially inferior people, telling me what to do."

Gordan had heard enough from this guy. "Probably for the best. There aren't many guys your size who can make it through any of the difficult training. You have to work twice as hard to get through the special-operations schools. I know only a few, and they are some of the toughest I ever met; you probably made a good choice."

"My MMA training is probably better than anything you guys ever received, and I'm not interested in running away much." He smiled again and then turned and headed out just as another door opened on the other side of the room.

Albert Perkins strode into the room, and the air changed. There was a crackling energy, as if lightning were going to strike. He was close to 6'5" himself and entirely grey, but it was that silver grey that seemed like a metal helmet. His frame was a bit slight, and Gordan remembered, seeing him on TV, being a very slim man, but he seemed to be a bit heavier out of office — still in good shape, though.

He strode across the vast room faster than Gordan expected and greeted him with the warmest of handshakes. His smile was worth millions, and he seemed genuinely happy to meet Gordan.

"My Lord, a real live war hero right here in my home. I've been so excited ever since the Secretary of Defense called and asked if you could come meet me."

He pointed over at some heavy-looking wood-and-leather chairs. "Come. Come, please. Take a seat and tell me about you. Oh, how about something to eat or drink after your long drive?"

"Thank you, Mr. Vice President. Really, I'm OK. Well, maybe some coffee, if that's OK."

"OK? I insist — and call me 'Al.'" He waved a hand at Gordan as he picked up the phone and ordered some coffee and cake brought to his study.

"Now, what is it you would like to talk to me about — something to do with charity work?" Perkins sat on the arm of the chair across from Hudde and gave him the full attention of a man engrossed.

"Well, sir..."

"'Al,' please"

"Well Al, I've been trying to help a small town with a problem, and we located some folks that may be hiding money or laundering money through a charity."

"Oh, no. I hate to hear about things like that." The former VP paused. "It's so difficult to regain the people's trust once you have broken it." He shook his head sadly.

"Well, I've been talking to an IT guy who thought it would be helpful to look at your charity's financial paperwork to see how funds are processed and then maybe see how some irregularities could be identified in the others. The concept is that we look at a charity that does it correctly, and then it will be easier to identify the frauds."

"Are you talking about the Perkins Foundation for Exploited and At-Risk Children?" Perkins looked a bit perplexed.

"Yes, sir. Everyone told me you wouldn't be able to open the books for us, but I thought it would be worth the chance, especially because this is for children."

Perkins put his finger to his chin. "We have financial documents that we must file every year, and it should be public... but you say this is for children?"

"Yes, sir. Our county has had a rash of abductions over the last few years, and our suspect is working for a charity," Gordan told him.

"Not mine! Tell me it's not a charity with my name on it!" He jumped off the arm of the chair and stood over Gordan, waiting for an answer.

"Oh, no, sir. But your charity may have provided some funds over the years, and my guy —well, we're just grasping at straws, but he was hoping to work with your people to figure out how best to look at this other charity."

Perkins pounded down happily on Gordan's shoulder. "Thank God. I'd hate to think it was any of ours. OK then…" He went back to the arm of his chair just as a woman brought in coffee and some little cakes on a silver platter.

As the woman set up the cups and coffee, Perkins leaned over toward Gordan. "Has your man got anything real to go off of yet?"

Gordan shook his head sadly. "No, nothing. And the info on the one suspect is very weak, but we don't want to just give up. We have the FBI working on it, too, and we're hoping she's gotten something over the last couple of days." Gordan took the cup that was offered and sniffed the coffee. "Smells good." Gordan smiled at the woman who offered him cream and sugar; he declined both.

"Listen, son. If there is anything we can do, our staff will assist you any way we can, including any access your IT guy wants to have. How's that?" Perkins slapped Gordan on the leg and then sat down across from him, sipping his cup of coffee.

"It's such a beautiful place," Gordan noted.

Just then Mrs. Perkins walked into the room. She was a tall woman about 5'10" and wispy thin. Her slacks and blouse were fitted, and she was lovely. Gordan thought he remembered that she had done some modeling in college; she was a good 15 years younger than her husband.

"I was just interested in going into town and wanted to make sure you wouldn't miss me much." She smiled and conducted a runway walk over, giving a small kiss on the left cheek of the VP and totally ignoring Hudde.

She turned and took in Gordan from head to toe and then spoke to her husband. "Are you changing landscapers, honey?"

"Not at all, darling. Meet Mr. Hudde. He is a bona fide war hero, and everyone in the service can't say enough good things about him." He stood during the introduction.

"Are you looking for work?" She frowned, not sure why this unwashed person would be in their study.

"Nice to meet you, Mrs. Perkins." Gordan stood and extended his hand. She looked at him as if he were a leper and pulled her hand to her own cheek.

"My husband, he loves veterans so much. Now please do not take advantage of his good nature." She said nothing else. She whirled out of the study as fast as she'd come in.

"Beautiful woman, isn't she?" Albert Perkins stood next to Gordan.

Gordan was a bit unsure how to answer. "Well..." Gordan didn't want to point out the obvious.

"Oh, go ahead, son. She's a vibrantly beautiful woman. You can say it. Everyone tells me how lucky I am, and you know what? I know it," he chuckled.

"Yes, sir, you are lucky," Gordan lied, "but can I ask you something?"

"Anything."

"Why don't you have some Secret Service protection? I mean, isn't that pretty standard?" He sipped his coffee after asking.

"You know, I don't think I've ever gotten a death threat — maybe because who threatens a VP? I don't know. We've done well for ourselves. Why burden the taxpayer? So we purchased our own people, and it's worked out very well so far."

Gordan pointed back at the front door. "Well, you'd have to be a bit crazy to try to get past your doorman."

Perkins nodded in agreement. "He's a good man — been around quite some time now. But you're right; nobody's getting by Leslie. I never go anywhere without him." He handed a business card to Gordan. "Here is our financial guru for the charity; I hope he can help your cause."

They began walking back to the front of the home, "Thank you again, sir, for your time, I'll let you know if it was helpful."

"Drive safely, son. It was a pleasure to meet you."

Gordan was traveling south and wondering if he could do the drive in closer to five hours instead of six. The light filtering through the trees made his eyelids heavy. He stopped for gas early to wake up and to call Ivan at CIA. He gave him the contact info and told him that he would get full cooperation from the Perkins staff to help him decipher the financial paperwork.

♦ ♦ ♦

Gordan couldn't believe that he had reviewed the paperwork for another full day without any other item falling out. He was sure of the Karen Barston connection, and he was fighting with himself as to what he thought was right or to follow the sheriff's instructions.

Gordan walked up front to see if Schmidt wanted to grab a sandwich with him, but he did not. To his surprise, Andrews had never called him back; John Schmidt called in to her boss, who seemed as surprised as they were that she couldn't be located. They ultimately decided to call this a cell-phone issue, and the boss put in a call to the West Virginia Branch to give him a call. He promised the sheriff that she would get back to him first thing in the morning.

Gordan drove home with some take-out. He parked and then got out and stretched before heading to the front door.

He unlocked his trailer and turned on the kitchen light and the TV. He flipped over to the news and pulled up a chair to eat but decided to walk up to the construction at the top of the hill with a beer.

Fifteen minutes later, Gordan was sitting on someone's toolbox in what one day would be his living room, having a beer, and watching the sun set on the valley down below.

He closed his eyes to better adjust to the fading light and thought about everything revolving around the missing children, Barston, Reavers, and the families. What he couldn't see while looking directly at the information at the sheriff's conference room but which was obvious from his thinking now was *organization.* This was not some random dirt-bag. This was well-thought-out and well-funded also; this had "Organized Crime" written all over it!

A vehicle slowing brought Gordan out of his temporary meditation. He set the beer can down on the concrete and walked over to watch the white-blue lights of the big vehicle slow at his driveway and then creep slowly past. About a quarter of a mile away, the lights turned into the woods before they turned off.

"Fucking Tolbert idiots," Gordan said to himself. *I may just kill one of them before this is over.* He slowly made his way to the switch-back part of his drive, and, then, out of years of training, he slipped into the tree line to watch for the advancement of the morons, who thought they could sneak up on him.

He made out the shapes as they came down from the east woods, where they would come out directly behind the trailer. The problem they would have was that Gordan was slowly making his way to get behind them.

Gordan made out the three forms; the silhouettes were slightly darker than the surrounding woods. They walked in a ranger file (straight line) through the woods, and, then, when they hit the edge of the meadow, fanned out in a three-man triangular shape. From the way they stopped and moved, Gordan knew this was not the Tolberts with Charlie; these were some kind of military-trained personnel.

These men were decked out in black, frog-walking across the open area in a modified weaver stance, handguns at the ready. Gordan reached to his back and saw an image in his mind of him walking in the door to the trailer earlier, when he'd set the sub on the table and the handgun on the counter. He felt nothing but the small of his back and the top of his belt.

Gordan had now snuck directly behind the three invaders as they got closer to his trailer. They stacked there. One of them tried to look into a window, but, while they were open, the men could see nothing, as the heavy drapes were closed, and the only noise they could hear was the TV.

The men were not wearing any night vision, and Gordan knew that the light emanating from the windows would limit their ability to look back at the darker woods, where Gordan now stood.

Gordan reached about until he found a rock the size of a softball. He began to creep slowly out into the open as the three men formed up and followed the side of the trailer around to the front.

The three dark men were so focused on making the final turn and approaching the door that Gordan crushed the skull of the back man and then punched the second man in the side of the head while kicking the first man in the ribs before they realized what was happening.

Gordan broke the first man's thumb, taking away his weapon, and that man ducked under Gordan's arms. Grabbing his right foot and driving hard, he took Gordan to the ground.

Gordan could see the second man getting to his feet, and Gordan used the silenced Glock to fire off five rounds; the man went back to the ground. The man who had taken

Gordan down used this time to crawl up, take a dominant position, and start raining down strikes at Gordan's head.

Gordan timed ducking a right-handed blow from above perfectly, and he leaned to his left. As it hit the ground to the right of Gordan's head, he violently twisted his hips and spun his shoulders, pinning the other man's right hand under his body. He grabbed that right forearm and pulled the man over onto his face. Gordan maintained a side position, which quickly became the man's back.

Gordan could feel that he was the bigger, stronger man, and he began putting the other man to sleep by stopping the blood flow to his brain.

Gordan crawled quickly over to the other two bodies and found that they both were dead. He lay flat in the meadow grass for a moment and looked up at the twinkling stars. He knew now that Andrews was not going to call. "I'm sorry," he said out loud.

Gordan took two deep breaths and then rose up from the meadow grass; he walked over to his truck and came back with two plastic cuffs, which he used to bind the unconscious one. He patted them all down and made a small pile of combat knives, silenced weapons, and one set of car keys.

He slid the living guy between the two dead ones. He'd always found that rather disconcerting when waking up from being knocked unconscious. Then he walked out to the big black Cadillac Escalade and drove it back to his place, backing it up near the pile of bodies. The men had nothing on them to identify them, but the Cadillac sure did: It was owned by

"Global Security Hawks — Every Security Need for Every Environment," or so said the business card in the glovebox. Gordan had to admit that it was catchy.

Gordan flipped the catch to the tailgate of the big black vehicle, and it popped open effortlessly.

"You can stop pretending to be out still," he said to the one man who he knew was conscious. "You've had to been awake for several minutes now."

Gordan bent and picked up one of the dead men, throwing the body into the back and pushing the legs up so that he could eventually close the door.

"If you want to live, I suggest you begin talking; I have things to do, and, frankly, torture was not on my list. You're either talking or taking up space with your friends." Gordan flicked the barrel of the Glock back and forth between the one living and the two dead.

"You don't know me, but I'm telling you I have no patience right now. Were you involved with whatever happened to FBI Agent Andrews?"

Silence.

"Is she or any of the children alive?" Gordan had now loaded both dead bodies into the back of the Caddie.

Nothing but silence from the one attacker. Gordan walked up and said, simply, "OK — the hard way it is." He then shot the would-be assassin with his own weapon, once in the chest and once in the forehead.

Gordan went inside and picked up his Wilson combat .45, replacing it in the small of his back. He went into the back and grabbed a boot knife for his backup — well, he always wore the belt with the buckle knife, but that was more for party tricks than a real weapon.

Gordan locked up everything and drove the Cadillac down to the sheriff's office, where he expected to find an empty office.

"What brings you down here so late, Gordan?" the sheriff said from behind his desk.

"Well, sheriff, I didn't think I was going to find you here, but I wanted to leave this." Gordan held up the Pine County Badge and then slid it onto the desk in front of the sheriff.

Big John Schmidt looked at the badge and then back up at Gordan. "I appreciate the help you've given me, son, and I know you're frustrated and all, but I'm asking you not to give up on the law yet." He pushed the badge back across the desk.

"Sheriff." Gordan paused, looking briefly at the floor "John, things have changed. Andrews is missing. The FBI either is aware and not telling or is as clueless as we are. It's time for me to do what I'm good at and see what kind of hornets come out of the nest." Gordan ran his hand down through his beard. "If you know what's good for you, you'll tell everyone that we got nothing on the abductions, OK?"

"What are you talking about, Gordan?" The sheriff stood up as Gordan began walking out to the front doors.

Gordan stopped and turned around in the nearly empty building. "John, this entire thing stinks, and it stinks much worse than any scenarios we've played out in our heads." He paused, looking up into Schmidt's face. "I'm telling you this: There is no single crazy guy out there taking kids. This is something larger, and we got somebody's attention, and it's not the good kind. You need to be safe, and I'll keep in touch." Gordan pushed on the first set of interior foyer doors.

"Gordan, you're kind of scaring me, son," Schmidt said.

"Good." Gordan didn't turn around.

"You get yourself a new car?" the sheriff said as he stepped out onto the concrete steps of the building.

"Yeah. Picked it up tonight," Gordan said as he unlocked it and started to get into the driver's side.

"Hey, Gordan," the sheriff yelled out.

"Yeah, John?"

"If you can, if there is the slightest possibility that you can save even one kid…" he paused, "…no matter what it takes." He turned and headed back inside without saying anything else.

Chapter Thirty-Five

Gordan drove the speed limit heading southeast toward the Barston residence; he guessed he'd be there by 0100hrs. What did he know about her? He ran his hand through his beard while driving.

She had worked for many years in a government agency. Politically, she would be accustomed to doing nothing beyond what was required; she would want things to go by the required steps. She was probably waiting for the next round of questions from the Sheriff's Department. Maybe she had already put an attorney on retainer. Maybe her first statement tonight would be, "Talk to my lawyer."

A 30-year bureaucrat would, regardless of their own opinions, be very used to the "1-2-3" style, the slow processes of all government agencies, the Sheriff's Department included.

Before pulling into the driveway, Gordan looped the neighborhood once, deciding that neighbors would not be much of a problem if he created a disturbance. He pulled into the driveway behind the now-familiar Ford. He guessed the odd hour would also be in his favor.

Gordan slipped on the sheriff's ball cap, black with the gold badge on front that he had taken while at the station.

He stretched and flexed his hands under the XXL mechanic's gloves a few times, feeling the materials stretch over his knuckles in a very satisfying way. He practiced his best smile in the mirror and headed up the four short steps to Karen Barston's front door.

On the third rap, Gordan noticed the lights coming on. A disheveled Karen Barston opened the wooden door and spoke through the gun-metal-grey screen door.

"Do you know what time it is?" She rubbed her hand through her hair. She was wearing pajamas that looked like a child business suit in pastels. Gordan thought they appeared very uncomfortable.

"Sorry, Ms. Barston, but the sheriff said it was important, and I came right over. Can you come out to the station with me?"

She looked at him like he was crazy and then looked past him for a moment. Gordan wondered if she was looking for his reinforcements.

"I've been driving that same piece of shit for years, and you guys are out getting Cadillacs?" She looked utterly sick at the thought.

Gordan felt very confident that his behavior analysis on the way there had been correct.

She shook her head, sad that he was wasting her time, and a bit annoyed that it was at this late hour. "Listen, um...." She looked for a name badge.

"Gordan." Hudde took off the ball cap and gave her his best "Aw, shucks!" look.

Barston shook her head, a bit disgusted. "Gordan, I'm sorry, but you're not even a real sheriff's deputy. Please tell the sheriff to contact my attorney the next time he wants to talk to me."

"Aw, gee, Ma'am. The sheriff's not going to be too happy. Do you have a number or business card of your attorney that I could give to the sheriff?"

"Hold on." she disappeared for a moment and then returned. She set a business card on the table, and she leaned over and began to write. "Here is my card with my attorney's number written on the back. I'll be glad to show up with him the next time."

Everything in order — *"1- 2-3,"* Gordan thought to himself. He also readied himself for a performance. She had been ready to piss herself when caught unaware at the station. Now she was poised because of the time she had to prepare. He balled his right fist and grabbed the handle to the screen door as she approached with the card extended in her left hand as her right reached out to flick the lock on the screen door.

As fast as he could, Gordan threw open the screen door with his left hand and punched Karen Barston in the stomach with his right. It was a blow meant to bring shock and pain. She whooshed out a big lungful of air and stumbled back into her kitchen. Gordan was in and locking the door behind him so quickly she had yet to come to a stop on her ass near the refrigerator.

Gordan pounced on her, grabbing her throat and dragging her inside to her own stairway to the second floor. Using his knees, he pinned her arms and began to choke her with two big hands. When he saw the light going out, he let go and threw her face first on the floor; using flex cuffs, he restrained her arms behind her back.

She coughed and then threw up, due either to the initial punch or the fear — Gordan didn't care which.

He walked around the small house. Locating her phone, keys, and a single laptop, he brought them all to the living room, where she lay crying.

Gordan stood over her and pulled her hair until her eyes met his. "First, shut the fuck up. Second, I know that you are guilty. If you want to survive this, you better start talking."

"I didn't do anything," Barston said through lingering tears.

It may have worked on others, but Hudde stepped up and gave a pretty good kick to Barston's ribs; she spit out the tears and tried desperately to regain her breathing.

Gordan knelt beside her head. "Every lie you tell me, it will get worse — do you understand?

"You are communicating to someone, telling them where they can find children who are at risk danger or are alone."

Gordan stood and acted as if he were readying another kick.

"Yes, yes, yes — that's what I do!" Barston was not going to offer that much resistance going further.

"How do you communicate?" Gordan made sure his boot toe was within centimeters of Barston's eyes as he hovered above her.

"The game station over there near the TV. I'm friends with that person, and I send them the address and the best time to be wherever. Listen, I'll tell you what you ask. Please let me sit up. I think you broke my ribs, mister"

Gordan roughly yanked her to a sitting position up against the sofa. "How did you know what this other person was looking for?"

"I have a web address that has 'orders' on it. If I can fill one, I send the message on the game messaging-thingy."

"How did you get into this?" Gordan toned down his voice.

"I borrowed money from someone that I never should have, and, when I couldn't pay, they made me reach out to someone, and they sent me the instructions. I didn't have a choice. I never wanted to hurt anyone, and I never have."

"Are you fucking delusional? You don't think you have ever hurt anyone? What do you think is happening to these children?" Gordan had to stop himself from doing worse to this woman.

"Maybe they are better off now." She looked down, to not make eye contact with Gordan. "Maybe I got them out of some terrible conditions, and now they are way happier than they would have been."

"You know they found a little girl dead in a river a little while ago. Was that one of your saved children?"

Barston continued to avoid his gaze; Gordan grabbed the laptop, phone, keys, and purse. He grabbed Barston's arm and yanked her to her feet.

"I've got someplace to be before it gets light."

"Wait!" she yelled out. "I've told you everything. What are you going to do with me?"

Gordan set her things on a small kitchen table and let her drop unceremoniously onto the floor. "Where do you keep the money they pay you?

Her eyes narrowed, and he saw some strength flow back into her face.

He kicked her in the stomach, and, when she next looked up from her position lying on her side, a large-caliber gun was in her face.

"I don't play games." Gordan said nothing else.

Through some moaning, she said, "Cookie jar under the cabinet," and she nodded her head in the correct direction.

Gordan looked under the cabinet through a bunch of pots and pans. A baby-blue, bear-shaped cookie jar was sitting in the back. He pulled it out and walked over to her other things on the table. He took the head off the jar and turned it over; a bunch of rubber-banded rolls of bills dropped out; a few made it all the way to the floor.

"Pretty full" Gordan said to her.

She had lost all ability to fight. "Each roll is a thousand."

Gordan found a cabinet with garbage bags and pulled one out, depositing the money in the bag.

He turned after tying it off and picking up her other things. "Let's go. This is far from over."

He helped her to her feet, and she gasped. He knew she would be in pain for weeks.

"Please don't kill me," she just about whispered to him.

"If you keep helping me, I promise you that I won't," he said to her. He had no real plan; he hoped he was telling the truth.

He locked the door behind them and then pushed her into the back seat. Before she knew it, she had her right arm cuffed to something in the back.

"Don't scream. Don't give me any reason to, and I will not kill you." He felt that, this time, there was some conviction behind it.

"I won't," she said to him, lying down in the seat. Her arm went up and between the middle seats to the back. She pushed hard and whatever her arm was cuffed to moved just enough that she was able to sit up a little.

Gordan turned the big vehicle over and readjusted the steering wheel. He flipped open his phone and made a call.

"Da?"

"Hey, Kid. I've got a laptop that has been used to receive messages from my kidnappers. Can you hack it?"

"You keep me at work until this ungodly hour and then call to insult me?"

"I'm sorry. You know what I meant — from where you are, right now?" Gordan said.

"Turn on your vehicle's satellite connection."

Gordan looked at the array of buttons. "What does it look like? Oh, never mind. Here it is."

"Now hit your emergency button"

"But won't that activate some search?" Gordan asked.

"Gordan, do I ask you how you find and kill people? No — I do not. Just do it."

Barston let out a scream from the middle seats. When Gordan turned, she was holding up the arm that was currently attached to a dead man.

"One more sound out of you, and *you* will be riding in the back," Gordan said, before turning back to the situation at hand.

"Sounds like a fun trip," Ivan said. "Now I turn off your GPS unit, and connect with the laptop. The laptop is on — correct, Gordan?"

Gordan flipped it open and then on. "It is now."

"OK," Ivan said, "you can hang up and drive. I've got it from here."

Gordan slammed his foot hard on the gas, and the big Caddie launched out of the driveway, now heading north; Mr. Reavers needed to answer some questions.

Gordan conducted the same thought processes about Reavers as he had about the Barston woman. He was a low-level thug; he'd done some time in a federal institution but was never the heavy. Maybe they could quickly get past the "I'm a tough-guy" attitude — a least Gordan hoped so. He also had to recognize that this was the last guy he knew to have contact with Andrews. Unless she had popped up in the last few hours, she had not been heard from in more than 24 hours now; this was no time to take someone lightly.

There was no need for Gordan to drive the block in South Carolina at the Reavers residence; there were no neighbors to worry about. Gordan went through the lawn, around the light-blue Chrysler parking behind the home. He found the button to the blue-and-white strobe emergency light on the dash and pressed it. The back yard became a light show. The lights made branches appear to move when there was no breeze whatsoever.

Gordan turned to Barston, whose nerves had put her to sleep, even in all the excitement. "Don't go anywhere." She didn't acknowledge him.

Gordan got out and began looking under bushes near the home and then behind the garage with a flashlight. He heard the back door open but didn't turn to acknowledge the noise.

"What the hell, hell?"

Gordan still didn't turn to acknowledge Reavers.

"Hey!" Reavers screamed out without repeating it.

"Oh, I'm sorry, sir." Gordan began walking to and then up the steps to the back door of the home, where Gary Reavers was leaning against the frame.

Gordan stood for a moment, taking in Reavers and the attitude he was exuding.

"Wait — didn't the home office tell you I was coming out?" Gordan scratched his head with his right hand that still held the lit flashlight. It flashed across Reavers' face several times.

"What is fucking wrong with you?" Again, Reavers did not repeat his words under duress. "And what are you looking for?" Reavers placed a hand over his eyes to protect them from the brilliant white light.

"Oh, sorry, sir. I'm looking for fellow Agent Sue Andrews. You remember her — correct?"

"I told the guys here earlier that she came and went. I didn't care then, and I don't care now, now!"

Gordan, who had been holding the flashlight high with his left hand, turned it so that the base was pointing down, and he now brought it down hard onto the top of Reavers' right shoulder. A closed switchblade knife dropped onto the floor at about the same time that Gordan bent into and drove hard with his legs, taking Reavers back into the home on his shoulder. He stopped suddenly, allowing Reavers to go flying backwards, falling onto his back. Gordan turned for a moment to kick the door closed and then spun back, kicking Reavers in the forehead, making his head snap back, slapping on the wooded floor.

Gordan was on Reavers, pinning an unmoving left arm and grabbing him by the throat. It was unnecessary, as he was unconscious. Gordan used his plastic ties to secure his arms in front; only then he checked to ensure that there was a slow and steady pulse. Gordan patted him down, looking for other weapons; he even checked his shorts and t-shirt to make sure there were no possible threats stitched into a seam.

Gordan then walked the home; he found keys, a laptop, and the game console that he would have used to communicate with Barston. Gordan believed that the two would have never met. Someone very devious seemed to be in charge of setting up this operation. He began looking for Reavers' hidden money when he came across a small card with some kind of web address on it; he pocketed it as Reavers began making some noise.

Gordan walked back and plopped down onto the worn brown sofa. It was too soft and too low.

"It's going to be a very long day." He rubbed his head and sat back. "Do you think you're going to live?"

"Fucking cocksucker — you're no FBI agent, agent."

"Can't sneak anything past you." Gordan sat up so that he could make eye contact.

"Yeah, you're from the company — aren't you, you?" Reavers rolled his head a little to make sure the kick hadn't broken a vertebra. "I told them that I told her nothing and I mean it. When she left, she knew nothing, nothing!"

Gordan believed him. "Well that answers one question. Where do you hide your cash?"

"Wait — you're not with them, either? Motherfucker, who *do* you work for for?"

Gordan stood over Reavers, pulling down on his beard, as he thought about the proper response.

"I guess I'm working for the kids you've abducted; I started out not caring much, like everyone else, it seems, and now I can't think of anything else."

"So, now what are you going to do, do?" Reavers held his hands up before his face, looking closely at the flex cuffs.

"I need to know what you did with the kids, and you're going to tell me. No — you're going to take me there." Gordan was thinking out loud.

Reavers was shaking his head "No." "I'm not saying anything to you."

"Here is the thing, Reavers. I'm a student of people. I know you're a survivor. I think you are a pretty tough guy, up here." Gordan tapped him hard on the forehead. "But what about pain? How do you handle *real* pain?" Gordan leaned down and watched Reavers eyes squint close at the thought. "I feel like I don't have a lot of time, so I apologize that I can't start with minor pain and slowly increase it to find out where your breaking point is."

Gordan stood back up and, as violently as possible, grabbed Reavers by the right ankle and yanked him down and over, putting him on his face.

"Wait — what are you doing?" Again in a moment of fear, Reavers seemed cured from his speech impediment.

"Have you ever had a dislocation, Gary? I think I'll start with your hip or your ankle or knee; it kinda depends on you, really, I mean: What will go first? Thing is, Gary, once something goes, it kinda ruins you for life."

Gordan began twisting Reavers' foot violently while placing his legs in a scissor hold.

"Noooo!" Reavers screamed out. "Jesus Christ! My life sucks enough already. I don't need to be crippled, too!"

"OK, then. First things first: Where do you hide your cash?" Gordan dropped Reavers' leg, and he relaxed a little, his head banging the wood floorboards under him.

Reavers' head rocked back and forth. He couldn't believe he was about to do this. "Freezer." He closed his eyes, defeated.

Gordan returned with Reavers' pillow case stuffed with the blocks of foil-covered cash. He wasn't as neat and organized as Barston. Gordan added the phone and laptop and placed the car keys in his pocket.

"OK, Reavers. Let's go." He helped Reavers to his feet and then locked the door behind them.

Gordan led him to the driver's door of the black Cadillac. Stepping aside, he asked, "Can you drive?"

Gordan could see the wheels spinning as Reavers started planning an escape.

Reavers, with his hands still flex-cuffed in front of him, reached out and pulled out the handle; the door popped open, and he slid himself into the seat.

"You going to cut these while I drive?" Reavers held out his wrists, showing the white plastic digging into the flesh of his pink skin.

"I don't know." Gordan looked inside the car a little. "Grab the wheel. Can you do it?"

Reavers placed his hands at about 11 and 1 and pretended to drive. "Not safe."

Gordan nodded at the windshield. "How about the mirrors — can you adjust them?"

He waited as Reavers moved the rearview mirror around and then looked at Hudde like he was crazy.

"OK. Buckle up," Gordan said, and he started to walk around the vehicle, the keys to the Cadillac still in his gloved hand. By the time he opened the back door and cut Barston free, Reavers had gotten the seat belt buckled.

"Who's she?" Reavers looked legitimately confused.

"Unbuckle and get out," Gordan said as he half dragged Barston back to Reavers' Chrysler. He unlocked the door, used another flex cuff to secure Barston's hands in front of her, and pushed her into the back seat.

"Well, at least tonight, you've been riding in luxury."

"Is that the guy?" Karen Barston looked back toward the Cadillac.

"He's like you — sold his soul for some cash; we're on a mission to find the top of this food chain."

Gordan walked back to Reavers, standing by the big black SUV. He showed Reavers the wallet and began looking through it. "Nice driver's-license photo." Gordan smiled at the confusion on Reavers' face. Gordan closed the driver's-side door and walked around to the back. As he hit the door release on the key fob, the gate slowly swung upwards, exposing a pile of bodies.

"What the fuck?" Reavers took two steps backwards.

Gordan threw the brown leather wallet forward. It probably fell between the front seats. Then closed the back lift gate and made a show of locking the vehicle with the fob. Gordan turned and threw the fob over into the empty field. Then he led Reavers back toward his own car.

"Looks like everyone will have some questions for you, Gary." He pushed Reavers into the back seat and then used an additional flex cuff to attach the two passengers together with their current cuffs.

Gordan climbed into the front seat. "Lots of room. I can see why this was a good choice," he said to Reavers. "Now" — Gordan turned to make eye contact — "if you want to live through tonight, tell me where we are going."

Chapter Thirty-Six

Abrahim Saied walked down the sidewalk from the main adults-only facility on the small island. The palms swayed with a steady breeze, the stiff branches making a racket above, while the waves tried to drown out that music from down below. He stood still, closing his eyes and facing the rising sun. Surely there could be no better way to pass your time on the earth. Maybe one day he would buy his own island for just him and a staff. This island was a construct of many different wealthy men, and part of his job was to gather information about the rich and powerful who frequented this place. When the Saudi government needed any of those who had used his services — whether it was to convince a famous celebrity to go to a wedding or a government official to change a decision — he was the one who held the necessary information. Yes, one day he would find his own beautiful place, and nobody would influence his own decisions.

But today, he had business to attend to. Saied straightened his back and strode forcefully out to the 12-year-old girl, with the younger one, sitting on a rock, sunning themselves like lizards.

"You know that your benefactor does not like you with a tan," he said to the older girl.

"Mister, is my mommy coming to see me?" the little one asked, squinting up through the sun.

"I'm sure she is on the way," he said.

Sarah squinted through the same sun. "So."

"He will be here later today or tomorrow, and I prefer him to be happy. Maybe you should ready your princess outfit. He likes that as well."

"I'm too old to play princess."

"Well you know what happens when something becomes too old to be useful; we throw those things out and get something new." Saied looked at little Debbie Tolbert to accentuate his point. "I bet Debbie here loves to play princess."

"Oh, I do!" Debbie looked up, hopeful of some new games to play.

"Soon, Debbie. I think you will have your chance soon." He patted her head as he walked back toward the main house.

Sarah wanted to tell Debbie about the horror that was one day going to befall her, but she was wise enough to allow her some more time as a child, her innocence still currently intact. It was enough that, for now, she was not crying about being away from her mother. She didn't need any additional monsters to worry about.

◆ ◆ ◆

"Slow down, slow down, slow down!" Reavers was yelling from the back seat. "I always miss it myself." He craned his neck, placing his face against the blacked-out window.

"Yeah, yeah — just around the next bend."

Gordan saw a spot that he could hide the big vehicle off the road in a tree line. He turned in, pivoted in the front seat, and looked back at his two captives.

"I'm going to be right back. If either of you tries to escape now, you'll have to drag the other's dead body for the rest of the trip."

"I have to go to the bathroom," Barston said, speaking for the first time in hours.

"When I get back." Gordan was gone, without any discussion.

He moved quickly at first until he observed an old farmhouse with a nice, new-looking steel structure behind it — just as Reavers had described it. He crept through the brush, lightly stepping toe first. Then he tested it to ensure nothing underneath would snap, and then he slowly applied his full weight. He repeated until he reached the edge of the clearing that made up the yard to the farm.

Gordan stood and watched the rising sun slowly creep down from the bright spot on the roof till it was lighting up half the house; there was no movement, no interior lighting, nothing that showed this to be occupied.

Gordan crept up to the back windows and risked peeking into the back of the house — nothing. He low-crawled up the back steps and looked at the screen door, inspecting it for booby traps, trip wires, or any other security equipment — nothing.

He slowly walked into a back screened-in porch and repeated the same thing with the back door — nothing. He shook his head and shrugged his shoulders. Taking a deep breath, he turned the knob — nothing.

He searched the entire house and found no signs that this had been occupied for anything other than temporary housing. There were no signs of permanent occupation, no toothbrushes or toilet paper, for that matter. No junk food, no coffee; this had not been used for anything other than a ruse.

Gordan snuck back and followed the edge of the steel barn all the way around — away from the driveway and the most obvious route. He stopped every two steps to listen; he heard no signs that any activities were taking place on the opposite side of this metal. He reached out when he arrived at the small concrete pad in front of the only man door. Wrapping his hand around the knob, he tried to make it turn; it was locked. Gordan pulled out the .45 and then thought twice; he replaced it into the holster inside his pants.

A loud *Clank!* notified Barston and Reavers that Gordan had returned as he unlocked the door with the key fob. He yanked open the back passenger door and told Barston to go the bathroom.

"Attached to him?" Barston seemed shocked.

"Or go right there. I don't care." Gordan slid into the car and turned it over, the big engine happy to be idling again.

"Come on, bitch. I gotta go too, too." Reavers began to pull Barston out the door.

There was a bit of a fuss as they decided how to work zippers and buttons, but they slid back into the back seat. Reavers kicked the door, and it bounced back and closed.

Gordan gunned the car in reverse, and it slid back out onto the pavement, the heavy front end sliding out a bit with the momentum. Gordan threw it into drive and slid back down the road until he came across the driveway. He pulled down around to the back of the barn. Slamming on the emergency brake and then stepping on the gas a bit, Gordan slammed the front right fender into the door at the back; it bent and then gave, popping inward.

Gordan was out of the vehicle with surprising speed, scanning the interior with the barrel of his handgun. There was no movement. He found a light switch and started a more thorough search. There were 10 small cells, each with its own sink and toilet all side by side straight down one wall. On the other side, there was a kitchenette and then a bigger bedroom, most likely for the English guy Reavers had described. A forensic team may be able to find something useful in here, but Gordan felt nothing but frustration. He contacted Ivan at CIA and informed him of the latest move on his part.

"I saw that you switched vehicles at the South Carolina residence. I could really use those laptops here to see what else I can dig into. This I know from what little I was able to do so far, Gordan: You are dealing with an international group participating in sex, body-part trading, and illegal adoptions — all of children." Ivan could be heard still tapping keys as he spoke. "The webpage is actually a menu for people like your Mr. Reavers to find what is most desired — to ensure that they aren't wasting time, I imagine."

Gordan was pulling down on his beard. "So how do I find the people in finance and who are making the orders? These are the bottom dwellers I'm dealing with."

"I'm still searching, Gordan. I just want to give you facts: There is one name that is always just three or four blocks separated from the places you've been at so far —The Perkins Foundation." Ivan paused. "And there's more, the men who attacked you in Georgia work for the same company that protects the former VP, Global Security Hawks."

"That's not good. How about their finance guy? Has he gotten back to you yet?"

Gordan heard Ivan sigh. "I've gotten nothing but the runaround every time I call. Look, Gordan. It doesn't mean anything. They are one of the deepest pockets that give to literally thousands of other charities, but..."

"OK, Ivan. Thanks for keeping at it. I may be offline for a while. I'm not sure what I'll have to do next. Ivan, I'll need the name and address of the guy who owns that security company."

Gordan climbed back into the Chrysler, slamming the door. "Where to next?"

"I'm afraid you won't want to go there alone." Reavers finally found a thought to smile about. "These boys play for keeps and I'm guessing they will not like seeing you knocking at their door, door."

"Tell me more." Gordan gritted his teeth and floored the Chrysler, looking for I-85N.

After about 15 minutes of driving and listening to Reavers, Gordan took a slight detour to a gun shop where he had made some purchases before.

◆ ◆ ◆

Rehan Tambe pulled the pager out of the pocket of his light-green hospital scrubs and stopped it from vibrating. He continued walking the emergency-room floor, looking in on the last patient to be admitted. This was one of his fears — that he would be paged while at work.

His supervisor did not understand and threatened firing him if he left. His pleading that this was a family matter of the most dire of circumstances did not matter to her. He drove out of the parking lot, cursing the gods for giving him the weakness that had brought him to this point in his life.

The nausea began to hit him the moment he got on the road, and he began to fight to keep breakfast down.

As he pulled into the abandoned warehouse driveway, he realized that he could not tell anyone how he had gotten there; in fact, he didn't remember driving there at all. He climbed out of his small car in a zombie-like trance. Tambe stumbled to the door and placed his forehead on the cool brick and steel of the door, hoping that it would ease the sickness that was nearly overwhelming him. He began to panic and thought that maybe he could tell Sasha to flee back to India, and then he could refuse to work for Alexei Orlov.

It was then that he noticed that the door was not fully closed. Tambe stood up and looked around; there were several vehicles, as there always were — nothing out of the ordinary.

Tambe pushed at the door and meekly said, "Hello." No one answered, and he pushed until the door was three quarters open. It suddenly stopped, and he looked down to see someone's feet.

Tambe knew that something was wrong. He understood that he should flee, but what if this was the reason they had paged him? What if there had been some kind of mob shoot-out, and now he was needed to help heal someone important? Yes, Tambe thought, maybe they would release him from his obligations if he did such a thing.

Tambe stepped past the man on the floor and immediately spotted Tock just a few feet further inside; he was chest down on the floor, with very dead eyes looking straight up at the ceiling. No need for an investigation on the cause of death.

Standing now in the relative darkness of the warehouse, looking over at his destination, the surgical room, just 20 steps away, his panic suddenly started up again.

What if the other bad guys were still here? Maybe they would kill him so that he couldn't help any of Orlovs' men. His heart was pounding so hard he knew it could be heard 10 feet away. He turned and looked at the door. He happened to glance up and observed a body on the metal walkway above him. The floor was tacky with the pooling blood, and now his sneakers were making a sickening squishing noise with each step.

He decided that he would find out why he had been paged; after all, this was not for the dissection of a child — this he knew.

Tambe opened the surgery-room door. Only the bright directional light that he had requested was on; it shined down on a still, fully clothed body. Tambe walked over and identified the very dead Alexei Orlov.

Tambe nearly jumped out of his sneakers when he heard a moan from the corner of the room, and he swung the light onto two individuals who were blindfolded and tied together in the corner. Tambe went over and began to reach down to remove the gag from the woman.

"I wouldn't do that!"

Tambe let out a scream and fell to his knees. "Don't kill me! Please — I beg of you." He squinted, but, after the bright light of the surgical lamp, he could see nothing in the darkness of the other corner. He heard the sound of a metal chair sliding across the concrete.

A very wide-shouldered, black-bearded man dropped the chair in front of Tambe and then sat backwards with a thunk.

"We've both made mistakes this morning. I lost my temper, and you were too slow," Gordan Hudde said to Tambe, using a very big handgun to accentuate this by pointing at himself and then Tambe with the barrel of the silver gun.

"I, I was at work; they never have paged me from work before," Tambe offered as an excuse.

"Do you know of a place they called 'Neverland'?" Gordan pushed with his legs, and the chair rocked forward, toward Tambe.

Tambe was frightened of where this was going to end, especially when he had to say, "No. These people never talked to me except to threaten and humiliate me or my fiancée."

"Did they call anyone 'The VP'?"

Tambe shook his head "No" several times, but he was very frightened to have to disappoint this man. "Are you going to kill me, too?" he finally asked.

"Tell me why I shouldn't Alexei filled me in on your relationship. I know what you did for them." Gordan stood up and walked behind Tambe, placing the barrel of the stainless .44 magnum on the back of his head.

"No, no, no! They forced me! I didn't care what they would do to me, but I could not bear to think what they would do to my Sasha! May Shiva strike me down if I am lying to you now."

"I guess I now own your debt, Rehan Tambe. What if you do one thing for me and then I wipe your slate clean?" Gordan holstered the big gun under his right shoulder and stepped in front of Tambe. "I keep my promises."

Tambe groveled at his feet. "Yes, yes! I would do anything that you would ask of me!"

"You being late allowed me to come up with something. Wait here." Gordan walked out into the main warehouse.

Gordan dialed his phone and waited. After three rings someone spoke in Spanish; Gordan asked to speak to the *El Jefe*, and then he said: "La mortalidad" Gordan waited several minutes, and then a voice he recognized as Luis Fernando Calderon, the biggest drug lord in all Mexico, came on the line.

"Is this really you?" he asked.

"Do you still like to drink Alquimia Reserva de Don Adolfo Extra Añejo Tequila with uninvited guests?" Gordan was referencing a time he'd called on Calderon last year.

"*Si,* my friend. Please tell me you have given up on your American bosses and are coming to work for me now!"

Gordan cleared his throat. "Maybe soon, but, for now, it is a favor I need."

"Anything!" Calderon was honestly pleased.

"Something told me that you would be better than Fed-Ex when it came to moving things." Gordan smiled.

About 15 minutes later, Gordan returned to tell Tambe what he would need to do to exorcise the demons from his shoulders.

"I will do this thing." Tambe nodded, looking over his shoulder at the two still tied together in the corner.

"Then you'll never see me again." Gordan turned and headed out to the daylight and the light-blue Chrysler.

Chapter Thirty-Seven

The 115-foot Christensen yacht came in at idle speed to the large concrete docks at Neverland Island. Abrahim Saied pointed, and his two men dropped the big rubber fenders over the side to add to the permanent protection of the rubber bumpers. Everything had been thoroughly thought out when they had designed the accommodations here.

The same two men then caught the thrown lines and secured the big seaworthy yacht to the deep end of the pier.

The tall, grey-haired man stepped onto dry land and bowed to the curator, Saied, who was nearly the same height.

"I am always so envious of your position here, Saied. What a beautiful day!" They shook hands, and then he concluded, "I have missed you, my friend."

Saied knew about politics; he was well studied when it came to the history of America and the Oval Office. Every time he spent a few days with Albert Perkins, he was shocked that he'd never made it to the Presidency.

"Mr. Vice President, you are always so kind, and the island itself welcomes your time spent here." Abrahim bowed deeply in return and made a grand, sweeping motion with his right hand.

Perkins looked every part the rich man on vacation, decked out in Bahama silk shirt and Bermuda shorts, with rich-brown-looking sandals. He turned and began walking toward the main facility. Perkins turned and observed Saied looking back up at the yacht.

"Saied?" Perkins called out to him.

"I wanted to greet your beautiful wife."

"Come." He held out his arm for Saied to catch up. "She was not able to get away just yet, however, maybe you could send down your man Malik to help out my bodyguard. We have a guest that is causing some...problems." He nodded to himself, thinking that "problems" was the correct word.

"It is too bad about your wife," Saied lied, "I will send down Saad and his mother to help with your things, of course."

"Maybe we could get a drink, and I'll fill you in on a few problems we have started having in the States. I don't think it will be a big problem; I have some people working on it, but it may slow our procurement for future endeavors a bit." He waved his hands in front of his chest, signifying "no problem." "We're going to have to depend on our West Coast operations for the time being. For safety, we shut down our East Coast operations."

They started up the slight rise over the concrete walkway through some palms and beautifully landscaped island flowers to the open, adult, side of the compound. "Come, Saied. Don't be a stranger. Tell me about the people who have been here since my last visit." Perkins put his arm warmly around Saied as they continued.

Chapter Thirty-Eight

Gordan traveled south, heading back down on the I-95, quickly approaching Baltimore. Ivan called him, and he hit the speaker to make it easier to drive.

"This guy, Ranks, was once a Colonel in the Army and became the Director of the Defense Intelligence Agency during the time of the Howles /Perkins administration." Ivan paused.

"What else?"

"He lives in a ritzy area outside of Baltimore — Anton North. I'll forward it soon. Anyway, he's built this very big security group, and the Pentagon has been leaning on his operators the last few years while everyone has been crying about "boots on the ground." He'd easily have the ability to pick some guys to go take you out while you were drinking beer and watching 'Wheel of Fortune.'"

Gordan remained quiet while the plastic keys tapped over the speaker.

"This guy's a real big deal, Gordan."

"So?"

"So, you make him go missing, and a lot of people will probably start looking."

"Stop thinking the worst. Tell me: Is there a family at this address?" Gordan made the correct turn onto the 695 West.

"Messy divorce, one older kid. Poor guy's on his own in his big mansion."

"See if you can find a security system and hack it. Maybe look at the home via satellite. Do something useful instead of harping on my bedside manner."

"Hey, who's helping who here?"

"You haven't told the boss what direction this whole thing has been going, have you?" Gordan suddenly felt that the Director of CIA, John Stevens, would probably frown on his current activities.

"No, and I won't. These people need to be ferreted out. I'll beg forgiveness later and, of course..." Ivan paused, wondering if he should continue.

Gordan nodded his head. "Blame everything on me. I know, and that works for me. Don't worry about it. Goodbye, Ivan. Call if anything big pops."

Gordan found the correct off ramp and the proper neighborhood: No fences, all brick, three-car garages, perfectly manicured green lawns with big hedgerows, and enough space between homes that he could expect some privacy. It was very fortunate.

Gordan found a hamburger place and brought his take-out into the parking lot of a golf course to eat and watch the golfers warming up while using the practice range. He was wondering if he should take up this game when some women in tennis outfits caught his attention. He got out and walked down to look at the courts and the good legs.

Gordan had to have answers from former Colonel Ranks and his Global Security Hawks. Had the three men currently napping at Gary Reavers' house been sent directly by him? Was it possible that the former Vice President, a big family-values guy from way back, could somehow be involved in something as heinous as the abduction and abuse of children? It was preposterous.

Gordan knew that the next step should be to get all the electronics to Ivan. Who knew what The Kid might be able to pull from the laptops, especially the one from the Russian mobster Orlov? But maybe he could get something of use from Ranks after they'd had a heart-to-heart later tonight.

♦ ♦ ♦

"Oh, my! How I've missed you, my lovey girl!" Albert Perkins hugged the 4'5" Sarah DeLucia, holding her tightly. "I think you've grown quite a bit since I saw you last." He lifted her chin to look at her face, and she pulled away.

"Please don't be difficult today. I've had enough troubles for a while, and you're supposed to be joyful, not bad."

"I hate this dress," Sarah said without looking up at him.

"You're a princess, my dear. Why not look the part?"

"I'm too old for this." She stood still looking down at the frilly white, pink, and gold gown, pulling the dress out from each side with both hands.

Perkins nodded his head in agreement and breathed out a deep sigh. "Yes, I suppose you *are* getting too old." He felt a little sadness as he realized it was time to get a new toy.

She smiled a little at the ground. "May I go change?"

"Yes, dear. You may do what you want...for now."

Sarah DeLucia walked quickly back to her room to change. Perkins searched out Abrahim Saied and draped an arm around his shoulders.

"It's time, Saied. Is it true that you have a new child I could meet?"

"Of course! Let us go meet her at once!" The two men headed to the children's quarters with freshness in their step.

Saied unlocked the door and stepped back, allowing Perkins to turn the handle and swing the door open.

"Oh, my God! What a beautiful little princess!" Perkins dropped to his knees and held his arms out, trying to get Debbie Tolbert to come to him. "Look at that beautiful platinum hair!"

Debbie stood in the opposite corner of the small room trying to figure out if she knew this man; he was really nice. She visibly made a decision, shrugging her shoulders and walking closer to the grey-haired man.

"Do you know my mommy?" She pouted immediately after asking.

"I do know your mommy, and she sent me on a mission to come and help take care of you. Would you like that?" Perkins began running his hands up and down her little body.

"Are you feeling well? Have they been nice to you?" He squeezed her legs and arms as if he was checking out a prized horse.

She giggled a little.

"Oh, my, Saied — we have a ticklish one!" Perkins began tickling the little girl's ribs, and she squirmed to the ground. "You be a good girl, and I'll see if we can play together later, OK?" Perkins patted the white ruffled bottoms that stuck out from the little smock as she ran back to her bed. Perkins shut and locked the door and then leaned into the wood, breathing deeply, as if he could still smell her.

"Yes. Saied. She will do just fine; charge my account accordingly." He closed his eyes, and Saied patted his shoulder.

"Oh, it is good!" Saied turned and began walking toward the bar, he was growing hungry.

Perkins' giant of a bodyguard brushed past Saied without a word. "Mr. Perkins — a call." He held out a satellite phone.

Perkins held it to his ear and said, "Yes." Then he listened for a few moments, making a few affirmative noises.

"Well, what does that mean?" Perkins went out into the early-evening darkness; palms were swaying gently, another calm night on the shallow-cove side of the island.

"Failure to establish contact? What the fuck are you saying to me right now?" Perkins' agitation was beginning to show.

Perkins ran his hand over his head and looked to the heavens. *Why do I always have to handle everything? Why is no one else ever capable?* "OK, listen. Burn everything about our association. Put out a press release saying that you have been having difficulty with these returning veterans being able to fit into civilian life, and then terminate those men. We will talk tomorrow." Perkins hung up the phone and handed it back to his man, Carver.

"Troubles, boss? Anything you need, I'll handle it for you."

Perkins slapped Carver hard on the shoulder. "I know that, and that's why you're with me. Don't worry. I'll fix it. Here — give me back that phone." He reached out and took the phone, dialing and then holding it back up to his ear.

"Yes, it's me. You're going to have to liquidate the entire East Coast operation, and maybe you should come spend some time here until we see how it all plays out." He paced again in small circles. "No, I'm not kidding. Yes, yes. Whatever needs to be done. Oh, my Lord! Just take care of it." And then he hung up and returned the phone to the big man.

Perkins slapped the giant shoulder of Carver again and shook his head. "You'd think I asked people to build a pyramid or something of such difficulty." He continued to shake his head as he led the way to the kitchen area. "Come on, Carver. Let's grab some dinner."

Chapter Thirty-Nine

"OK, Ivan. I think I can hear an engine coming up the drive-way. Go ahead and disable the garage CCTV camera now." Gordan hung up the phone and slid it into a pocket.

Headlights flashed across the yard, stopping on the ga-rage door closest to the house and the farthest from where Gordan lay, in the dirt, under a hedgerow near the Ranks home.

The big BMW slid into the garage, and Gordan began creeping toward the door. The taillights suddenly went bright as Henry Ranks stepped on the brake as he placed the ve-hicle into park; then he pressed the button to turn off the en-gine. The headlights remained lit for a few minutes until after Ranks was inside the house.

Gordan dove down through the door and rolled up to the back of the car, careful to not touch the hot exhaust. He wait-ed until he heard the car door open and saw two pair of black shoes touch the pavement.

Ranks was just telling someone on the phone, "Not to worry. I'll take care of it." The moment the phone started going for a front suit-jacket pocket, Gordan had Ranks in a sleeper hold.

If Ranks had ever been a field soldier, if at one time he had been in great physical shape, with the reflexes of a combat veteran, those days were long gone. Gordan put him to sleep with no great satisfaction.

Gordan patted him down and took the slim .380 auto in his right-hand pocket. Gordan slipped it into his own back pocket. Gordan placed the keys, wallet, and cigarettes into a small pile at Ranks' feet and waited for him to return to consciousness. His hands were zip tied in his lap as he leaned against his own vehicle.

Ranks' head began to rock back and forth, and it appeared that he tried to touch his neck with his right hand alone before he realized that both hands were tied together.

"What is this?" Ranks had not yet recovered his full senses; he opened and closed his eyes and rubbed his forehead with the back of his tied hands.

"Oh, it's you; I guess that means my men will not be checking in."

"Not unless you use a crystal ball. So tell me how this thing works out." Gordan stood over the man, waiting for a response.

Ranks looked a bit confused. He glanced left and then toward the garage door that connected to the house. "Where are the FBI agents" Will I be secreted off to some federal location, maybe Guantanamo?"

"Speaking of the FBI, what happened to the woman — Andrews?" Gordan knelt down to be level with the older, tired-looking man.

"Oh, I think I'll just wait for my attorney," Ranks said, and then he relaxed, allowing his chin to rest on his chest.

It was Gordan's turn to look confused. He looked left and then right. "Oh, I get it: You think this is some kind of *real* investigation. You know who I am — correct, Colonel?"

"I read your jacket."

"Oh, I'm so disappointed then. You sent three wannabe's to take me out, to kill me. Do you really believe they are being held somewhere, too?" Gordan leaned in to look at the man's eyes. "No, sir. They're out there bloating as they reach room temperature. You should have sent many more."

Ranks frowned, thinking.

"You sent them. I'm here to find out why and to return the favor. There's nothing official about this business." Gordan flicked his wrist, and a deadly knife blade appeared before Ranks' face.

Beads of sweat began forming on Ranks' forehead; his chest was moving rapidly. Gordan prayed that his ticker would hold up.

"I don't like repeating." Gordan smacked Ranks with the flat of the blade on top of his head. "Where is the female FBI agent?"

Gordan watched a bit of panic take hold. "Wait! What do I get if I tell you what you want to know?"

Gordan stood up and walked out in front of Ranks. Wrapping his fist around his chin, he pulled down on his beard, thinking.

"You're going to cooperate?"

"Yes."

"Anything I ask, you're willing to tell me?"

"Yes."

"Wow, I didn't plan on this outcome." Gordan paced back and forth. "I promise to leave you here alive and well when I get everything I ask."

Ranks looked up at Gordan, wiping the sweat with the back of his two hands again. "I'll be fine. No need for paramedics and you're not calling the police or anyone?"

Gordan nodded his head and ran his hand down through his beard one last time. "OK. You have a deal." Gordan wheeled back and to his knees with incredible speed; he held the knife at eye level. "But you'd better be telling the truth."

"I will." Ranks looked up at Gordan defiantly as if he were saying, "Try me."

"The female FBI agent?" Gordan stared into Ranks' eyes.

"I don't know. Perkins had some questions, and I helped them… meet. Look, it was a few days ago. I assume she's gone."

Gordan's stomach tightened. Another woman he had gotten close to had probably died a horrible death.

"How did you get mixed up in all this?"

Ranks sighed and leaned his head back into the door of the black sedan "It's a long story, but Perkins had some info on me, and then he helped me get Global Hawks into operation."

"So now you're beholden to his every whim?" Gordan felt relieved that he'd never had to serve under this pushover.

"No, now we are so intertwined that it would be mutual destruction. So what's the point?"

"Are your people helping with the kids?" Gordan was taking a chance that he had any valuable information on this.

"Oh, please. No. I mean — sure, I know what Perkins likes, but..."

"So you're the muscle, and that's about it."

This got under Ranks' hide a bit. "No. I've traveled with him and all that. I mean, I might not be part of his inner circle, but I'm important. I've even traveled to Neverland with him."

"What?"

Ranks seemed upset. "No — not to do little kids. I mean, they have older girls there, too — much younger than me maybe, but it's not what I meant." Ranks didn't mind being a murderer or looking the other way and assisting with pedophilia. He just wanted Hudde to know he didn't participate in defiling little kids.

"Can you point this place out on a map for me, Colonel?"

"Sure. It's in the South Caribbean, north of Venezuela — not much more than two square miles, but it's perfect for their purposes."

"What exactly is that?"

"Anything and everything to do with kids: Rich kid in Morocco needs a heart transplant? You call these guys. Like to fuck six-year-old boys? These people. And if you want to adopt a healthy American baby, but you live in Belarus, these people get you what you want."

Gordan stepped back, as if Ranks had the plague.

"What? You don't know these people exist out there? Don't blame me, pal. I just play the hand dealt to me."

Gordan looked about the garage; he looked at the BMW, the Land Rover, and the Mercedes in the last stall. "Looks like you have played your hand pretty well."

"Whatever, I wasn't going to live on a Colonel's pension. Now, I'll do just fine."

Gordan squatted down next to Ranks again, sticking the knife into the soft flesh just under his eye. "Last thing before I go: Who else is involved?"

Ranks carefully shook his head "No" before speaking. "Look. I dealt only with Perkins. Other than the island staff, I don't know anyone else."

"How many staff on the island?"

"Oh, eight to ten, counting everyone, I presume."

"How many hostages?"

"Oh, they call them 'guests' there, and I really don't know; I just saw a few adult women when I was there."

"Are they armed? Do they have weapons?"

Ranks sighed deeply.

Gordan moved the knife to Ranks' throat. "Am I boring you?"

"No... I just don't know. I assumed that his two men are armed. They do have occasional Caribbean pirates, you know, and those two were very-serious-looking Middle Eastern men."

"So, there is a connection to what country?"

"I believe Saudi Arabia. But it could be somewhere else. You've got me guessing at things now."

Gordan stood up, as satisfied as he could be. "What assurances do I have that you won't call in more of your men and cause me a great deal of trouble?"

"None, I suppose. But I did hold up my end of the bargain."

Gordan stood over Ranks, thinking. "Do you drink?"

"Doesn't everyone?"

"Does your medicine cabinet have some sedatives or pain killers?"

"Yes, but…"

"OK. Get up, and let's go into the house. You down a few sleeping pills and take a couple slugs of the drink of your choice, and I'll feel like a have a few hours' head start, at a minimum."

Gordan helped Ranks to his feet. Ranks flipped open the access panel on his security system and allowed the two entry.

"Why such a lousy system when you're a security expert?"

Ranks looked at him. "The wife hated them."

"Say no more," Gordan told him.

Gordan had Ranks lead him through the house, finding first some prescription pain meds and then a bottle of good bourbon. Gordan poured a good pint into the glass and then laid out four tablets on the counter.

"I'm guessing at your body weight. This should put you out until late tonight."

"As long as it doesn't kill me." Ranks looked at Gordan from the side of his eyes.

"I made a promise; you will be fine when I close the door behind me."

"Well, let's get started." Ranks reached out and popped pill number one, washing it down with several sips.

Gordan started looking about at the fine things Ranks and his family had accumulated over the years.

"Going to steal some things on the way out?" Ranks asked between sips.

"I'm looking for a pen and paper, actually, but that's not a bad idea. If I end up on the run, I may need some cash.

Ranks looked at him, already beginning to find it difficult to focus. "The pad and paper are in the drawer nesht to the window," he began to slur. "Money in the only sneaker shoebox in my wife's closet."

Ranks looked down at the fourth pill. "I don't think I'm going to need this."

Gordan plopped the pad of paper in front of Ranks. "Before you take that, I need some additional assurance. Write down that you know the former VP is a pedophile and that you have killed to cover it up. Then sign it."

Ranks followed directions; he finished with a grandiose flourish of a signature. "Duressshh," he almost yelled out.

"Sure. Under duress — I get it." Gordan had to wait only a few more minutes until Ranks slid into a medicated stupor.

Gordan ran up the stairs, finding the correct closet on the third try. Only one Nike box was in a pile of approximately

200 others. Gordan opened the box and found it packed with bundles of $100 bills, maybe close to $20,000. Gordan took the entire box out to the garage and laid it near the door.

Pulling out his phone, he contacted Ivan. "I've had to be inside for a while. Can you do something with the CCTV system?"

Ivan laughed. "It's connected through the cable. I'll reroute it and have it recording HBO. By the morning, the memory will be full."

"Later, then. Wait in your office." Gordan hung up. He walked over and looked down at the sleeping Ranks. He reached down, flicking open the knife as he did, cutting Ranks' hands free. He then pulled his limp body over his shoulder. Taking him out, he set him in the BMW.

Gordan returned to the kitchen and took the other two sets of keys. Walking out into the garage, he started the engine to each vehicle — the BMW last. Gordan folded the note he had just made Ranks write and set it on the passenger seat.

Closing the garage door with the remote, Gordan made his way to Reavers light-blue ride and headed off to see Ivan in person.

Never let it be said that Gordan Hudde didn't keep his promises. Gordan knew that everyone lied; he hoped he could believe the eyes looking back at him in the rearview mirror when this thing was over.

Chapter Forty

Traffic was light, and Gordan stuck to just under 10 miles faster than every posted speed limit. He arrived in the basement of CIA headquarters and made it to Ivan's cave in very good time.

Could Perkins really be involved in something so sick while being so close to the most important position in the world? It would be a possible answer as to why he never reached for the highest office in the land, but this goes well beyond what people have ignored in the past.

Everything could be worked on after they rescued any children; that was the priority.

"Ivan, I've got an electronic stash for you to check out." He held up the pillowcase now stuffed with phones and laptops.

Ivan was holding up one finger, seeming to ask for a moment. Gordan set the bag down and waited. As always, Ivan was working faster than Gordan could read.

"Yes." Ivan put his fist in the air and then pressed a button; a printer began warming up a few feet away.

Ivan spun in his chair to face Gordan, a big grin on his face. "I was doing everything I could to find out who'd purchased these buildings, what banks were used, and where down payments came from. I've been hacking so many systems over the last day." He shook his head sadly.

Gordan was nodding his head "Yes."

"I was being too tricky; I took a list of properties that the foundation had invested in and then cross referenced with who was paying the utilities. Presto!" He pushed off the floor, and his chair rolled to the printer.

Ivan stood when he presented it to Gordan. "One dozen properties owned by The Perkins Foundation, with utilities paid by one law firm."

Gordan took the page and began looking at the locations. Ivan couldn't wait, and he pointed at the page.

"Reavers' house right here, the Virginia holding cell, and the New Jersey warehouse." Ivan stood back beaming.

Gordan looked up from the page. "Could it really be that simple?"

"Oh, wait." Ivan motioned for Gordan to follow, tapped his screen, and brought up a face.

"Who's that?" Gordan asked.

"The guy at the firm who writes all the checks." Ivan was still smiling.

"Should I know this guy, Davis?"

Ivan shook his head "Do you know Cheryl Perkins' maiden name?"

"No shit! Ivan, you're a genius!" Gordan paused. "But you're not done. I need everything you can get on an island off the coast of Venezuela, satellite images, distances from US Virgin Islands, and then maybe Florida."

"Taking a trip?" Ivan's hands began flying over the keys.

"Probably. Maybe you can see if we have any assets, including military, anywhere nearby."

Ivan nodded. "Sure."

Gordan looked back at the paper for a moment. "Hey, Ivan. Did you notice that there are six locations east and six west of the Mississippi?"

"Oh." Ivan rolled back to the printer and took the next page from the tray. "I printed you a map."

"That location is about 20 minutes from the Perkins home in West Virginia."

Ivan nodded at him. "Or you're going to have to go to Louisiana or Florida."

"All right. I'm just saying 'Fuck it" and heading right to Perkins' place." Gordan started walking to the door.

"And say what?" Ivan asked. "'Hey, are you running a child-abduction ring? Oh, no? Never mind. Gee — thank you, Mr. Vice President, sir'?" Ivan turned back to his keyboard. "Good luck with that one, Gordan."

Gordan found a gas station and filled the Chrysler up; he planned on getting the worst gas mileage possible for the next few hours. He made one last call to Dam Neck, Virginia to check on some Navy Seal friends he used to know. He was told that they were not available, which meant they were deployed, as far as Gordan was concerned.

Then he set his mind to driving and put the gas pedal to the floor to see what the big sedan could do.

◆ ◆ ◆

The distinguished-looking gentleman from Virginia was not at his home. He was 2,000 miles away, leaning over the petite form of Sarah DeLucia right now. He currently was doing everything possible to shove his manhood down the young girl's throat. He squeezed her neck while he thrusted.

"Don't you throw up on me!" he warned as he was nearly there.

He pulled on her ponytail with his free hand as he tilted his head back and finished. She rolled over, crying and gasping for air.

"Now, now honey; you made me feel good, and you should be very pleased." He patted her exposed pink, ruffled panties while he glowed in his own pleasure. Her fear and anger did not register anywhere in his mind.

"Yes, you should be very happy because I think this will be an extended stay this time. We should really be able to enjoy each other on this trip." He gave her his biggest campaign smile and kissed her forehead as he stood up. He replaced his now limp penis in his shorts and shook his head.

"Oh, you're really growing up into a beautiful young lady." He smiled as he exited her room; she heard the lock turn after his exit.

Perkins strode confidently into the bar area on the adult side of the island. He slid onto a bar chair next to Saied.

"You're looking good tonight," Saied told him something he didn't need to know.

"Oh, she is such a beautiful child," Perkins noted.

Saied saw some sadness in the smile. "She's nearly as old as the last one."

Perkins nodded. "Soon, maybe," he pondered. "Oh, that little Debbie is a cute one, though." His big smile returned.

"Indeed. But didn't you need to tell me something?"

"Oh, Saied. I'm sure it's nothing. I have many people working on our behalf back in the States. I'm sure I'll get some good news in a few days. If not, I'll fill you in."

"Be it so." Saied got up and excused himself, patting Perkins' shoulder as he left the room.

"Oh, hell!" he heard Perkins say to the bartender. "Make it a double. I'm not driving."

Chapter Forty-One

Gordan thought he could have done the five-hour trip in fewer than three under the right circumstances but was pretty happy with getting there before 0330hrs. The button on the gate went unanswered. Gordan was tired. He hadn't slept in days. He knew he was closing in on something big and bad. He suddenly felt angry that he had to worry about the importance of Perkins. He put it in gear and rammed the gate. It was not really for security, and Gordan went through easily, following the long, winding driveway to the circular drive in front of the stately log cabin.

It was dark — not a window lit, no vehicles to be seen. Nothing but the wind and a horned owl somewhere close by. Gordan walked up and banged hard on the front wooden doors — nothing. He walked to the back and looked into the windows — still no signs of life. Gordan had stepped back and was looking up at the second-floor options when he heard a vehicle approaching.

Gordan ran to the corner of the home just in time to see one of the big Cadillac Escalades slide to a stop on the gravel of the driveway.

Gordan was surprised to see Cheryl Perkins get out of the driver's-side door. Gordan surprised her more when he stepped out from the shadows.

She let out a small scream, "Oh, my Lord! What are you doing here?"

"I was looking for your husband, Mrs. Perkins. I'm sorry to have startled you."

Gordan noticed that the normally coifed hair was a mess, her white blouse was untucked, and she seemed to be missing a button; she was carrying her shoes.

"Are you OK, Mrs. Perkins? Where is your security detail?" Gordan instinctively reached for the big magnum grip tucked firmly under his right arm. He stepped backwards into the shadows looking for some unseen threat.

She totally ignored Gordan and walked directly to her front door. Her keys jingled and she stepped in and turned to Gordan.

"I suggest you make an appointment for the next visit. Now, leave before I call the police." She slammed the door, and Gordan heard the dead bolt slam home.

"What the fuck?" Gordan said out loud. He was startled when his own phone rang.

"Ivan, what's going on?"

"Gordan, I don't know where you are right now, but you better hurry to the first address. There is fire reported there right now."

Within seconds the Chrysler was throwing stone as Gordan screamed out of the driveway heading south. He blasted past the broken gate like an intercontinental ballistic missile breaching the surface above a submarine.

Gordan did the 20-minute trip in 10; he would have driven past the wooded driveway if there had not been emergency vehicles already on the scene. As it was, he slid a hundred feet past the access road. A police officer ran up to the car as he pulled over.

"You trying to kill somebody, mister?" he yelled at Gordan as Gordan ran past him toward the structure.

The fire crew was just getting hoses set up from a tanker truck and starting to put down a spray on the fully engulfed building. The heat was intense, and an official from the local fire department started to approach Gordan with a hand up to stop his advance.

"Wait a minute, son. This is as unsafe as it gets, and we need to get those flames down before the entire forest goes up."

"Has anyone gotten in there?" Gordan screamed at him over the roar of the flames and the sound of other fire trucks arriving.

"Just get back — that's an order," the man yelled at Gordan.

Gordan ran past him toward the front doors and kicked them in before he could be stopped. Smoke billowed out, and Gordan knelt, holding a forearm over his face as the heat intensified. The nozzle man on the ladder saw him and sent a spray of water over Gordan as he went through the door.

Staying low, he crawled, trying to keep under the smoke. His way was well lit by the fire on nearly everything on the back wall. To the right were the bodies of two men. Gordan could see that one had been shot; there was a cane sword through the chest of the other. Gordan could smell the gasoline soaking their clothing as it burned away and cooked flesh. If he weren't so badly burned, Gordan may have recognized the always-dapper Reginald Theodore Lenard from the description Reavers had given him.

Gordan coughed and spat. He low-crawled a bit farther. He could see a small cell, like some jail in a small town. In it, Gordan could see a still, smaller body. He fought everything in his mind that was screaming at him to retreat to safety, but he had to continue forward. Somewhere, part of the roof collapsed. Gordan was about to turn back when a small hint of silver caught his eye. There, in the protection of a fire-blackened child's hand lay the ornate silver button from the blouse of the killer.

Anger got Gordan out the door; a couple of emergency paramedics dragged him to the back of an ambulance. They poured water over him and gave him some oxygen until he returned to full consciousness. Gordan coughed and hacked, spitting. His lungs still felt like they were burning.

"What kinda fool are you?" the man from earlier was standing over him, yelling.

Gordan looked down into his own left hand; he had retained it, the evidence. He staggered to his feet, gaining strength as he got farther out to the road. Gordan got into his vehicle and turned it around, heading back the way he'd come. He rolled down the windows to try to clear his head; the only thing burning more than his lungs was the vengeance in his heart.

The big sedan fought around the last corner to the Perkins driveway. Gordan thought he saw some tail lights up ahead but needed to be sure. He launched up Perkins' long drive-way. Several hundred yards before getting to the house, he got a good glimpse of the empty parking spot.

Gordan spun the wheel hard, the front wheels tearing up the manicured yard and flowers lining the driveway as he got back out to the road.

Gordan pointed the vehicle north and kept the pedal to the floor. The suspension was soft for a comfortable ride, and he risked bottoming out at a few locations but kept his speed as high as he could reasonably control.

As he sped down the hill toward the stop sign at Route 16, he saw the Cadillac making the turn toward the small town of Fayetteville. She must have seen him coming, because she suddenly sped up, putting extra distance from him as he slowed to make the turn. He was just a few miles an hour from being totally out of control, and he swung wide around the corner, tires screaming. The big sedan was not the car of choice for the drifting crowd.

Gordan was happy for two things: One, it was still too early for morning traffic, and, two, Cheryl Perkins hadn't been driving much for 30 years now. He gained on her to within the length of two football fields as they seemed to fly past the small shops and stores that made up the main street. He was doing near 90 in the 25 mph residential and commercial area.

She nearly didn't make the turn onto Route 19 heading northeast. The Caddy screamed for a moment on the two outside wheels, precariously; it looked to be flipping over. Gordan took a right through the yard of an Exxon on the corner, taking out several signs but sliding beautifully onto the street, heading in the right direction and losing very little speed. Perkins was now just a half-dozen car lengths in front of him.

The US Route 19 was straight and relatively smooth. The two vehicles now opened up. With the top speed of the Chrysler slightly faster, Gordan was now two car lengths behind as they rocketed past the sign for the New River Gorge. He got behind the bigger vehicle and bumped the back. Both vehicles lost some road grip, and Perkins slowed considerably as she got onto the west side of the New River Gorge Bridge.

Now, Gordan struck the Cadillac hard, and it nearly turned sideways before over-correcting and bouncing off of the center concrete barrier before coming to rest, facing the wrong direction, nearly against the bridges outside lane, directly over the river.

Gordan ran up to the driver's-side door, stealing a glance at the big drop to his right. He opened the door to a clearly dazed Cheryl Perkins; the airbag had deployed, doing its job.

"What the fuck do you think you're doing?" she demanded — even in all this, giving off the air of authority.

"You just killed a kid, maybe a couple. I don't know — maybe more. Who the fuck do you think you are?"

"You'll never prove it, and nobody will ever put me in jail. Do you know who I am?" Spittle flew from her mouth, and Gordan stepped back.

She began to unbuckle her seatbelt.

"You know all about what your husband is doing, don't you?" Gordan watched her eyes; they narrowed, and her lips curled into a sneer.

"He's helping those kids. Without him, they'd all probably end up dead, anyway."

Suddenly Gordan remembered the ornate button, and he pulled it out from his pocket.

"Do you know where this was found?"

Her eyes locked onto the small silver orb, but she didn't say a word.

"This was in the hands of the little boy, a little boy who must have reached out and grabbed it while you poured gasoline all over the place." Gordan's chest was heaving as hard as if he had run to catch her.

"Fuck you and your evidence!" she suddenly screamed and kicked at the back of his hand.

Gordan watched, horrified, as that little button flipped and tumbled, sparkling in the remaining moonlight like a small tear making a graceful arc over the guardrail, slipping off into the complete darkness 800 feet below. Gordan imagined the tiny splash into the New River.

"Your word against mine," she sneered.

Gordan reached over and took her by the neck. Snatching her from the car, he picked her up over his head, her 130 pounds nothing in his current state.

"Go get it," and he hurled her with all his might over the railing; he hoped she'd hit a rock, so he didn't bother imagining a splash.

Gordan got back into the Chrysler, a bit stunned at everything that had happened over the last hour. He set his jaw, spun his car around, and started heading south, making phone calls to contacts past; he estimated the next leg of his journey would take him near 10 hours.

Chapter Forty-Two

Albert Perkins sat on a rattan chair, back to the rising sun, on the veranda, overlooking the small cove at the center of the island. Despite the already-warm, moist air, his coffee steamed.

Perkins heard the big man approaching from behind him.

"What's happening this morning, Leslie?"

Carver stepped around to the front of Perkins. "I've heard some news from stateside. My boss committed suicide last night."

"What, Ranks?" Perkins stood up and walked out to the end of the concrete, rubbing the back of his head. He turned back to the giant.

"How, how did he do it? Did he tell anyone? Did he leave a note? Come on, man, speak!" Perkins' mind was racing.

"All I know is that he was found in his garage this morning by one of the guys who were supposed to pick him up for an early flight. That's all I know. The police are there now. I knew you guys were close. I'm sorry, VP."

Perkins looked up at Carver. "It's not just that. My wife called in a bit of a panic last night. She said she would call back, but I haven't heard anything; I'm worried." He pressed his temples and then walked over to get his coffee.

Perkins tapped his nose with his forefinger and then shrugged his shoulders. "It can't be related — could it?"

"How?"

The big man had no idea.

"Are you sure that FBI agent didn't get a message out somehow?"

"On that, I'm positive. No, no. It's impossible. I made sure of it." He waved a big, open hand out in front of his chest. "No way."

"OK, then. Maybe I'm just being overly paranoid." Perkins patted the giant's shoulder as he headed back inside. "Maybe I need some breakfast."

"Sure, VP. Nothing to worry about. I'll let you know if I hear anything more about Ranks. I know he was pretty upset about the divorce."

Perkins turned back to face Carver. "Yes, you're right. We did speak once about that — now I'm sure you're right."

◆ ◆ ◆

Just past 1400hrs. the same afternoon, Gordan Hudde turned into the dirt road just outside of Troy, Alabama, that led to the small home of Charlie Kent Chester, former Special Forces, and former CIA operative.

The old wooden house was nearly overrun with greenery. Chester was sitting on the wraparound porch, wearing torn khaki pants and a dirty white dress shirt with the sleeves torn

off. His unkempt, dirty blond hair was pulled back into a ponytail; he was perched on an old stool, a paintbrush hanging
out his mouth, looking at a canvas on an easel.

Gordan rolled to a stop and quickly got out of the car,
making his way to the porch.

Chester stood and watched. "Mr. Hudde. It's been a long
time."

"Charlie, you don't know how much I appreciate this. Did
The Kid forward you anything? You get Internet service here?"
He stood back looking for any signs that Charlie even had
electricity here.

Charlie nodded his head at the easel. "What do you think?"

"I hope you can still fly better than you paint. Come on,
Charlie. No fucking around, man. I have a clock ticking."

"Alright, brother. This way. Follow me. No need to be hos-
tile, man."

They walked around the side to the back of the house. As
they headed back farther, it was like a small aircraft junkyard.
All kinds of helicopter and fixed-wing pieces were strewn everywhere. There was a fuselage of a small plane with plant
life growing out of it. The closer they got to a very large steel
structure, the more the aircraft looked useable.

A small helicopter with a tarp thrown over the rotors looked
good, and several single-engine, small fixed-wings were also
in good-looking shape, tied down and covered.

Gordan took it all in. "Hey, Chuck — any of this stuff going
to work?"

"Man — I told you I could do this. Don't worry about it."

They reached a door to the steel barn. A key appeared in Charlie's hand. He unlocked the door, and they were in a very clean and modern-looking office. The walls were covered in maps from around the world. There were several model airplanes on the top of the desk and file cabinets.

Gordan couldn't help taking a step outside and looking about before heading back into the modern, clean, concrete-and-steel structure.

"You should live in here," he said to Charlie, with no malice.

Charlie just grunted as he printed a page from the desktop computer. "Here is your island man." He held the page out for Gordan to review.

Gordan looked down at the satellite photo of the boomerang-shaped island nearly two miles long. It was thicker at the center, with a small quiet-looking cove facing west. Two large structures were at the center of the island, with a smaller, thinner structure extending away from both, looking a bit like two exclamation points. There appeared to be a very large dock and pier extending into a deep-water channel at the north end.

"Somebody has some cash," Charlie noted over Gordan's shoulder.

"These sons of bitches are abducting American children for all kinds of nefarious reasons."

Charlie looked at Gordan for a moment. "So where's the cavalry, man. Where are the Famous But Incompetent?" Charlie tilted his head. His faded blue eyes bore into Gordan's green ones. "What's the real story, man? Why are you trying to MacGyver this thing on a shoestring budget?"

Gordan returned the gaze without blinking. "I'll be glad to fill you in during the flight. I'm not telling you're going to get a reward, but nobody is coming after me right now, either. I just don't have the evidence to prove it to anyone important enough to get the support. I don't have the time, and I'm all out of patience. Do you have the things I asked for?"

Charlie patted him on the shoulder. "I've never let anyone down before, and I'm not starting now."

He led Gordan through a door. There was momentary blindness in the total darkness. Charlie flicked some switches, and lights began buzzing overhead. In the middle of what turned out to be a hangar, there sat a Fokker F-127 Friendship dual-turbo-props aircraft, in perfect-looking condition.

"Sweet," Gordan nodded. "Where did you steal this beast?"

"Yeah, but what's mine say?" Charlie was beaming. "It's my baby, and I stole it fair and square from our brethren in the 'Christians In Action' when they had me flying in and out of Honduras a few decades ago."

Gordan ignored the movie reference. "Very nice. How about everything else?"

"This way." They walked to the back, and Charlie pointed at a work table full of some of the items that Gordan had requested.

Charlie walked the table left to right, placing his hand on each item as he went.

"This here Dash-1-Bravo parachute hasn't been jumped in 25 years. I took it out, and there wasn't too much rot, so I repacked it."

Gordan looked a bit skeptical. "What is *'too much rot'*?"

"Fuck, man. Not all the panels will blow out, I guess."

Gordan shook his head. "That's comforting."

Charlie stepped to the next green bundle. "Standard reserve chute, in about the same condition." Charlie stepped over to a duffle bag and opened it. He pulled out the items as he called them off: "One Uzi with folding stock." He turned to look at Gordan. "Sorry, I've never been as much of a gun nut as you. Five full thirty-round magazines and two additional boxes of fifty rounds, and I had one box of hunting rounds for that hand cannon you're dragging around under your arm. I think we can rig this web belt and ties so that you can jump the duffle." He stopped to look over at Gordan for approval.

"You did good, man — really good, especially under short notice." Gordan was pleased.

Charlie led Gordan over to the aircraft, opening the door near the tail, from where Gordan would jump. The back of the aircraft was empty, and there were only two rows of seats to the front.

"I've entered a flight plan to Miami to refuel. I'll get you to the right spot and then wait four days in the US Virgin Islands. If you don't show, I'll make the return trip."

"That's it, Charlie. I've got about twenty thousand for you to at least pay for fuel and the stay in the islands." He set a pillowcase down in front of Charlie.

"Shit, man — I'd do this for free. But I won't. Thanks. I've got a bit stashed around for rainy days." He grinned at Gordan and folded the excess pillowcase around the stacks; he took it to a toolbox and placed it inside.

"That your safe?" Gordan shook his head sadly.

Charlie gave Gordan his best "crazy" look. "Nobody around these parts going to mess with "Charlie-Charlie." He noted his old call sign from years ago.

"I never thought you were crazy," Gordan said, grabbing the back of his neck. "Maybe...Unstable Charlie, but Charlie-Charlie sure sounded better over the radio than Uniform-Charlie."

Charlie grabbed the two chutes and threw them into the back of the plane. He walked over and hit a switch; the entire front of the hangar began to roll up. A hard dirt track led out to a large, open field that served as the runway.

"Impressive," Gordan noted.

"Come on. If we get started, I can get you there in total darkness, just like you like it."

Charlie climbed in and closed the door. Walking to the front, he offered the co-pilot chair to Gordan and then buckled into the pilot's chair. By the time they were airborne, Gordan was sleeping soundly.

Chapter Forty-Three

West Virginia Police were still searching for signs of the occupants of the abandoned vehicle on the New River Gorge Bridge. The first responding trooper was being asked by an investigator for the tenth time about each and every aspect of him showing up early this morning and finding the accident scene as it was.

No one had been able to contact anyone at the Perkins home, and no one had been found walking up or down the highway. A search was still being done for limo and cab services to see if anyone had been picked up nearby. All the local airports were being asked to review their manifests for either Perkins. It was not out of the realm of possibility that the Perkinses would continue on a scheduled trip and leave a minion behind to deal with some traffic-related incident.

The Perkinses' publicist told the police that the couple was vacationing outside the US and most likely would be unable to receive calls — a real vacation, a first in many years.

There was luggage in the back of the SUV. Was it to be shipped to her vacation location? If so, where was the driver? A meeting was scheduled for the following morning to determine what the best course of action would be if they could not locate the vacationing couple.

♦ ♦ ♦

Charlie reached over and woke Hudde when they were approximately 30 minutes from Time On Target. Gordan shook the cobwebs from his head and climbed into the back to don his equipment.

Gordan put on the main chute and snapped the reserve onto the big D rings on his chest. He struggled to attach the duffle bag to the same D rings. Everything seemed ready, with no open zippers or pockets. He wrapped a couple of feet of duct tape around the handle of his K-bar, securing it securely to the right-side suspender of his web belt; he did the same to the .44 magnum under his right arm.

Charlie called out at five minutes to TOT.

Gordan went to the back door. He pulled up on the handle, and the door rolled into the aircraft, providing clearance for Gordan to exit.

Gordan grabbed both sides of the doorframe and leaned out as far as he could, looking forward; he could see some lights in the darkness approximately 5000 feet down below. Normally, Gordan would have suggested a HALO – High Altitude Low Opening-for an operation like this, but he didn't have the equipment. Five thousand feet would give him a bit of time in the air to try to make adjustments if anything happened. A shiver ran down his neck as he thought about everything lurking in the darkness beneath the surface.

Gordan took the static line and attached it to a cable that ran the length of the airframe. Gordan knew that, after he jumped, Charlie would increase the airspeed and climb so that he could come back to pull in the static line and close the door. Gordan heard the engines slow. He looked forward and saw Charlie hold up five fingers, then four, then three, then two; then he pointed, and Gordan was out into the slipstream. He heard the engines immediately grow louder as Charlie sped up away from the stall speed that a jumper required.

Gordan counted in his head and felt the full shock that a chute catching air brought to a jumper. Gordan did hear a ripping noise and looked up, trying to observe what damage had been done; he could not see anything obvious.

And then there was only the sound of the wind across the nylon of the chute. Gordan found the island lights down below and pulled on the proper toggle to adjust his angle of descent. He wanted to land as close to the beach in the cove as he could; there he could remove the chute and lock and load to start his mission.

The silence was interrupted with some tearing noise that soon became a thunderous, ripping noise. Somewhere near 3000 feet, Gordan was once again in near freefall as a catastrophic tear ripped his old chute into two pieces!

Gordan reached up to his shoulders and opened the clasps to the chute's quick releases. He grasped the two wire loops, one in each hand, and pulled; nothing happened!

Gordan yanked with all his might. The release worked on the right, and the riser flipped up out of sight. The left release wire pulled from the mechanism and did nothing. The chute, still attached to Gordan's left shoulder, was now streaming behind him, causing him to spin wildly as he fell.

Chapter Forty-Four

"This isn't right." Albert Perkins began to pace again. He turned to Saied. "Call to my boat, and make sure they are prepared to leave tomorrow if needed."

Saied put down his drink and reached for a blue phone. He listened briefly and then spoke: "Please inform Captain Kashon to have the Vice President's yacht prepared to leave at first light." He paused to listen. "If necessary, yes," he said, and then he hung up.

Leslie Carver jumped up from his seat. "I'll check on them." And he walked out of the bar and lounge area.

Saied looked over at Perkins. "Albert, you will probably find that these are two unrelated incidents. Right now, your beautiful wife is probably on a flight to Miami."

"I can buy that Ranks putz offing himself. He was a sap for that family of his. He actually believed my "family values" speeches." Perkins rolled his eyes in disgust. "But Cheryl would have called me back — she sounded concerned."

Saied took another sip from his crystal snifter. "Maybe she was tired, frustrated, or maybe she was behind schedule?" He threw his free hand palm up about chin high as a "What-if?" gesture.

Perkins went over and looked across the beach. "I guess it's possible."

"Relax, Albert. Have another drink, take a walk on the beach, or go visit your girls. I'm sure they would like a visit."

"Yes, I think I will." Perkins poured another few fingers and then headed out to the beach.

◆ ◆ ◆

Gordan Hudde knew that the drag of the chutes was keeping him from terminal velocity, but slapping the water at 80 mph wouldn't be conducive to a successful mission. Gordan knew there was little time and reached down, grasping the reserve handle. He pulled the release handle and threw the reserve as far away from his body as he could under the circumstances, praying that it wouldn't immediately become entangled with the main chute.

There was about a second between the chute filling with air and slowing Gordan's descent — for which Gordan was very thankful — and Gordan's slapping the surface of the water, nearly flat on his back.

The force of the water under him and a duffle bag on his chest caused Gordan to cough out his breath. Then the weight of his equipment began to pull him down. To make this entire situation worse, the reserve began to fill with water and catch the current, pulling Gordan down and away from the lights approximately a quarter mile away.

Gordan fought to the surface and found one small breath of air before he could no longer fight the forces pulling against him. The best course of action now was for him to allow the water to take him wherever it wanted to while he focused on removing his harness. He slid deeper and farther away from the island while he struggled with the harness quick release. When he finally wriggled out of the harness, it and his duffle bag slipped away with the chute, following the current.

Gordan realized that he would drown or pass out very shortly, and he dug for the surface. His lungs, which still burned from the fire in West Virginia, now burned with a desire for oxygen. He had to ignore his brain and fight past what he believed his body could do.

Gordan burst out of the water, taking in a fair share of salt water with his first breath of air. He unsuccessfully fought the urge to cough and slipped to his back, trying to make his way to the cove. The current continued pushing him away, and he tried to swim with it, but he ended up getting to one of the large yachts at the pier, missing the cove entirely. He pulled himself up onto the rocks and lay flat, catching his breath and thanking God for another successful jump — not pretty, but he was alive. Off in the distance, lightning flashed across the sky; Gordan took that as a "You're welcome."

He peeled the tape off of the K-bar handle and the rubber grip of the big stainless-steel Smith and Wesson 629 .44 magnum. Gordan flicked open the cylinder and looked at his precious six rounds. *It had better do,* Gordan thought — *it's all I've got.*

Gordan climbed to pier level and could hear voices on the big boats; he hoped these would be workers with no real devotion to the owners. He crept silently towards the first cabana, not sure what or who he would find.

Nothing in the first room. It appeared to be a room for the help, and he worked his way to the next room; listening, he could hear voices. When he opened the door, a woman screamed and jumped naked out of the big window over the bed. Gordan allowed the barrel of the .44 to sweep the room, stopping at the open bathroom door.

Malik Saad dove from the room, thrusting the big blade he always carried at Gordan's chest. Gordan back-pedaled and fired a round that caused a bloody crease from the half-shot-off ear to the back of Saad's head; but this did not cause him to pause.

The blade swept past Gordan's neck, and Saad continued driving forward. Gordan used the heavy gun to slam the top of Saad's head, and he spun away and fired another shot at center mass. Blood and guts added to the brightly colored bedroom wall.

There was no need for sneaking about now. Gordan ran to two other rooms, kicking in the doors and looking about. He tripped barging into the next room and found a light; the room was littered with toys. Gordan knew it was not a fun, happy place and set his jaw before heading to the final room in the hall. After that, there was the larger structure at the center of the island.

Gordan kicked in the door and headed in. His arm was grabbed in the darkness, and a wrestling match for the handgun began.

The person was taller than Gordan but was lighter and weaker. Gordan would not give up the grip he had on the .44, but the stranger caused Gordan to pull the trigger two more times rapidly. The roar of the gun and flash in the darkness caused Gordan's ears to ring and spots to appear before his eyes. Gordan pulled down on the handgun and drove his legs forward, carrying the man into the wall. The man caused Gordan to squeeze off another round that went right between Gordan's arm and chest, the muzzle flash burning off the hair on the inside of his upper arm. But Gordan used this moment to pull the gun away, and he put a round into the forehead of the man, ending the stewardship of the island by Abrahim Fazal Saied.

Gordan ran around to a door at the back of the larger structure and entered into a kitchen area. A woman screamed, and a man was holding a chef's knife, waving it before him. The woman ran from the room while the man screamed out, "I'm just the cook."

Gordan pointed the big gun at him and said, "If you're a worker and want to live, stay out on the beach."

The man with the blond ponytail looked for the woman and, when he didn't see her, dropped the knife and took off running after her; Gordan followed. The vast room they entered was empty, and the two workers exited in the direction Gordan had just come from.

Gordan ran into the next large building, which was a carbon copy of the one he had just come from. Again, nobody was about. Gordan continued out and into what was a long hallway, green doors on both sides, looking a bit like a hotel hallway.

Gordan walked to the first door. It was locked with a simple deadbolt from the outside, he turned the knob and opened the door. A boy about five years old with frightened eyes was standing in a small room. Gordan holstered the gun and tried to calm the boy by putting his hands out, palms up.

"Are you OK?" Gordan knelt as he asked.

"I want my mommy and daddy," the little boy said.

"I'm here to take you to them, OK?"

The little boy nodded vigorously.

"OK. Then stay behind me." Gordan turned back to the other door.

He turned the lock and repeated the sequence with a boy closer to seven or eight. Gordan asked him to take the other boy's hand.

Gordan looked at the exit doors. They were still alone; he turned back to the next door and opened it. He was amazed to find a face he recognized.

"Debbie Tolbert — I know you!" Gordan couldn't help himself as he dropped back down to both knees.

She stood silently in the room, sucking her thumb.

"I can take you to your mommy. I know her, too." He gestured for her to come out.

"Come on. We're all going home." She came out and looked the other two boys up and down; she did not allow her thumb to leave her mouth.

Gordan turned to the next door. This one had a bar across the center and a padlock holding it all together. Gordan gestured for the kids to step back and then sent a vicious kick at the hinge side of the door. He followed it up with two more before the hinges failed; he pushed through the door, stooping under the bar and broken door.

"Gordan?" the bound woman on the floor said.

Gordan dropped down and began to untie the ropes binding Susan Andrews. She began to cry with relief, and she hugged Gordan once her arms were free; she sobbed uncontrollably.

"If I called ahead, would you have picked up your room a little?" Gordan asked.

She said, "Fuck you" through some tears.

"Look, we're going to have to do this later. I don't know how many bad guys I'm dealing with here, and now I got some kids in tow. Do you think you could do some babysitting while I'm trying to work?"

He felt her immediately stiffen up. "Funny. Sure, Gordan…"

Debbie screamed in the hallway.

Gordan came out with the .44 pointed up the hallway. Leslie Carver, a giant that took up the entire doorway, was standing at the end of the hall with a sawed-off shotgun pointing back at him.

"I'll survive your shot spread, but you won't mine," Gordan called out to him.

"I guess I'll have to take my chances," Carver yelled back.

"Let Andrews and the kids past and I'll give you a shot: Man to man, hand to hand."

"Seriously?"

"You think you're a tough guy, you disparaged my brothers in arms before, and I'll kill you with my bare hands...unless you're afraid."

Carver tilted back his head and laughed. "Your funeral. Go ahead. Bring them up. I'll just go down and grab them when you're dead."

Gordan looked back into the room where Andrews was huddling with the three children. "Can you get them to the yachts?"

"Yes," she whispered. "Just *shoot* him — he's an animal."

Gordan turned back to Carver. "Back up!" He kept the handgun leveled at his chest.

They walked up the hallway; in the big lounge, Carver stood near the bar. He nonchalantly set the shotgun onto the top of the bar, waiting.

Andrews and the kids shuffled off, all holding hands, taking the shortcut across the beach toward the pier at the other end of the island.

"Now you," Carver called out; he kicked a couple of chairs aside and pushed the sofa, creating room.

Gordan held up the handgun. He slowly dropped the hammer and made a big show of setting it on top of a table.

He unsnapped the sheath of the K-bar and slammed the knife into the top of the wooden table. He held up a finger in the "wait" sign and then pulled his boot knife from his right ankle and set that next to the .44.

"Fair and square," Gordan called out.

"Oh, I'm going to fuck the FBI bitch on your cold corpse tonight," he smiled, "and then I'm going to drag her to the beach and drown her in the moonlight." He laughed. "What can I say — I'm a romantic." He laughed hard now.

Gordan advanced his hands up into a modified boxing stance. Carver strode very upright into the center of the floor he had created as if he had no cares. Gordan fired a right foot straight up the middle to kick Carver in the groin. Carver turned into it to catch the kick mostly on the inside thigh and put both hands down to try to block it. Gordan then threw a switch kick, landing his left foot perfectly across the right cheek of Carver's face.

"Keep talking," Gordan smiled, "if you can."

Carver felt his face and wriggled his jaw. "You're faster than I thought you'd be. I'll give you that. But if that was your best shot, you're finished."

With surprising speed for a man that size, he closed the gap. Gordan tried to backpedal. Gordan threw a knee straight up the middle; it seemed to connect, but Carver ignored it.

Carver got both hands around Gordan's neck. He began to push him back, first *into* the wall and then *up* the wall. Carver had Gordan a foot off the floor, trying to strangle the life out of him. Both of Carver's arms were fully outstretched.

Gordan felt like he was about nine feet off the floor.

Exactly where he wanted to be.

Gordan threw his right leg up and around the shoulders of the big man. He wrapped his left around, hooking his ankles and then he began to squeeze. Gordan reached with his right hand over the fully extended left arm of Carver. Grasping his right wrist, he pulled just enough to ensure he was still getting some blood and air.

With his left hand, Gordan reached down and felt for the belt-buckle knife that was always there. Getting it between his knuckles so that it stuck out from his fist, Gordan began striking Carver in his very exposed neck.

Gordan rained blows. Carver rained blood.

Finally Hudde stood over the dying Carver. Blood was dripping from Gordan's hair and beard. He didn't care. It wasn't his own.

"No soldier wants a 'fair fight' — we just want to win." Gordan stood and stretched; his neck already felt like it was tightening. Gordan looked at the little two-and-a-half-inch blade sticking out from between his fingers. "No shit," he said to himself, never thinking he would really ever have to use the thing.

"Very impressive, Mr. Hudde. You really should be working for me, you know. Your talents are wasted on the government," Albert Perkins said from behind him.

Gordan turned to see Perkins pointing a big silver handgun at him — Gordan's own.

"That's right. In all the excitement, look what I found." Perkins smiled at Gordan waving the handgun for a moment, like a fan. "What a big gun you have. But, don't worry. I know how to use it."

"Can I ask you something?" Gordan said and paused.

Perkins tilted the barrel of the gun up and down as if giving the go-ahead.

"You have everything. You have money and power. What the fuck is wrong with you?"

Perkins' brow furrowed. "There is nothing wrong with me. I'm perfectly normal, and everyone I work with here is normal." This, obviously, was not a line of questioning that Perkins had ever been subjected to, and he was not happy.

"Fucking little kids is not normal, there, Grandpa." Gordan shrugged his shoulders. "Like, come on, old man. You already have a wife who's 25 years younger than you."

"This is something a Cro-Magnon man like you could never ever understand."

Gordan was amazed that Perkins was still trying to maintain an image of being totally in control.

Gordan laughed at him. "What's to understand? You're an old, perverted fuck who likes to diddle little kids!"

Perkins lost it a bit for the first time. He stomped his foot and yelled back, "Love! It's about love! I love that child down there!" He pointed with his free hand back down the hall.

"That's rich! You abducted a kid to *love*. I bet that kid hates your guts down there. I bet that kid would love to see you dead."

"She loves to make me happy..."

Gordan interrupted. "Oh, you're a demented, perverted, sick old fuck."

Perkins was now seething. "I should just shoot you where you stand."

"How about a bet?" Gordan asked and paused. "I bet that kid down there hates you. If you win, shoot me where I stand. If I win, we get to go free."

Perkins was thinking. Gordan could see his brain working, except his brain was not working properly. Albert Perkins believed what he said more than anyone in this world.

"Fine!" Perkins began to motion Gordan to the hallway. "Don't reach for that knife," he warned as Gordan approached the table where he had left his weapons.

Perkins led Hudde by gunpoint down the hallway until they reached the last unopened door.

Perkins stood, shaking, near the green door. He flicked his wrist to the right and, with the barrel of the magnum, ushered Gordan to the opposite side of the hallway. Gordan leaned back against the wall and kept his hands at chest level, showing no signs of resisting.

"Stand still, and don't move!" Sweat was rolling down from his grey hairline into his eyes, but Gordan did not move when the barrel left his center mass as the Vice President wiped his forehead with the back of his hand.

Perkins reached into his pocket and retrieved a key. Knocking softly on the door, he called out to the prisoner inside.

"Sarah, honey. It's your daddy, I'm coming in now."

He turned the key and then the door handle, and he stepped aside, allowing Gordan to see into the room. A pillow flew out at the same time as a scream. "Leave me alone!" cried Sarah DeLucia, who was in the far corner of the room; Gordan recognized her from the two-year-old photo in her case file.

Gordan caught the pillow and held it under his arm. Blood from his earlier fight rubbed off onto the pillow case.

She cried out more, seeing the bloody visage that was Gordan Hudde. "Who are you? What do you want?"

Perkins stepped into the doorframe and then into the room, so that he could see both DeLucia and Hudde.

"Honey, this evil man wants to take you away from me. He wants me to let you go. I told him that I would...you would... never allow it. Tell him that it's true." He looked expectantly at the twelve-year-old girl; his brows furrowed when she didn't respond right away.

Gordan knelt in the hallway. "Are you Sarah DeLucia?" He shook his head in awe when she nodded in the affirmative. "I met your dad not too long ago. I'm Gordan. I walked from your farm up to your friend's house, just like you must have so many times."

She nodded at him again.

"What do you think you are doing?" Perkins pointed the big gun at him like it was a stick he could poke him with.

Gordan ignored him. "Men have tried to kill me to get me to not come here and ask you this. I almost didn't make it, but here I am." He sighed. "I was beaten as a kid, Sarah; it was a 10-foot monster that haunted my every day...and night. I can't promise you that it will go away — only that the monster gets smaller every day. To me, now it's a pea, and, when the monster comes up, I smash it." He smashed his fist into his other, open hand. He closed his eyes and then opened them. "And then it's gone for a while." He smiled at her and raised his left arm, inviting her to leave. "Would you like to get away from here?"

When she didn't move or answer, he continued.

"You can come with me, and this I promise: I'll check on you often, make sure you're doing OK. Your dad is now doing well, by the way; I think you being home would be real good for both of you." He opened his large hand, looking for her to come put her hand in his.

"What the fuck do you think you're doing?" Perkins walked over and placed the barrel to Hudde's forehead.

Hudde never flinched. His eyes never wavered from Sarah's, and she rose up and then began walking across the small room, extending her hand, reaching for Gordan's hand as she did so.

"What the fuck do you think you're doing?" Perkins turned the gun back over to point now at Sarah, standing in the center of the room, her little schoolgirl outfit not matching the rest of the scene.

"You'd best point that thing at me." Gordan stood, and Perkins quickly swung the barrel back, cocking the hammer. "Don't test me, son."

Gordan reached across Perkins and touched Sarah's hand, tiny in comparison to his. "It's OK," he said as she walked past Perkins. "We made a deal, and now you and I can go."

"You son of a bitch!" Perkins screamed, spittle flying out his mouth. He stepped up and placed the .44 against Gordan's temple and *Click!* went the gun.

"What?" Perkins started pulling the trigger over and over, driving the hammer repeatedly into the previously fired primers. Every time he pulled the trigger, it resulted in pushing him backwards, as if a force was striking him in the chest each time. Deep in the room, he looked up and saw Gordan standing in the doorframe, blocking any escape. His face twisted into terror, and the gun dropped from his hand.

"That's right. I tricked Leslie into a fight because my gun was empty, and now I've tricked you." Gordan allowed Sarah to walk under his arm out into the hall. "You know," Gordan continued, "that's about the same look your wife gave me just before I dropped her off the New River Gorge Bridge."

"Impossible," Perkins said, but his eyes and shoulders slumped, showing that he knew it was true.

"Wait here, and don't listen," Gordan said, looking down at Sarah and stepping into the room, closing the door.

Sarah heard the bloody man offer to play a game with her "daddy" — something he called "One flew over the cuckoo's nest." He told him that he was going to play "Chief." Sarah didn't know what that was, but there was a lot of commotion. She heard her "daddy" yelling, *Do you know who I am?* and

"*Stay away from me!*" She started to put her fingers in her ears but then stopped. She *wanted* to listen.

Then there were some crashes and then…nothing. Sarah saw her hand floating out and away from herself, grasping at the door handle. She turned it and slowly opened the door as if she were no longer in control of her actions.

The bloody man — he called himself "Gordan" — was sitting on the chest of the Vice President, who was flat on his back on the floor. She looked at the thick muscles and tendons straining out of his neck; his large, rolling shoulder, under the blood drenched dark t-shirt, led down to thick arms. The Vice President was holding on to the triceps of a big left arm, a large "U" shape of muscle above the elbow, leading down to thick, hairy forearms that were holding a pillow and hiding the face of the Vice President.

Perkins hand at first tried to push him away; then, he grasped at Gordan's arm. Finally, his hand dropped to the floor. But Gordan did not stop pushing. He wanted to drive the head under the pillow into the concrete that made up the floor. He began punching the pillow, one vicious blow after another. Gordan roared with each blow delivered.

Gordan grew tired well after the death of Albert Perkins. The blood and brain matter that was leaking out from under the pillow told the story. Gordan didn't realize the door was open until he felt a light touch on his shoulder. It startled him.

"The monster is gone. We can go now." Sarah offered Gordan her hand; he reached over and picked up the handgun, returning it to under his arm. He took her hand, and, standing, he hulked over her, but she led him to the hallway and up and out of the beautiful and deadly place.

The dark, starlit sky and salty ocean air brought Gordan out from somewhat of a trance. A group of children and adults were standing on the pier near the yacht. Gordan pointed Sarah at the group and told her that he would be right back.

Entering the extravagant room of Abrahim Saied, Gordan found the light switch. The item that most caught his eyes was the large safe. Gordan approached and looked at the double dials and large ship's-captain wheel that would open the heavy steel doors.

Gordan stood for a moment. looking at the mechanisms; shrugging his shoulders, he grabbed the big wheel and turned it.

It was open.

The safe was filled with cash but also held some ledgers and a laptop. Gordan found several large duffle bags and filled them to the max; there was still cash in the safe, but Gordan had to go.

Reaching the pier, Andrews introduced Gordan to Kashon, captain of the former Vice President's yacht, the *Tiny Princess*. He was told the ship had been topped off and ready to go. Captain Kashon, of Jamaican descent, said he could get them to the US Virgin Islands. "No problems, mon!"

They all boarded, and Andrews took the children below deck for the ride. Gordan looked over at what he guessed to be the island staff, standing on the small private beach. He shrugged his shoulders and sat on a comfortable cushioned loveseat near the bridge. The engines began purring, and the yacht moved quickly out into the darkness. A scream was heard and then some yelling. *No rest for the wicked*, Gordan thought; He slid down a ladder and ran below deck to check on the commotion.

A yellow-haired, small, dark woman was holding her hands up and yelling in Arabic. Andrews and all the children were huddled together on the opposite side of the cabin; the children all seemed to be frightened or agitated.

Gordan was busy trying to determine the woman's dialect and whether she was from Syria or Palestine when Andrews approached him, pulling him over to whisper.

"She was some kind of 'nurse" on the island, She basically administered a lot of sedatives, me included. The kids are all very upset that she is here; we won't be able to gain their trust with her present."

Gordan frowned and rubbed his forehead. "What do you want me to do with her now?"

Andrews suddenly looked very tired, like maybe she would slip to the floor and sleep right there. "I just don't care I think she is the mother of one of the guys running the island." Andrews went over and huddled back up with the children; they moved as one to the sleeping cabin behind a door.

Gordan approached the woman with his palms up, not looking for a scene. "Listen. The children are very upset by your presence; why don't we talk on deck?" He took the small set of steps up, and she followed.

The water was very calm, and the ship was motoring along comfortably. Gordan walked to the stern and put a foot on the railing. Gordan turned to the woman: "The children certainly don't like you."

She smiled, which made everything worse; a dentist could have spent several weeks trying to fix the gnarly yellow grin.

"I did what was required. Children don't understand," she said.

Gordan tilted his head. "But, your son — where is he?"

"I imagine you killed him." She continued to grin at Gordan, but her eyes narrowed, and he could see the hate emanating from her. He suddenly remembered an old *Phantom of the Opera* movie photo he had once seen.

"Why would you help him?"

"It was Allah's will" She looked at Gordan and saw that this answer was not sufficient. "There is no good or bad. There just is what is required of one."

Gordan shook his head and reached out, grabbing the woman by the neck. He hoisted her up over the bulwark and railing and, for the second time in as many days, he threw a woman into darkness.

"I'm sure you'll understand that that was required of me," he said as he walked back below deck.

Gordan swept the rest of the yacht, and, except for the captain and his first mate, there were no other surprise stowaways.

Chapter Forty-Five

Two weeks later, Gordan Hudde was sitting in a chaise lounge on the concrete patio of his not-quite-finished "bunker" home. He sipped a beer and watched the sun, slightly off to his right shoulder, dip into the tree line, casting very long shadows.

He sat up to look over the south side when he heard a vehicle stop near his driveway. The dark, official-looking sedan then pulled in and continued up and around the switchback, making its way to the top of the hill.

Gordan padded barefoot over to the two steel doors painted to look like wood that made his front doors. He stepped to the side and lifted the bronze eyepiece that made up his secret door peephole.

Susan Andrews walked confidently to his door and then looked around for the doorbell. Gordan waited until she found the cord to pull. Immediately the sound of a submarine diving alarm began: *Ah-ooh-gah!*

Gordan was smiling when he opened the door.

"What the fuck is that?" she said, eyeing Gordan up and down.

"Coming in for a beer, or is this official business?" Gordan asked.

"Here's your mail." She handed him a pile of envelopes that he started shuffling through.

She came in and began looking around. "Wow, what a surprise. You like early-man decorating. What the hell, Gordan" It's kind of like being in a cave."

"Does this mean you won't sleep over?" Gordan looked sad.

"I guess it depends on how much liquor you have." She smiled/sneered at him.

"I see you found a sense of humor." Gordan came back from the kitchen with a beer and held it out for her to take. "Even at my own expense, I like it." He walked out onto the concrete patio and pointed to another lounge chair.

"Thanks, Gordan." She took a swig of the beer and raised up the brown-and-gold labeled bottle. "*Negra Modelo*. I've never tried it. It's pretty good on a warm night."

"I've got some good memories tied to it." He turned to look at her. "So, is this really business?"

"No it's really personal, and I hope to do you a bit of a favor — nothing like saving your life, but I'll work on that."

"OK, then. Shoot."

"I've been talking to all the parents, and almost every family has said in confidence that somebody has given them all a good sum of cash; that 'somebody' is you — right?"

"So." Gordan drank from his bottle and then sat up, putting both feet on the floor, facing Andrews. "Don't tell me you're going full-on bureaucrat, contacting the IRS or something?

That money was from ill gains — ill gains from abduction, rape, and worse for those kids and their families!"

"Whoa, big fella, I'm asking just for me." She put both hands up in the universal "stop" sign.

"Another thing: We were looking at Reavers and the Barston woman."

Gordan made a face like he'd smelled something bad. "Should I check you for a wire or something?"

"Gordan, stop being so paranoid. I'm your friend. I'll always look out for you. I need to fill in the gaps...just for me."

Gordan stood up and drained his beer. "Another?" he asked her as he headed back inside.

"No, thank you," she looked at him pleadingly, waiting for his answer.

Gordan smiled at her when he came back, enjoying this moment in which she appeared so earnestly interested.

"I made them both a promise that, when I was done with them, they would be alive and well, just like the children that the two of them dealt with. They swore they were not responsible for any harm to them."

She nodded.

"So I came across this young doctor who owed me a favor. I used him and a contact to ship them south of the border." He smiled at Andrews.

"How far south, Gordan?" She tilted her head, and he noticed that she had gotten a haircut — too bad, in his opinion.

"See, this doctor kept the pair unconscious the entire trip, so that they would wake up sitting in one of the cheap plastic chairs, like these, somewhere up the Amazon; I mean, *way* up the Amazon." Gordan grinned. "Alive and well when I last saw them! Get it?"

"And you're serious?" Her brows furrowed.

"Hey, short notice. I thought it was pretty good!"

Andrews shook her head. "What if they come back?"

Gordan shrugged his shoulders. "I'd better never see them."

Andrews took a deep breath. "Gordan?"

"I'm still here."

"The Bureau has been reviewing the information that you provided from the island."

"Hey, I was never there."

"This is just you and me talking here. The Bureau has no clue what really happened. They don't believe me — I can tell you that — and some of the kids gave a description of a crazy, bloody man who saved them."

"Alright."

"I'm sure that you duplicated the information and understand that Perkins and his crew had a West Coast operation going on at the same time." She was looking at him with concern.

Gordan didn't say anything. He just shrugged his shoulders.

"Gordan, the entire East Coast operation was wiped out — you did that. Please let the Bureau handle the rest of it. Promise me that you won't head out west."

"I should make you promise me that the FBI won't fuck it up." Gordan opened one of the envelopes and started reading the enclosed letter.

Andrews got up. "Gordan!"

"What do you want from me, Andrews?" Gordan got up and walked inside. He opened a drawer and used a highlighter on the letter, placing it on the kitchen counter when he was done.

"I want you to promise me! Promise me that you will stay on this side of the Mississippi river!" She was pleading, sincere in trying to keep Gordan from becoming an FBI target.

"That list contains some very high-profile child killers," Gordan pointed out.

Andrews was growing frustrated. "Gordan, you can't continue to take things into your own hands. You'll end up on the wrong side of all of it."

"Aren't there some people out there who deserve justice, not a courtroom and lawyers?"

Andrews raised her voice. "I'm not leaving until you swear to me; I know that that's very important to you — not breaking your word." She stood still, folding her arms over her chest.

Gordan was still looking down at the letter. He looked up and made eye contact with Andrews. Sensing her frustration, he strode over and took her hands into his left while holding his right high. "Susan, I Gordan Hudde, vow to stay on the east coast and allow the FBI to handle everything west of the Mississippi." Gordan put his arm down. "OK — feeling better?

I understand what you are trying to do for me. I do, and I appreciate it very much."

He took her in his arms and gave her a big bear of a hug. "You staying? I'll take the couch, and we can watch movies all weekend."

She kissed him. "Maybe another time, Gordan. Thanks for listening and... everything."

They walked together to the front doors and said some goodbyes; Gordan had the feeling that they would see each other in the future only if it concerned business.

Behind Gordan the form letter laid open on the kitchen counter. It read in part:

> *Dear Super Fan,*
> *We are pleased that you have an interest in the incredible works of Harvey Golem. The following is a list of dates and locations for this year where you can hear a lecture and maybe even meet the famous director and producer of great films like...*

There were five locations listed; now highlighted was:

> The Four Seasons
> July 9th and 10th
> New York, New York 10022 USA.

Gordan Hudde will return in: ***AN EMERALD ABYSS***.

What is being said about Gordan Hudde novels?

A Deep Purple Hue-
"With an extraordinary conspiracy story, this book is perfect for fans of 24 as Hudde reminds me of a bearded Bauer - he doesn't always play by the rules and never bows to authority." -The Book Magnet.

"The perfect conspiracy, well-suited characters, a beginning that hooks you right away..." – Serious Reading.

An Angry Orange Sky-
"With plenty of shocks and surprises, An Angry Orange Sky does not disappoint and I have no doubt that we will be hearing a lot more from Gordan Hudde, at least I certainly hope so!"- The Book Magnet.

"...Hudson expertly narrates what a single man driven by determination and courage can do to counter the evil forces around him." – Serious Reading.

"This violent, cinematic second entry in the Gordon Hudde Novel Series shows promise, with its surprisingly original plot, and despite a dauntingly large cast of characters..." – BookLife Prize in Fiction.

A Hint of Silver-
"...Graphic and violent, the gritty manuscript powers along relentlessly... it's hard not to root for a hero like Hudde." – BookLife Prize in Fiction.

Words being used by other reviewers-

"Addictive, interesting, dark, disturbing, brutal, brooding, and exciting.

One reviewer said: "This novel would make a great movie!"

A Retail Investigator- Many 5 star reviews!

"The book clearly outlines the excitement, risk, and exasperation that is part of the deal being in the investigation business. The stories narrated are fun to read and extremely informative for anyone who is currently serving or interested in anything related to the investigation industry." – Serious Reading.

Don't forget to leave your own review at the location you purchased this book!

Please visit me at my authors' blog: http://www.markhudsonofficialsite.com/

You can also find me on Facebook: https://www.facebook.com/markhudsonauthor/

Mark Hudson lives in Arizona with his wife Darlene and two rescued cats, Scotty and Chance. He spent his youth in the Army as a combat engineer and in the infantry with Bco 4/325 in the 82nd Airborne. In the civilian world, he became a professional in the retail-security field, specializing in employee fraud and embezzlement.